8/5/2018
To Jeff, a fellow history buff!

THE WOLF
OF
BRITANNIA

VOLUME II

Best wishes,

JESS STEVEN HUGHES

Jess Steven Hughes

A Historical Novel

MILFORD HOUSE

n imprint of Sunbury Press, Inc.
Mechanicsburg, PA USA

S0-EKK-397

MILFORD HOUSE

an imprint of Sunbury Press, Inc.
Mechanicsburg, PA USA

For information about special discounts for bulk purchases, please contact Sunbury Press Orders Dept. at (855) 338-8359 or orders@sunburypress.com.

To request one of our authors for speaking engagements or book signings, please contact Sunbury Press Publicity Dept. at publicity@sunburypress.com.

ISBN: 978-1-62006-563-1 (Trade Paperback)

Library of Congress Control Number: 2015932529

FIRST MILFORD HOUSE PRESS EDITION: May 2018

Product of the United States of America
0 1 1 2 3 5 8 13 21 34 55

Set in Bookman Old Style
Designed by Crystal Devine
Cover by Lawrence Knorr
Cover art by Tal Dibner (www.dibnergallery.com)
Edited by Janice Rhayem

Continue the Enlightenment!

VOLUME II

BRITANNIA
AD 43-60

DRAMATIS PERSONAE
(IN ORDER OF APPEARANCE)

THE BRITONS

* Caratacus – king of the Catuvellaunii and Trinovantes
Rhian – Caratacus's wife
Clud – iron maker and master craftsman
Havgan – arch-Druid priest
Fergus ap Roycal – clan chieftain
* Tog (Togodubnos) – king and brother of Caratacus
Dana – young Brigantian woman
Adminios – brother of Caratacus
* Verica – deposed king of the Atrebates
Fiona – young female warrior captain
* Venutios – Brigantian prince and warrior
Owen – Druid priest
* Cartimandua – queen of the Brigantes
Crone – medicine woman
Brath – king of the Silurians
Macha – Caratacus's daughter
Alfyn – young warrior
Kyncar – clan chieftain
Uric – clan chieftain
Gadeon – clan chieftain
Donaut – clan chieftain

THE ROMANS

Marcus Valerius Bassus – centurion
Gaius Flavius Porcius – emissary and senator
Cyrus – Persian freedman and Porcius's steward
* Aulus Plautius – general
* Titus Flavius Vespasianus (Vespasian) – general
Marcus Severus – military tribune
* Hosidius Geta – general
* Marcus Ostorius Scapula – general
Figulus – Roman tribune
* Claudius (Tiberius Drusus Claudius Germanicus Nero) – emperor
    (AD 41-54)
* Caligula (Gaius) – emperor (AD 37-41)
* Tiberius (Tiberius Claudius Nero) – emperor (AD 14-37)

* historical character

CITIES AND GEOGRAPHICAL LOCATIONS

ANCIENT NAME	MODERN NAME
Bononia Gesoriacum, Gaul	Boulogne, France
Britannia	Britain (England)
British Ocean	English Channel
Caleva	Silchester
Camulodunum	Colchester
Dubris	Dover
Durobrivae	Rochester
Durovernum	Canterbury
Eburacum	York
German Ocean	North Sea
Maugh-Dun Castle (Maiden Castle)	Dorchester
Noviomagnus	Chichester
Portus Rutupis	Wantsum Channel
Regulbium	Reculver
River Colne	Colne River
River Danubus	Danube River
River Rhenus	Rhine River
River Tamesis	Thames River
Rutupiae	Richborough
Tanatus	Isle of Thanet
Verulamium	St. Albans

CHAPTER I

AUGUST. AD 43
THE SOUTHERN COAST OF BRITANNIA

In the glare of midmorning sunlight, Caratacus spotted the approaching rider. He galloped from the direction of the observation post on the bracken-covered ridge rising behind the camp. The rhythmic thumping of hooves kicking up chalky dust grew louder as the horse approached Caratacus's headquarters tent from where he had just stepped outside.

Wearing a tartan tunic and home-spun breeches, longsword at his side, the warrior drew up in front of the tall, broad-shouldered, thirty-four-year-old Celtic ruler of the Catuvellaunii and jumped from the foaming mount. The pungent odor of horse sweat reeked from man and beast. '

Gasping, the dusty rider stepped before the king and took a deep breath. "The Romans are crossing the channel, Sire—hundreds of ships."

Muscles tightened in Caratacus's back and arms. *So, it's finally happened. Damn!* He kept his scarred, weather-beaten face impassive, but pulled on his long, drooping moustache. "How far from shore?"

The horseman glanced in the direction of the coast. "About fifteen miles. Right now, they look like water bugs skimming a pond, but they're coming sure enough."

"That's a long ways to see so well."

The warrior nodded. "The channel is so clear, you can see the ships crossing from the Gallic coast—it ain't the usual haze."

"Where are they heading?"

"It looks to be Rutupiae," the warrior said.

1

Caratacus nodded. The fishing village with its small harbor was north of the white cliffs less than twelve miles away. Its wide beach an ideal place to land with a trackway leading to the interior. "They can only sail as fast as their slowest ship. We still have four to six hours before they reach us."

As he thought about how he would defend his people, Caratacus focused on the encampment surrounded by the woodland of ash, pine, and hazel scrub that dotted the surrounding hillside. His army was bivouaced on the expansive grasslands, a hodge-podge of tents and lean-tos, plus the larger tents of clan chieftains and captains. The camp sat at the base of foothills east of Dubris to the south and Rutupiae to the north. The ridge jutted more than five hundred feet from the plain below. From the observation post on the summit, his men had an unimpeded view of the British Channel to the southeast and the farmlands in the Great Stour Valley to the west.

The king's headquarters tent was the largest multi-room, goat-skinned tent, situated in the center of the temporary base. Posted before the front entrance stood a dozen streamers, representing tribal clans, and as many guards surrounding the shelter.

Arms were stacked before the warriors' tents. The smell of baked bread, porridge, and roasted meat drifted from cooking fires. Hundreds of warriors milled about, talking, cursing, and coughing, which mixed with the bellowing of cattle, whinnying horses, and bleating goats from surrounding pens. The laughing calls of green woodpeckers and chirping of warblers drifted from the nearby trees.

Dozens of wagons carrying grain, water, and weapons had been gathered in a protective circle near the headquarters tent with a posted guard.

Through this wide expanse of meadow ran a series of streams and a small river used to supply the camp's water.

The king turned when he heard the whisking sound of the tent flap opening. Rhian, Caratacus's flaxen-haired wife, clothed in a bright-blue and yellow, tartan tunic and blue, striped breeches, joined him. Three fingers shorter than her husband, she raised her head slightly and peered into his midnight-blue eyes. Her bowed lips curled into a frown as she touched his muscular upper arm. "Did I hear right, Caratacus, the Romans are crossing the channel?"

"You did."

She pulled her hand away. "Mother Goddess, I must prepare my warriors at once."

Caratacus stayed her with a detaining hand, palm outward. "We have plenty of time to prepare your cavalry and my infantry and chariots." He turned to the nearest of twelve guards posted about the tent. "Find Clud. Tell him to bring twenty of my retainers and meet my wife and me at the observation post on the ridge. See that arch-Druid Havgan meets us there as well."

The guard saluted and left.

Caratacus shook his head. Earlier that morning he had conducted a staff meeting with his friend and advisor, Clud, his senior clan chieftain, Fergus ap Roycal, lesser chieftains, and captains. He had dismissed them about a half hour before the messenger arrived. *Too bad he hadn't arrived while we were still gathered. They could have heard the news firsthand. Still, I need to see for myself what the invasion force looks like before making further plans.*

Caratacus turned to another sentry. "Tell the groom to saddle our horses at once."

* * *

An hour later from the summit of the ridge, Caratacus sat on his Gallic mount looking toward the British Channel, bordering the coast about ten miles away. It was midmorning, a clear sunny day. As he inhaled the salty, sea air, a light breeze caressed his face. Thin wisps of clouds drifted overhead. The messenger was right. The usual gunmetal glint of the ocean caused by overcast and fog had given way to a peerless blue. Appearing in the distance, as dark specks dominated by square sails, hundreds of Roman ships, rolling on gentle swells, slowly sailed toward the British Coast. The invasion Caratacus had long feared was upon them.

Although grinding his teeth, the king forced himself to keep a placid face. But his hand slowly reached down, fingers tightening around one of the leather pommels of his saddle. He fixed his blue eyes on the invading fleet. *Damn! Why didn't you come a moon ago when I had one hundred thousand warriors in place? We would have slaughtered you!*

Caratacus had placed the army in position along the southeastern coast where it had remained from the middle of May until the beginning of August. Then his spies had informed him that Roman troops had mutinied and refused to board ships for the crossing. At that point, he had sent most of his warriors home to harvest the summer crops. Caratacus figured if they had not invaded by August, they wouldn't until the following year.

Unfortunately, he had learned from spies that Emperor Claudius's secretary, a Greek named Narcissus, had disguised himself as an officer of the Praetorian Guard and persuaded the legionaries to come to their senses. After that, the ringleaders were rounded up and executed. The message was clear—board the ships or else.

Caratacus heard the pounding of dozens of hooves on the chalky trail. He turned to see his balding friend and close advisor, Clud, approaching on his gelding, followed by twenty of Caratacus's retainers. Right behind him, Havgan followed on his mount. A long, white robe, girdled by a copper belt, draped his short stature. A dark thin beard covered his gaunt face, and a silver triskele, symbol of his authority, hung from a chain down the front of his scrawny chest.

The bodyguards fanned out behind Caratacus as Clud pulled up to his left side with Havgan next to him. Clud raised a hand in greeting to the king and Rhian while the Druid bowed.

"Sire, why didn't you wait for me and your retainers?" Clud asked.

Havgan sniffed. "And why am I here?"

Caratacus nodded toward the channel. "I needed to see this for myself and quickly. It was important you two saw it, too. Take a look."

Havgan stared out to sea, his face expressionless.

Clud slightly bent forward squinting his gray eyes, deeply set beneath bushy eyebrows in a wide face. He grabbed the hilt of his longsword. "So the messenger was right. Shit! We don't have enough men to stop them—you sent them home."

4

Havgan tugged his thin beard. "By the gods who I dare not name, the dream I had last night has come true."

Caratacus and Fergus ap Roycal turned toward the Druid.

"Yes, I was planning to inform you this morning, Great King," Havgan said, "but your retainer found me, as I was about to break my morning fast, and gave me your message."

"Tell me about the dream," Caratacus said.

"It was short, but in my vision I saw thousands of eagles flying in a shimmering light across a great sea. I did not know where they came from or where they were going before I suddenly awoke. It's obvious what the eagles meant."

"Aye, the eagle is the symbol of Rome and its army," Fergus said. "Thousands of birds mean invasion."

Caratacus arched his eyebrows sharply, and a frown crossed his lips. "It doesn't make any difference, they're coming now, but we know the terrain, they don't—we'll ambush them."

Rhian lightly touched the gold torc circling her neck. A mischievous smile brightened her rosy face. "I like that. We shall fight them on our terms."

Havgan shook his head. "The Roman menace must be stopped, or our people will be slaughtered as were our cousins in Gaul."

"And they will slaughter the Druids," Caratacus said.

Havgan exhaled. "Yes."

"We'll stop them, I promise," Caratacus said. "But if the Romans are wise, they will establish a beachhead and dispatch a probing force inland before sending their legions."

"It would be the smart thing to do," Rhian said. "Only a fool wouldn't send cavalry ahead to scout the countryside."

"When Julius Caesar invaded our lands ninety years ago," Caratacus said, "my great-grandfather, Cassivellaunus, knew he couldn't defeat his forces, they were too many."

Clud scratched an armpit and gestured with a thick, calloused hand toward the sea. "How did he fight 'em?"

Caratacus touched his chest with a fist. "Like us, he knew the land and sent four thousand chariots to attack the Romans where they least expected. We will do the same."

Rhian turned and focused her apple-green eyes on her husband. "We have no more than five hundred chariots."

"I know. That's why you will supplement what chariots we have with your cavalry detachment."

Rhian tossed her head, golden hair flying about her shoulders. "I only have four hundred."

"We have no choice," Caratacus said gruffly. Then, in a more conciliatory tone, he added, "Besides, you have trained your women well. I have no doubt they will prove their worth in battle."

"Have faith in yourself and your riders, Lady Rhian, you shall do well," Havgan said. "I will conduct a sacrifice in the Sacred Grove."

Slowly, Rhian inclined her head to Caratacus and Havgan. "They will, wait and see."

Havgan nodded and touched the triskele medallion.

Caratacus grinned. Since she was a child, Rhian had trained to fight as a warrior. However, she was only allowed to prove herself as a fighter after she had become his wife.

Then there was Dana, his younger, second wife. She was staying safely inland at Caleva, his secondary capital and home of the Atrebates. She had moved there from Camulodunum back in May when the Roman invasion seemed imminent. She was due to deliver in two months. Would he be home for the child's birth? He couldn't think about it now.

He nodded to Rhian and then in the direction of the women's bivouac. "In the meantime, you will send scouts ahead to reconnoiter Roman troop movements."

She smirked. "With pleasure. I will send my best scouts, led by Fiona."

"Good. Once we know where they're going, we'll strike them hard. Then we'll withdraw, taking the livestock and burning all crops in the Romans' path."

"I will place a curse upon them. They will sicken and die from the pox," Havgan said.

6

A black-toothed grin erupted beneath Clud's drooping, brown-and-white-speckled moustache. "Aye, we'll pollute the well water with dead animals and shit. That's bound to make 'em sick. The Romans will have to bring in all their supplies."

Caratacus didn't believe in curses but prayed in this instance he was wrong.

"Shouldn't it drain their manpower?" Rhian asked. "They will have no choice but to escort their supply columns."

"They won't," Clud said. "That's when we'll surround and crush 'em."

"If my spies are correct, it will confirm what the messenger told me," Caratacus said. "The Romans will go ashore near Rutupiae and probably the Isle of Tanatus."

Clud spat. "That's a mighty small area, Sire—seems to me they'd be landing at other spots, too, if the reports are right about them bringing four legions."

"They will," Caratacus said. He scratched the scar running across the right side of his face, an old wound received in an earlier battle. "The spies said there are about forty thousand troops, split about half between Roman legionaries and the rest auxiliaries."

"Piss on the numbers," Clud growled. "The Romans will learn to fear us."

Rhian's nostrils flared. "I wonder if your cowardly brother, Adminios, is on one of those ships. After all, didn't he ask the Romans to invade our lands. The pig!"

"No doubt he is," Caratacus said. "Only through the Romans can he reclaim his kingdom, but we'll defeat them. If he had not betrayed my father, we wouldn't be dealing with an invasion."

"What about the other traitor, that so-called king, Verica?" Clud asked.

"Probably," Caratacus said. "The bastard wouldn't stand with his army when I challenged him to battle for the Atrebatic Kingdom, which he had stolen from my dead Uncle Epaticcos."

Clud laughed scornfully showing his black, jagged teeth. "He ran like a dog with his tail between his legs, and he'll run again."

"Now, that beast and Adminios return with Roman backing," Rhian said.

Caratacus glanced seaward and again back to Clud, Havgan, and Rhian. "I've seen enough—back to camp. Havgan, not only will you sacrifice for Lady Rhian's warriors but for the entire army while we prepare for battle."

* * *

By early afternoon, Caratacus received word the Romans were landing on the wide, rocky beach and estuary near Rutupiae and the Isle of Tanatus, as he had expected.

Outside his headquarters tent, beneath a goatskin canopy, Caratacus, Rhian, and Clud were surrounded by his officers, including the senior clan chieftain, Fergus ap Roycal, minor chieftains, and captains, discussing strategy against the Romans. To one side, a cow-hide map stretched between two hardwood poles. A messenger had just informed Caratacus that his scouts discovered an advance Roman force, a cohort of between 450 to 480 men marching inland on the trail to Durovernum to Rutupiae. The trackway ran roughly in an east-west direction. He dismissed the rider.

"Are they mad?" pock-faced Fergus ap Roycal asked. He jabbed a dirt-encrusted finger toward the map. "They're moving only a small detachment inland without deploying a screening force."

Caratacus turned to the gathering. "It's called Roman arrogance. They believe all they need is to appear, and we will wilt away."

"What foolishness." Rhian twisted the two silver bracelets on her left wrist with her other hand.

Fergus wiped the sweat off his ham-like hands on the sides of his breeches. "The bloody bastards are asking to be slaughtered."

"And they will be." Clud pounded a fist into the palm of his hand.

The rest of the group voiced their agreement.

"I know just the spot to strike the Romans," Caratacus said. "There is a huge meadow surrounded by a pine forest. It's a cross-roads for the east-west trackway from Rutupiae to Durovernum and the north-south road from Portus Dubris in the south to Regulbium in the north. It's ideal for springing an ambush. The area allows for maneuvering of our chariots and cavalry."

Caratacus pointed to the cow-hide map. He touched the road to the north of the crossroads and then to the east and south. "That's where we will place the chariots. Then they can sweep in when the Romans march up from the west end of the road into the meadow. The chariot assault should give the infantry enough time to emerge from the forest, form up in companies, and be ready to attack once the charioteers finish their run."

"The place is perfect," Rhian said.

Caratacus gave orders to the leaders to move out the ten thousand warriors who had been ready to deploy at a moment's notice.

"All right, see to your warriors," Caratacus said.

* * *

Less than an hour later, as the afternoon grew hot and muggy, Caratacus's forces arrived at the edge of the forest dominated by ash trees and hazel shrubbery. Beyond them lay the broad meadow, its chalky turf covered with thyme, rock rose, and a variety of wild orchids.

Caratacus turned and motioned with his head for Clud and Fergus ap Roycal, who had been riding behind him, and Rhian to move up on his other side. The two leaders approached. "Clud," Caratacus said, "take your three thousand men and deploy them on the north side of the forest at the edge of the meadow."

"Done," Clud said. He turned and rode away.

Caratacus gestured to Fergus ap Roycal. "Place your three thousand men to the north side as well, but to the right side of the north-south road. Split your three hundred charioteers along the north and east roads down to the forest's edge. You'll attack the north side of the Roman column."

Fergus narrowed the raven eyes set in his pocked face. "By Teutates, we'll crush the fucking lot, we will." The hulking warrior turned his mount and cantered back to his position at the edge of the forest.

9

Caratacus motioned to four minor chieftains and as many captains forward, and they encircled him. He gave them instructions to place infantry in the woods along the south edge of the forest, but to keep the north-south trackway clear. In addition, chariots were to deploy along the south and east roads just out of sight of the meadow. The chieftains and captains saluted and departed. Caratacus's forces of almost ten thousand infantry, cavalry, and charioteers were now in position among the widely spaced trees surrounding the meadow.

Sitting on his mount, Caratacus wore a checkered, green and yellow, short-sleeved tunic covered by protective, ringed chain mail, topped by a red, painted helmet. On a ringed, iron belt hung a steel longsword, sheathed in an ornate scabbard.

Rhian sat next to her husband wearing a long, gold and green, tartan tunic of light wool and blue-and-red-striped breeches, feet adorned in deer-hide shoes. Hanging from her shoulder down to her right side at the waist ran a leather baldric, which held an iron longsword sheathed in a cow-skinned scabbard, decorated in multi-colored, paisley patterns.

Adorned with tattoos on their faces and torsos, most of the warriors were equipped with iron-tipped spears, long, slashing swords, and their heads crowned with iron, conical helmets. A few, like Caratacus, the clan chieftains, captains, and his retainers, wore woolen or linen tunics and breeches cross-strapped from knee to ankle above leather sandals. Long moustaches on otherwise clean faces proclaimed their nobility, and gold torcs circled their necks. The rest wore pelts of wolf or beaver above leather kilts, and many were stripped to the chest.

Commanded by Rhian, the four hundred cavalry riders rode small, Spanish mounts. They wore soft, short-sleeved tunics over ankle-length kilts and were armed with longswords and javelins.

Under Caratacus's immediate command, the nearly three thousand infantry were deployed in dozens of loose companies, numbering from one to two hundred each, led by captains or minor chieftains. On the right flank, Rhian's cavalry stood in ready. Nearly two hundred chariots, each holding a driver and a warrior armed with three spears, waited out of sight on the south road.

Caratacus turned to his wife. "Rhian, once the chariots have attacked and passed beyond the Roman column, I will signal you to split your cavalry to attack the enemy. Hit them at the head and rear of the column where they are most vulnerable."

"I will." She turned and trotted to where her unit waited among the ash trees.

Both knew the legionaries would face outward with shields in front to defend against the infantry, their sides exposed.

From his mount, Caratacus viewed the crossroads through a gap in the trees from the south side of the east-west trackway. He had a clear view of the meadow. To his left he surveyed the north-south road as it disappeared into the woods in the direction of Regulbium. Silence enshrouded the forest. No sounds of a gentle breeze whisking through the branches. The air grew heavy, and the sky seemed to be as close as the top of the trees. Not even the birds, such as the shrilling nuthatches, called to their mates.

About ten minutes later a couple of scouts galloped towards him up the east-west road from the direction of Rutupiae. They drew up before Caratacus and reported that a column of Roman infantry were approaching. He acknowledged and dismissed them. The king called for his runners and dispatched them with orders to Clud, Fergus, Rhian, and the rest of his commanders to prepare for battle.

Despite being a veteran of many campaigns, the tension of impending battle always caused his muscles to tighten. His throat dried, and his tongue felt like sand. His stomach churned and growled. Perspiration ran down the side of his neck. He spat. *Fear is normal. If I weren't afraid, then I would be either stupid or a mad man.* He grinned and remembered the words spoken to him by his uncle, Epaticcos, many years ago when as a youth he took his first head in battle. "Being scared is half the fun. If you weren't, I'd send you to the stables to shovel shit for the rest of your life!" *Well, Uncle, as usual, I'm scared to death!*

Soon he heard the muffled sound of hob-nailed sandals tramping, kicking up dust along the trackway.

The Romans emerged from the woods to the clattering of articulated body armor, which covered knee-length tunics, with short swords and daggers strapped to their waists. Each legionary carried two javelins, *pila*, which rested on their shoulders, blades glinting in the bright sunlight. In their other hand, the men carried a partially curved, rectangular shield, *scutum*. It was tall enough to protect their bodies from shoulder to knee. Entering the meadow, the legionaries changed from columns of two and regrouped into columns of four, strung out in parallel lines of eighty men each.

The Roman commanding officer, a centurion, marched at the front of the formation. The scarlet transverse crest of horsehair on his iron helmet, metal greaves, and the long, vine cane he carried identified his rank. He was followed by a standard bearer, holding upright a tall pole bearing the cohort's number X emblazoned in silver, signifying the tenth cohort. Along the column at intervals of twenty men, marched junior centurions, standard bearers on one side, and on the opposite side, an *optio*, assistant centurion.

Caratacus tightened his sweaty hand around the hilt of his sword. He turned about, glancing at his retainers and beyond at the warriors scattered through the trees. Caratacus looked in the direction of the south and then east roads where the chariots hovered out of sight. He turned towards the Romans, and an evil grin crossed his lips. *I'll make these shit-eaters pay for invading my country. May Teutates be with us.*

As the Romans moved across the meadow, the commanding centurion gave the signal to take a break. The troops halted but stood in place, leaning against shields that pointed outward on both sides. As the dust disappeared, the soldiers wiped away the grime from their faces, sighing in relief, and pulled out canteens for a drink to quench their parched throats.

Caratacus peered around the low-lying scrub and smiled. *This is better than I expected.* Quietly, he raised his sword and gave the signal for his men to get ready. He turned and nodded to the trumpeter next to him. Using an upright, wolf-headed carnyx, the warrior sounded the brassy signal for attack.

Chariots stormed down the roads from their hidden place into the meadow. Warriors yelled at the top of their lungs as they bounced, and bumped over the uneven meadow floor kicking up dust. They rode light, two-wheeled, wicker-framed chariots with spoke wheels pulled by two ponies. Each car contained a driver and a warrior armed with three throwing spears.

The commanding centurion looked about and cursed. Instantly, he turned and barked orders to his other centurions. A split second later, the legionaries kneeled, javelins jutting between the shields of the outer two ranks. The inner two ranks raised their shields, turned them crossways, and formed a protective cover over the formation known as the turtle.

Caratacus watched as wave after wave of his and Fergus ap Roycal's charioteers hurtled through the roiling dust, working opposite sides of the Roman column and hurling spears at the Roman shield-wall. Several penetrated and a few soldiers went down screaming. But the wall instantly closed around the dead men.

Despite the churning earth that partially obstructed his view, Caratacus watched as about a dozen charioteers drove their cars headfirst into the Romans, attempting to break or ride over the formation. The line buckled but held as Roman swords gutted the undersides of the hapless ponies and shoved them back onto the bloody field.

Caratacus slapped a hand on his thigh, realizing the Roman defense was far better than he had expected. *We must destroy their column!*

When the riders had exhausted their supply of weapons, they returned and rode behind the infantry companies Caratacus and Fergus had held in reserve. The dust finally drifted upward, forming a gray-white haze as it disappeared into the sky. They halted behind the footmen, dismounted, and unsheathed their swords, ready to reinforce the units. Caratacus nodded to the trumpeter, who sounded another command and the infantry of Clud, Fergus, and his men drew swords and raced toward the

Roman defenders. The warriors yelled, whirling swords above their heads or waving spears at the Romans.

"Kill the bastards!" Caratacus shouted.

Within the space of a heartbeat, the legionaries stood and raised their shields and javelins. Upon command of their centurions, the first column of Romans locked their shields, protecting the spearmen behind them. Those soldiers set their feet, placing one foot to the front. In unison, they hurled a volley of hundreds of javelins at Caratacus's attacking horde. Dozens of the deadly missiles found their marks as screaming, dying Britons rolled onto the ground, dead. But many survived, hurling their spears into the Roman ranks. A few found their marks, but most struck only the wall of shields. Then the lines hurled another volley of spears. More British warriors fell to their deaths.

A second later, the shields of the front line opened and the rear line, which had expended its javelins, moved forward and formed a shield wall as the former line stepped backwards, stopped, and hurled their weapons.

Fighters jumped over their dead comrades and rushed toward the Romans. The enemy hurled another volley of spears.

Hundreds more went down before reaching the Romans. After expending their javelins, the Romans again locked their shields in place with an echoing slam, forming a near impenetrable wall. The legionaries raised their shields to eye level, protecting their upper bodies, from the onslaught. They readied their short-swords to thrust between the narrow gaps at the sides of the shields.

Caratacus watched as the screaming warriors slammed into the wall of Roman shields.

"Break them, dammit!" Caratacus shouted. "Crush them!"

A growling uproar soared from the defenders. Cut and parry. Guard and thrust by the legionaries as wave after wave of Britons hurled themselves against the defenders only to be slaughtered in their tracks. Blood curdling screams echoed among the sounds of steel upon steel swords and crunching of bones by crashing Roman shields. Using the domed, iron bosses in the center of their shields, the Romans smashed into the Celts faces, followed by the deadly thrusts of short swords aiming for chests, armpits, bellies, and the groin.

Appalled by the losses of his warriors, Caratacus raised an arm in Rhian's direction signaling her cavalry to attack the Roman flanks.

Rhian rode with her women into the frenzy, screaming like banshees.

Despite the fierce Roman defense, their shield-wall wavered. Small breaches appeared in the Roman column. Caratacus's warriors punched more holes through the shield wall. The legionaries closed up, fighting savagely, slicing off heads, arms, and legs of their assailants even as their losses mounted. Agonizing screams, splattering of blood, and the gaseous release from bowels and bladders soared above the carnage.

Rhian's female cavalry struck the flanks, hurling their spears, striking Roman soldiers along the unprotected sides of their formation. One soldier after another died, and the defenses gave way.

Even from three hundred yards, Caratacus observed that upon initially seeing woman riders, the Romans appeared hesitant to fight them. *Good, they don't like fighting women. That will work in our favor.*

Unfortunately, as soon as a couple of legionaries took spears to their chests and another lost his head to a longsword, they fought the women as savagely as their male counterparts. The Romans gutted their horses, toppling them to the ground, and slayed dozens of Rhian's riders. The Roman line crumpled, but not before at least two thousand of Caratacus's warriors had been slaughtered. The chalky ground, now a pinkish, oozing mire littered with what seemed like endless piles of hacked and mutilated corpses. Flocks of wing-fluttering magpies, jackdaws, and thousands of buzzing flies dove and feasted on the putrefying dead.

Caratacus spotted one lone Roman, a tall centurion, hunkering within his bloodied, partially ripped shield as he was encircled by a dozen warriors. Caratacus and Clud rode to the scene. The king raised his sword and shouted, "Stay your weapons!" He turned to Clud, who had drawn his sword, and shook his head. Clud sheathed his weapon.

Using his legs and feet to command the horse, he guided the restless mount forward through scores of slain Roman soldiers and British warriors. The centurion stood guard despite his wounds, silent against a circle of taunting warriors. The Britons parted as their king rode through their circle.

They expected him to kill the Roman. Caratacus measured the young man, a junior centurion, and knew him as dangerous, even now with a headless, Celtic warrior lying at his feet.

"I am Caratacus," he called out in halting Latin. He slowly guided his snorting gelding around the centurion. Caratacus glanced sideways to see if he had heard. The soldier turned slowly, following his movement, and nodded as if surprised to hear a barbarian speaking his tongue.

About twenty paces away, Caratacus spotted a blood-spattered, riderless horse standing by a dead, female warrior. He turned to a nearby captain and motioned with a hand. "Bring that mount here."

The captain brought the gelding next to the king. Caratacus nodded to the Roman and then the horse. "You are free to go ..."

A dissenting murmur rippled among his men. Caratacus glanced back at them, and they fell silent.

"Go and tell your general how easily I destroyed your cohort!" he told the centurion. "Take the horse, now!"

The centurion looked up at Caratacus and, for the length of five or six heartbeats, fixed his eyes on him. Then he turned away, lowered his sword, and shoved it into his scabbard with a hiss. He stepped to the animal and mounted hastily. The circle of warriors parted, and the Roman picked his way through the body-littered ground. He halted beyond the edge, as though questioning that he was still alive.

"Your name, centurion?" Caratacus called.

"Marcus Valerius Bassus!" And he was gone.

This minor victory has not been easy. More than two thousand of my warriors lie dead. Like disciplined fire ants, the Romans literally fought to the last man. This is just the beginning of a long and bitter fight.

I won't stop until we have wiped out every last Roman.

16

CHAPTER 2

The evening after the Romans landed in Britannia, Senator Porcius sat in his brightly lit tent above the rocky beach writing a secret report to the Emperor Claudius, his Persian freedman Cyrus beside him. The corpulent Roman was a self-proclaimed expert on British affairs. *I may have to endure the discomforts of camp life, but I am determined to at least have well-lit quarters. My eyes deserve that.* He surrounded himself with twelve candles and olive oil lamps. Although a bit smoky, the light burned to his satisfaction. In his midfifties, his eyesight was growing weaker, Porcius pushed the parchment farther away from his eyes, almost at arm's length, as he wrote upon it. He had been writing for more than an hour before he looked up from the document and blinked. *Soon, I will be forced to dictate all my correspondence to my slave-scribe. Gods, I hate the thought. There are some matters that are better left from their prying eyes. Who knows if one of them is a spy for my enemies.*

Cyrus snapped his fingers, and a slave immediately refilled Porcius's silver cup, wine from his private stock of Sentenian.

I'm not about to drink the vinegared swill issued to the army. He took a long swig and turned to Cyrus. "It doesn't seem possible we have returned to Britannia after more than three years. Where has the time gone?" For a moment, he stared at his goblet.

"Aye, Senator," Cyrus said. "When you learned Caratacus was elected king and had deposed his father, you saw what the Jews called, *the writing on the wall.*"

Porcius exhaled. "All too true." He hated fleeing to Gaul, but knew Caratacus would invade the lands of the Atrebates ruled by King Verica, especially after Caligula and the Roman legions had withdrawn from the Gallic coast.

"Still, you were fortunate when we arrived in Rome to escape the homicidal wrath of Emperor Caligula," Cyrus said, interrupting Porcius's thoughts.

"Thank the gods," Porcius replied. "How could I forget? I was nearby when that monster was assassinated by officers of the Praetorian Guard."

Cyrus smiled. "I, too, was grateful, lord, and how we drank a toast when you received the news."

Porcius nodded as he, too, remembered the day as if it had occurred only an hour ago. The Praetorians had killed Caligula as he strolled down a dark corridor beneath the palace on Palatine Hill the afternoon of January 24th, two years before the invasion of Britannia by Emperor Claudius, Caligula's successor and uncle. "And it was also about the same time I came to the attention of the new emperor," he added.

"Events only turned for the worse, did they not, Senator?" Cyrus asked. He paced back and forth in front of Porcius's table, shaking his head and scratching his trimmed, black beard.

Porcius sipped from his cup. "For Caratacus, yes. He made a horrendous mistake in overrunning King Verica's lands. Then, along with Adminios, Verica begged Claudius to invade Britannia and restore them to their rightful thrones."

The Roman huffed and shook his head. *I still don't understand why Claudius waited so long. He needs this campaign to strengthen his power and credibility with the army and Senate. This is no dynastic struggle between petty, barbarian kings. Caratacus and Verica are fighting for control of southern Britannia!*

He smiled as he rubbed the rim of his wine cup with his forefinger.

"But now we are back in Britannia, sir," Cyrus said. "You have always seemed more comfortable here than in Rome."

"Indeed, I am, and yet I found it puzzling that the initial landing had been unopposed. No resistance? That was strange indeed." The commander of the Roman

Expeditionary Forces, Aulus Plautius, had refused to allow him to disembark until late afternoon when the support units of the invasion force went ashore and until he was certain there was no danger from an enemy counterattack. *Spurned, mind you. General Plautius had the brass balls of Jupiter to deny me anything, a Roman, advisor of British affairs to the emperor.*

After the first wave of five thousand heavily armed infantry, Legion Fourteenth Gemina, had landed in early afternoon along sandy Stonar Beach near the fishing village of Rutupiae, Gemina's Tenth Cohort had been immediately dispatched inland to reconnoiter the countryside. Behind Fourteenth Gemina landed legions Second Augusta, Ninth Hispana, Twentieth Velaria, and a host of auxiliary support troops, forty thousand in all.

Within three hours the Romans had established a defensible beachhead. Finally allowed to land, Porcius was oblivious to the shouts of a hundred tyrannical beachmasters directing the landing. He watched the endless streams of barges and transports sail up the doglegged channel of Portus Rutupis. They passed the treeless Isle of Tanatus and unloaded along the sandy shore. Here they disgorged thousands of troops, horses, mules, and tons of supplies, a process that would go on for days, if not weeks.

The gods couldn't have picked more perfect weather for the landing. A contrast to the cursed weather in reports of Julius Caesar's landings a century before. A balm to Porcius's painful arthritis, the warm sun hung like a blinding, gold coin high in the west. A slight breeze blew off the British Ocean barely rippling the aqua surface. Despite the present circumstances, he was happy to return to Britannia. Porcius and General Plautius, escorted by a detail of forty Praetorian Guardsmen, strolled to the huge scarlet, leather tent, Plautius's temporary headquarters. Confusion reigned as the general's aides directed slaves and servants in the placing of trunks, maps, and other equipment around the spacious shelter. A *contubernium*, squad of eight Praetorians, surrounded the tent.

Short and compact in stature, the remaining hair on Plautius's balding head was more gray than jet-black.

Alert, lime-shaded eyes peered beyond the tumbling, wide nose, overhanging a firm mouth and strong jawline, in a weathered face. He loved the outdoors and ordered two chairs, a portable table, and a map of Britannia's south coast set up outside near the entrance covered by a protective canopy.

Before Porcius sat down, he scanned the ridge above the distant fishing village, straining to see if Caratacus or his warriors were watching the Roman landing. He spotted jagged dots upon the distant saw-tooth ridge, certain they were Caratacus's horsemen, if not the king himself. *Why hadn't Plautius's scouts discovered them?*

As Porcius was about to inform General Plautius, a trumpet signaled the approach of the rider, a centurion. He glanced toward the sea and its carpet of a thousand ships and then to the hill, now empty and smooth.

The commander heard a noise from behind. He turned and saw one of his aides approaching at double-time.

"Sir," the red-faced tribune puffed, "Gemina's Tenth Cohort has been annihilated!"

The general winced. "Survivors?"

"Only one, sir."

"Bring him at once!" Plautius ordered.

"Four hundred eighty men dead! In the name of bloody Mars, how?" he fumed at Porcius. "Are these men demons? I'll see what this cowardly survivor says before I plan a counterstrike."

He slammed his gilded helmet on the table then wiped beads of sweat from his broad forehead. He tossed his scarlet and gold-edged cloak to a servant.

"It had to be along the trackway to Durovernum," Porcius said. "There's a heavy forest on the other side of that ridge." He pointed to the unfolded parchment map on the table. "It's thick enough to conceal an entire army." Porcius pointed his index finger to a place in the center of the map. "It's not marked, but there is a crossroads here, which is surrounded by a huge meadow. I'd wager a gold *Aureus* that is where the cohort was attacked."

"If we could afford to lose men, I'd say good riddance, but we can't—not even troublemakers!"

20

The general's startling remarks dismayed Porcius, but he knew what Plautius meant. The cohort had been directly involved in the mutiny when the invasion forces were still assembling in Gaul. Fortunately, the uprising had failed and plans continued for the landing.

Porcius shook his head. General Plautius had told him he would never forgive the Tenth. The general ordered Fourteenth Gemina's commander to use them for shock troops. Besides the fact the legionaries had been mutinous, it was also appropriate. The Tenth Cohort, in all of the army's legions, contained the newest recruits plus troublemakers reassigned from each legion's other nine cohorts.

The young centurion approached, halted before Plautius at attention, and saluted. His face and segmented armor were smeared with dried blood, his tunic in shreds, a dent on the side of his helmet. In his late–twenties and lanky, the Northern Italian of Ligurian stock stood well over six feet, his ruddy complected face peering out beneath thick, chestnut hair. A thin scar crossed from the base of the right ear lobe to the bottom of his squared chin.

"Your name, Centurion," Plautius said.

"Marcus Valerius Bassus, sir." He stared straight ahead.

"Why is it that you are the cohort's sole survivor?"

"Because their king wanted me to give you a message, sir."

"And what is the message?" The general refrained briefly from asking the obvious question, noting a sword gash in the man's iron-armored *lorica*.

He must have fought like a madman to have survived, Porcius thought. *There is too much blood smeared on his face and body to be his own. Despite what Plautius said earlier, this man is no coward.*

Bassus nodded. "He said to me, 'Go and tell your general how easily I destroyed your cohort of five hundred men!' I'm trying to remember exactly, because he was hard to understand, 'Tell him, so will all Romans die by my hands ...'" The centurion's eyes glazed. "And, '... all Romans will die in my sea of warriors.'"

Plautius stomped his foot onto the beach sand. "Arrogant bastard! We'll deal with him, you can count on it."

"Did this king have a name?" Porcius asked.

The centurion hesitated.

"Answer Legate Porcius, he is in our confidence," Plautius said.

"He said his name was Caratacus, he speaks Latin."

Porcius exhaled as he shook his head. "I might have known. Only he would have the brass balls to challenge Rome."

"Now, explain the circumstances of your cohort's slaughter, Centurion," Plautius ordered.

Bassus relayed the story and more. "Priscus, the senior centurion, led us into a trap, sir." His blood-smeared hand gripped the hilt of his short sword.

"Trap? Great gods! Give me details, Centurion," the general ordered, impatience growing in his voice.

"Yes, sir," Bassus huffed. Slightly swaying from fatigue, he wiped the sweat from his blood-stained face with a calloused hand and continued his report. The day had grown hot and muggy, and Centurion Priscus, impulsive at best, had grown impatient waiting for a troop of Spanish cavalry. The unit was to accompany the infantry and reconnoiter ahead for signs of the enemy. But he ordered the troops to march without them. The other centurions, including Bassus, who had only been assigned to the cohort a week before the invasion, advised him to wait. Priscus called the officers a "bunch of cowardly bastards" and ignored their counsel. Discovering the little village of Rutupiae deserted, scouts from the Tenth found the trackway to Durovernum and continued inland. They plunged into the valley and were quickly swallowed by the choking forest.

"And?" Porcius asked stone faced.

Still staring straight over the head of Plautius, Bassus narrated. The cohort had been on the march for two hours when they came to a large break in the forest, a meadow with a crossroads running through its center. They halted for a brief rest, still no cavalry. Suddenly, hundreds of chariots with screaming warriors swarmed from the north, south, and west parts of the crossroads hurling spears and themselves at the force.

The general narrowed his eyes. "Chariots?"

"Yes, sir," Bassus answered.

"How many?" Plautius asked.

"I'm not sure because of the dust they kicked up, but there must have been almost five hundred."

The general glanced to Porcius, who shrugged, and back to Bassus. "Continue."

"The legionaries instantly formed into four close-knit, shield-to-shield files forming the turtle defense. The Britons raced along both sides of the columns, hurling their spears like the furies, but failed to penetrate our defenses." Bassus exhaled and continued. "The chariots retreated but were replaced by thousands of warriors on foot. They sprang from the underbrush and trees and charged us like demons from the underworld."

Standing taller than before, Bassus said in a voice full of pride, "Although badly outnumbered and with little chance of escape, we held our ground and hurled our javelins before the Celts were upon us. Through a wall of tightly packed shields, we used our swords to slaughter those undisciplined savages. It was a vicious cycle of thrusting and parrying, and we butchered warrior after warrior.

"We didn't retreat a foot, sir," Bassus spoke through clenched teeth. "Hell, there wasn't any place to withdraw. There were thousands of them. Why, there were even women cavalry!" He exhaled.

"Women? Are you sure?" the general questioned, his thick eyebrows raised.

"Yes, sir."

Plautius glanced to Porcius and back to Bassus. "I had heard stories about women fighters, but I dismissed them as tall tales. Proceed, Centurion."

"Yes, sir. They picked off troops at both ends of the cohort's formation," Bassus continued. "A few of the men hesitated at the idea of fighting women, especially when they looked so young, and some were even pretty. You could see that even through their face paint."

"The fools," the general growled.

"Not for long." Bassus narrowed his eyes. "After a couple of our men were stabbed by their javelins, the rest didn't have any qualms about killing those amazons. The savages pressured us where our defenses were weakest, but we kept fighting, not one of my lads gave ground."

Plautius nodded in approval.

"We desperately attempted to keep a tight formation," Bassus said, "but defenses started crumbling until finally our ranks were pressed and consumed by hordes of blood-chilling, screaming demons. I knew we would all die," Bassus finished.

There is no doubt in my mind, Bassus fought with the skill and cunning of a warrior in a Homeric poem.

Porcius nodded slowly.

Bassus wiped the sweat running down the side of his blood-smeared face and wiped it on the exposed part of his tunic beneath his segmented armor. He exhaled.

"Don't stop now, Centurion, continue," the general ordered. "If he's Caratacus as you say, why would he spare you?"

"That's what I'm coming to, sir. In one hellish nightmare of killing, it was over. I was surrounded by wild men—half-naked, cursing, screaming, dancing, laughing," he said raising his voice. "At first, I thought I was just cut off from the rest of my century. Then I knew they were all dead, except me. I pulled myself closer to my shield waiting to be rushed by them. By the gods I was determined to slice up as many of the bastards as I could before they killed me." Bassus swallowed and took a deep breath. "But they halted, and this king, because that's what he was, commanded them to stay their swords."

"How do you know that's what he said?" Plautius asked.

The centurion nodded. "I was raised in Northern Italy near Placentia, sir. A lot of Gallic people live there. I picked up many of their words from my boyhood friends."

"Go on," Plautius ordered, impatience creeping into his voice.

"Yes, sir." Bassus explained the king had ridden his Gallic stallion forward through scores of slain Roman soldiers and British warriors.

"As their leader approached," Bassus said, "I looked about and saw the carnage spread over the wide meadow on the trackway we were taking to Durovernum. We were along the edge of a thick forest about ten miles from here. Despite my wounds, I stood silent against that circle of taunting warriors. I wasn't going to give those bloody savages the satisfaction of asking for mercy.

"I should have died with my men," Bassus said. "But the Britons parted as their king rode through their circle. Next to the leader rode some hulking warrior, I expected him to kill me. He drew his sword and looked to the king, who shook his head. The big man slid it back into a scabbard as the king seemed to take my measure. I believe he knew I would fight to the death. He saw the headless warriors lying at my feet. The king called out in Latin, 'I am Caratacus.' He slowly guided his snorting mount around me and glanced at me sideways. I wasn't letting him out of my sight, and I turned slowly, following his movement. I was surprised to hear a barbarian speaking my tongue, although haltingly. Then he surprised me again."

"In what manner?" Plautius asked.

"This Caratacus said I was free to go."

Porcius cricked an eyebrow. "Indeed?"

"Yes, sir," Bassus answered. "I could tell by their angry voices, Caratacus's men didn't like it a bit. But he gave the lot an ugly glance, and that shut their mouths."

"I believe that," Porcius said. "He is a powerful leader. Then what happened?"

"Caratacus motioned for a warrior to bring me a horse, which he did. He told me to saddle up. I found myself sheathing my weapon, and mounted hastily.

"He asked me my name as I made my way through the dead bodies," Bassus continued. "I halted beyond them and looked back, thinking it was a miracle I was still alive. Not trusting they wouldn't come after me, I shouted my name and galloped away."

General Plautius stood up and, for a few seconds, studied the young centurion, his grimy face, eyes full of hate.

Porcius broke the silence. "Sounds like the work of Caratacus. It's just like that scoundrel to spare a man to bring a message to his enemies. The tales he'll spread about camp by nightfall is more than worth this centurion's life to Caratacus."

"Describe their king, Centurion," Porcius demanded.

"Yes, sir," Bassus answered. "He's tall for a barbarian, well over six feet, in his early-thirties. His face is scarred and sunburned, and his muscled body riddled with tattoos. An iron helmet painted bright red covered long, brown hair. He wore a fancy scarlet and purple cloak open in front and green and gold, tartan trousers, same as the Gauls wear. His weapon was a bright, steel sword, the biggest I've ever seen."

"The physical description and broken Latin fits perfectly," Porcius said. "Few Britons speak the language at all, but Caratacus is one of them."

"You're a brave man, Centurion," the general conceded. "Is there anything else?"

A frown crossed Bassus's chapped lips, and he balled his fists. "Sir, I want revenge! I want a chance to fight them in the open. I lost too many good men today, some were friends." He unclenched his fists. "But that's not all. I learned a lot about the British while growing up. Begging the general's pardon, I don't mean to sound like a braggart, but I know more about them than most Romans."

Porcius raised his eyebrows at that remark. *A Roman who knows the Britons? This could be interesting.*

"And how did you come by this store of knowledge?" the general inquired, his eyes narrowed as if skeptical of the remark.

The centurion returned Plautius's glare. "My great-grandfather was a legionary in the Fighting Tenth Legion, sir. He served under Julius Caesar on both his expeditions to Britannia. Stories of his adventures were passed down from his time to mine. My father was a retired centurion who settled in Placentia on the River Padus. He was a prosperous blacksmith, and I served as his apprentice. We shoed horses and repaired many wagons belonging to the traders returning from Britannia. They taught me well, for I pointed out several geographical sites, including the crossroads, to Centurion Macro when we first landed here and later during the march, which had been described to me." He shook his head. "They didn't lie!"

General Plautius's apparent reserve had begun to melt, Porcius noted, though his granite face didn't reveal it. "Thank you, Centurion." He clapped, and a slave appeared. "Have my personal physician attend to this man's wounds."

After Bassus departed, Plautius spoke to Porcius. "What do you think? Is his professed knowledge of any significance?"

"Folklore and war stories, I suspect. But if channeled in the right direction, he may prove to be of some value." Uncertain of the young officer's knowledge or political connections, Porcius deliberately downplayed the importance of this rare find, a Roman with knowledge of Britannia.

"Was he right about the geographical locations?"

"For one who had never set foot on British shores before today, it was as if he had been bewitched."

"Before the army moves inland, I'll verify his report. I'm sending a detail of scouts to check the area now." The general signaled for a runner and gave the order. After the soldier departed, he turned back to Porcius. "The legions will pass the way of the Tenth Cohort tomorrow."

"But Caratacus may be waiting with his army."

Plautius arched a bushy eyebrow. "No. If he's wise, and I don't believe he's stupid, he'll not want to risk a battle too soon and dispel his invincibility among our troops. But if he's a fool ... all the better. I doubt he'll be there if what you've said is true. He'll take up more defensible positions until he can regroup his forces again."

"Yes, upon reflection, I believe he would." Porcius pinched his thin eyebrows together.

"And I have a good idea where he'll be. By then we'll know if Bassus told the truth. I'm curious to see if that pile of supposed bodies is still there."

"Caratacus won't stay around once he has stripped all bodies of their armor and weapons."

"Senator Porcius, you must know we landed unopposed only because Caratacus chose to fight us on his terms."

Porcius grunted. "I had long feared otherwise. You know Caratacus can command a combined army of more than one hundred thousand men, savages, but men dedicated to die at his word."

"And yet we may, Senator ... and yet we, too, may die. Meanwhile," the general continued, "I'll make inquiries as to this Bassus's background and what part, if any, he played in the mutiny."

"You sacked the ringleaders before we sailed, and he only joined the cohort last week."

"He could have been another troublemaker transferred to the Tenth Cohort, that's where all of them are sent."

"If that were the case, wouldn't he have been broken from the rank of centurion?" Porcius asked.

"Not always," Plautius answered. "In any event, I learned to watch my back many years ago, Senator, just like you. Otherwise, neither of us could have survived, could we?" he answered with a sinister grin.

He was right. Porcius decided to send one of his agents to Northern Italy to make discreet inquiries about the young centurion. *My gut feeling tells me this young man will prove to be invaluable.*

* * *

"Lord, you were sitting there staring blankly at the parchment for a long time. I was beginning to worry." Cyrus twisted his fingers.

Porcius rubbed his bloodshot eyes and scratched his fleshy forehead. He looked about his well-lit tent, realizing he had dozed off while reflecting on the events leading up to the invasion and the slaughter of Centurion Bassus's cohort.

"I was thinking about our next move against Caratacus. And more importantly, where his next attack will come. He won't wait much longer."

* * *

Caratacus, along with Clud and a small scouting party, crouched among the rocks, watched from a cliff as tens of thousands of Roman soldiers landed on Stonar Beach near the fishing village of Rutupiae about half a mile away. In the noonday sun, the glaring surface of the British Channel's blue-green waters nearly blinded the king.

Perched like a seagull on a ledge, he watched the activity with growing fascination as he contemplated his next move. Beyond the shoreline, hundreds of ships rode at anchor, rising and falling on gentle swells. Barges and lighters sailed back and forth between them and the land, bringing more troops and supplies. He feared his small triumph would only stir their anger.

"Why didn't you come a moon ago when I had one hundred thousand men assembled, you son of a sow?" He cursed the unseen general.

"Aye, the filthy bastards," Clud spat, sitting on his mount next to Caratacus. "Now we'll have to wait until the rest of our warriors have been recalled, and that takes time!"

"Patience, Clud," Caratacus said in an even tone. "We'll drive them into the sea when the hour is right. No Roman Army will overrun my lands."

"May the Great Teutates damn your brother, Adminios, and the traitor, Verica, for bringing the Romans to our shore!"

CHAPTER 3

Eleven days had passed since the Romans invaded his lands. Caratacus's army had taken all the livestock with them, leaving a scorched path of burning crops and farmsteads as they withdrew thirty miles north from the landing site of Rutupiae to the River Medway. There he waited for the rest of the disbursed tribal armies to reassemble. In the meantime, Caratacus received reports from his scouts and spies that the Romans had not been able to forage. They were becoming more dependent on ever-lengthening supply lines and were vulnerable to attack.

On the evening of the twelfth day Caratacus and his brother, Tog, King of the Trinovantes, received word that the Second Legion had landed and was marching north to reinforce the Ninth and Twentieth Legions at Durovernum. The Cantiacian capital was now in Roman hands, plus the legion camp on the coast.

The following morning Caratacus, along with Rhian, had seen his brother off before dawn with a force of one thousand of his best horsemen and eight thousand spike-haired infantrymen from their joint encampment. Before Tog departed the three huddled together outside the goatskin headquarters tent. Brightly colored streamers and banners representing the various tribes and clans hung limply on poles planted in the chalky ground.

"Good luck, Brother," Caratacus said to Tog. Narrow faced and nearly as tall as Caratacus, his younger brother wore a crimson cloak. Over his wide shoulders was his best mailed armor, and a new silver helmet topped by a broad winged eagle. Besides his great longsword, Tog carried two javelins with spiked butts, and a bright, red-and-orange-striped shield with an iron center boss.

The two brothers reached across and clasped hands briefly before Tog mounted his gelding.

Rhian kissed Tog on the cheek and murmured a blessing of the gods.

"This is an opportunity I can't afford to pass up," Tog said. "It isn't every day I can smash a legion."

"Tog, we discussed that last night," Caratacus said. "You're to hit the center and destroy the supply wagons, not the entire legion."

"As king, I make the final decision, Brother, and I will kill every Roman maggot crossing our lands," the younger brother replied.

Caratacus jabbed a scarred forefinger in Tog's direction. "Aye, you're a king and a good one, but we must fight together as allies. Yes, butcher the Romans, but concentrate on destroying their supplies—that's your first priority—it will set the Romans back further than slaughtering the entire legion. You must understand that allows time for our forces to reassemble."

Tog's face turned florid. He growled through a mouth full of crooked teeth. "I hate running and so do my men."

"You're not." Caratacus shook his head. "If you engage them in a full-pitched battle, they will defeat you! You don't have enough men to destroy them head-on. There is nothing kingly about wasting good men."

Tog motioned to the warriors waiting a short distance from them. "We're not cowards!"

"You have never been a coward, my brave Brother-In-Law," Rhian said. Briefly, she placed a hand on his scarred forearm.

"Bravery has nothing to do with it," Caratacus said. "Right now we can do more damage by wearing them down and spreading their supply lines so thin they are forced to bring replacements from Gaul. By the time those arrive, we will be ready. Patience."

Tog crossed his brawny arms in front of his chain-mail-covered chest. For the span of ten heartbeats, he stared menacingly at Caratacus. He relaxed his arms and lowered them to his sides. He exhaled and looked toward his awaiting troops and back to Caratacus. "All right, Brother and Rhian. Farewell, pray to the gods that I return victorious."

The younger brother mounted his horse, turned away, and signaled the trumpets to sound the order for the march.

As the warriors departed, churning up the chalky dust in the early morning light, Rhian turned to Caratacus. "My band of women riders and I will pray for Tog's success."

"It wouldn't hurt, but I'm certain he will succeed."

She sniffed. "So long as he listens to your advice."

Caratacus tightened his lips and nodded.

* * *

Caratacus jabbed a finger in the direction of a clump of elms. "Not here you fool!" Caratacus ordered the young warrior driving his chariot. "Take the horses to the spring. This water is too salty, it'll kill them!" He stepped from the car, picked up a smooth, flat stone and skimmed it part way across the muddy River Medway. A whisper of a breeze blew through the bushes lining the water's edge.

"Clud!" he shouted.

"Aye, Great King?"

"Replace that idiot." He motioned to the young warrior driving his car away. "Anyone who would lead my horses to salt water has no business driving my chariot." He wiped the dust from his face then spat on the muddy embankment.

Clud raced off in the wake of the vehicle with a puzzled look on his face.

Caratacus shook his head. Not wanting to enter his stifling, hot headquarters tent, he sat on a small boulder protruding into the river, oblivious to its hard surface digging into his backside.

He had just returned from Durobrivae, the small fortress on the Medway's west bank. After holding a morning war council with his chieftains, where he relayed information on the Roman's weaknesses, his stomach was still in knots and his face hot. *War council, indeed! I spent most of the time settling disputes about who would lead which warriors when they next fought the Romans.*

Clud, who had been present, confided later what he thought of the meeting. "It was more like which fool would lead what fools upon Roman swords. They don't come close to the warriors of the old days."

"About some of them, you're probably right, but there was much face-saving at stake."

Caratacus's scar-faced friend looked about. He slapped one of his huge thighs with an equally big hand. "Aye, but it'll cost us a lot more lives when we face the Romans again. It could decide the fate of the kingdom."

Caratacus glanced across the river knowing the enemy was somewhere on the other side, no doubt making plans for a crossing. A servant approached, stepped upon the big rock, stooped down, and offered a huge, earthen bowl of beer. After dismissing the man, Caratacus drank the corma and reflected on how the chieftains, in some ways, reminded him of little children with petty jealousies and swelled heads. He complimented, persuaded, and bullied them when necessary, but determined to deploy his warriors where he saw fit.

Refusing to confront General Plautius until he recalled his scattered forces, Caratacus had dispatched companies of infantry and cavalry squadrons to destroy the slow-moving, Roman supply columns, in turn bogging down their advance. He received news that Plautius was slowly advancing, consolidating his gains as he did so. Upon landing in Britannia and occupying Durovernum, capitol of the Cantiacians, Plautius had placed Adminios back on the tribal throne, *no doubt with a Roman leash around his scrawny neck!*

Soon Caratacus's forces would outnumber the Romans nearly five to one. He was confident he would defeat them. He hadn't forgotten the losses in destroying the Tenth Cohort. As he waited for enough reinforcements to drive the Romans back into the sea, he planned to change his tactics.

Now he tossed the empty bowl to the servant, who waited nearby. Another approached to remove his dusty cloak and handed him a towel. As he wiped the grime from his body, Clud returned.

"I sacked the driver with a boot in the arse, Caratacus, and replaced him with a better man." Clud stepped upon the boulder and stooped down next to his long-time friend.

"You said that about the last one." The king's voice trailed off as he looked eastward across the river. He waved away a cloud of gnats swirling about his face. The sun was high, but he spied dark clouds gathering in the distance. White caps erupted on the Medway's sluggish waters, and a cold wind reeled its way across its broad surface. In the distance, outside Caratacus's command post, banners and streamers fluttered and snapped as the breeze gradually built to a stronger wind.

Clud peered toward the southeast, the direction Tog and his men had traveled earlier that morning. "You suppose Tog's men have hit the Romans yet?" Clud asked.

Caratacus nodded as he ignored the breeze that tossed strands of long, sandy hair about his face. "Soon, if he hasn't already. Surprise will be the key element."

His friend scratched an armpit. "He's destroyed Roman supply columns before."

"Aye, but this time he is going after the advance elements of the Second Legion, who are escorting another pack train." Caratacus tossed the towel to the ground and motioned to a nearby servant for two bowls of beer for Clud and himself.

"They must be desperate if they are using legionaries instead of their stinking Gallic auxiliaries as escort."

Both men held their silence when the young slave brought their drinks and moved out of earshot. Clud partially guzzled his.

Caratacus took a sip and continued, "That works to our advantage. They won't expect Tog and his men to attack by way of the marshland." Unlike the Romans, Caratacus and Tog knew the pathways through the choking, mosquito-infested area near the River Medway. The Romans were forced to stay to the area's major trackways if they weren't to lose their way. The plan was to hit the rear guard and then destroy the baggage train carrying vital supplies, positioned in the middle of the vanguard, before the advance units could turn about and counterattack.

"If Tog's warriors inflict enough losses in men and material, the Romans will have to wait for reinforcements from mainland Gaul," Clud said and finished his beer with a gulp and loud belch.

"Aye, that gives me more time to gather forces for a major confrontation with the Romans," Caratacus answered. "Now, old friend, I need time alone to think. Keep everyone away from me unless they have news about Tog."

Clud grinned through snaggled teeth. "I can do that."

* * *

As he brooded by the river bank, Caratacus yawned, barely keeping his eyelids open. He had slept little since the beginning of the invasion. He planned to make a stand against the invaders along the twisting Medway. The king decided against holding Durovernum, because the unfortified town rested on a flat plain in the valley of the River Stour. The Medway, twenty-five miles to the west, was far easier to defend. Only one narrow rickety bridge, which he planned to burn, crossed the river.

From information gathered by his spies, Caratacus learned the main objective of the Roman Army was the capture of Camulodunum. This meant crossing the meandering Medway and the wide, swift Tamesis further north. The large Roman naval presence in the estuary posed a threat not only to his left flank, but to supplies flowing into Camulodunum by sea.

Relinquishing Durovernum had been a soul-wrenching decision but a strategic necessity. Caratacus had met fierce opposition from the chieftains, but he refused to bend, and his will triumphed. *The fools would have needlessly wasted lives and met with certain defeat, leaving the road to Camulodunum wide open and certain destruction of the kingdom.*

Cartimandua, his cousin and sister-in-law, now reigned as queen of the Brigantes, ascending the throne upon the death of her father, King Dumnoveros. Dana, who was Cartimandua's older sister and Caratacus's second wife, along with Venutios, Cartimandua's husband, and Caratacus's friend, urged her to send troops to aid Caratacus. Much to Caratacus's anger, the politically astute and self-centered queen, along with the king of the Iceni, had refused after being paid handsome sums of gold by the Romans to remain neutral.

Before the Romans landed in Britannia, Dana had warned Caratacus about Cartimandua. "My sister serves only herself. She'll use any man to advance her interests. She has many lovers besides Venutios. He's a fool for staying with her. Don't trust her, my love, don't trust her!"

Caratacus knew Durotrigians, a tribe to the southwest, would fight the Romans, but only if their lands were threatened. In the meantime, their king refused to send an army to the Medway. *The three rulers are fools if they believe neutrality will stop the invading Romans.* Exhausted, Caratacus sat upon a boulder protruding from the river's bank and drew his knees up to his chest. He yawned so hard the muscles in his jaws ached and stared blankly toward distant black clouds.

* * *

"Caratacus ... High King, wake up!" Clud shook him from his slumber on the rock. "Please get out of the rain before you catch the fever," his friend pleaded. Spears of lightning flashed across the late-afternoon sky, followed seconds later by thunder and torrential summer rain, the first in more than a month. The chalky countryside had been reduced to a slimy quagmire within two hours of the first drops.

"Thanks be to Taranis for the rain." Caratacus rubbed his eyes as he looked about. He had slept so soundly, he hadn't felt the rain running down his body and soaking his clothing. "It'll bog down the Romans for a while."

Clud, also drenched, agreed. "Your brother should be returning soon," he added, a slight hint of concern in his voice.

"Anytime."

Caratacus stood, facing the twisting bank of the river, and glanced at the bonfire near the front of his headquarters tent. Several of his officers and shield bearers were gathered in a circle, warming themselves.

Clud motioned towards the men. "I ordered them to keep their distance while you sat here, my friend," Clud said.

Caratacus yawned again. "How long have I been asleep?"

"A couple of hours."

"You should have wakened me sooner." Caratacus shook his head.

Clud huffed. "Sire, you have slept little these last few days."

"I'll decide when to rest. I'll get little sleep so long as the Romans are here."

Big, soothing raindrops ran down Caratacus's tattooed, sunburnt back, and he was reluctant to cover himself lest the burning pain return. He risked catching pneumonia, but hated greasy ointments and stinging vinegar concoctions that Dana and the healing women had applied over the years. He considered water the best medicine. The slackening rain would soon end, as clouds broke apart in the distance. He refused to take any further rest until Tog's force returned with news of victory.

* * *

Caratacus retreated to his quarters to escape Clud's constant harping to guard his health. He sat in a high-backed chair near the center of the brightly lit, goat-skinned tent. The rain stopped and night fell, clear but moonless. A short time later, a messenger brought him news that survivors of Tog's army were straggling into camp.

"Do you have any further details? Is King Tog still alive?" Caratacus asked the haggard courier, his clothing muddy, but sweat running down his narrow face.

"All I know, my lord, is that a captain is on the way to your quarters with more information. He should be here soon."

Caratacus dismissed the warrior. *Tog defeated? Impossible! But if true, the wild boars were feasting.* He cursed to himself for not being with his brother and prayed he was still alive. Caratacus exhaled heavily, then admitted it was Tog's battle.

He called for one of his servants to fetch Havgan to headquarters tent.

While he waited for the Druid to arrive, a surviving captain, broad faced, covered in purple tattoos, and smeared with blood, entered and stood before Caratacus.

"We were badly beaten, High King," the captain said.

37

Caratacus's muscles tightened. "My brother, King Tog, what news of him?"

The captain hung his head. "Your brother is ... dead, High King."

No, not Tog! His throat tightened and stomach churned, ears filled with a roar as if by an avalanche. He clamped his mouth shut, forming a straight line, face expressionless. *As king I can't weep, especially in front of my chieftains.* He placed his elbows on his knees, hand clenched, the muscles on his forearms rippling like angry snakes.

"Did I hear right, King Tog is dead?" Havgan asked as he entered the room, staff in hand.

Caratacus gave him a terse nod and waved him to his side. "Just listen."

"Explain from the beginning," Caratacus ordered the captain.

The captain swallowed. "As planned, our warriors approached the Romans by way of the marshes and reached the forest ahead of the Second Legion. Lord Tog placed a line of archers to the front of the advanced troops and along the flanks. The archers fired volley after volley, totally surprising the Romans. At first, they scattered, but soon regrouped and formed battle lines. But they couldn't advance in close order, because the trees and bushes were too thick."

He explained how the Celtic infantry ran forward in open ranks and engaged the Romans. As they did, Tog's cavalry struck the supply wagons in the center of the vanguard, butchering troops and pack animals, setting fire to the wagons.

"But then the situation changed," the captain went on. "We heard trumpets, and quickly, another legion came running up the trackway, their cavalry in the lead. We were outnumbered two to one," he said. "The Romans battled us like demons."

"How many did we kill?" Caratacus asked.

The captain hesitated. "Maybe six to seven hundred at the most."

"How many did we lose?" Caratacus asked.

The warrior bowed his head. "More than four thousand."

Havgan gasped and clenched his yew wooden staff.

"Out of ten thousand. Gods," Caratacus hissed and shook his head.

The captain scanned the room and continued, "But Lord Tog refused to disengage as you ordered. He was determined to fight them to the last man."

The Druid frowned and shook his head.

"Fool!" Caratacus said.

"The Roman dogs formed a group of tight shields that looked like a tortoise shell. They circled shields around the side and top, bristling with spears and short swords." He jutted his arms upwards for effect. "They pushed right through our men. We couldn't penetrate them."

Caratacus glanced to Havgan and the captain. "I know the tactic." From his battle with the Tenth Cohort.

"Every time we'd try and prick the dogs, they'd gut our men. Mine got so angry, they threw themselves on the Roman swords and were slaughtered. I couldn't stop them."

"Then?" Caratacus sighed.

"Lord Tog rode right into their middle," the captain continued, "wielding his great sword. He slew many, but then he was wounded and fell from his horse. I heard someone shout, *Kill him! He's one of their chiefs!* And it was all over. One after another, the stinking Romans hurled javelins into his fallen body." The warrior paused as though reluctant to continue.

"Go on, don't stop," Caratacus ordered.

"Yes, lord. If that wasn't enough, they hacked his body to pieces with their swords. Even if we could have driven them away, there wasn't enough of King Tog left to bring home for burial."

Havgan banged his staff to the floor. "No!"

Caratacus sat straight, swallowed a scream, but caught himself digging his fingers into his palms.

"King Caratacus," Havgan said. "I must consult with King Tog's arch-Druid, and together we will sacrifice and beseech Andraste and Teutates to take your brother beneath the ground. Otherwise, his soul will wander forever. With your permission, I will leave now."

Caratacus barely nodded.

The king thanked the captain and dismissed everyone else.

Tog, his brother and friend, was gone. Caratacus wept. He damned Rome and swore he would avenge his brother and slaughter every legionarie that set foot upon his lands. *You will pay dearly for the deaths of my brother and all of my people!*

* * *

Later that evening when Rhian heard the news, she left her women riders and came to Caratacus's quarters to console him.

"I never dreamed that I would lose my brother, even in battle," Caratacus said.

Tears came to her eyes. "Nobody thinks they'll die," she said. "I never thought my father would die either."

"Aye, Donn was a good man and great warrior." Caratacus briefly recalled how Rhian's father had died from a stroke just before the confrontation with cowardly King Verica, who, instead of fighting, fled to Rome.

Caratacus returned his attention to Rhian.

Despite her own sorrow, Rhian gently stroked Caratacus's arm as they sat together on the bed-pallet in the corner of the tent. She rested her head against his muscular shoulder. "If we did believe we would die, then all of us would flee the battlefield before the fighting started."

"Tog died a warrior's death, but they didn't have to hack him to pieces like a piece of meat," Caratacus said.

"The Romans are barbarians, that's all. And they claim *we're* savages?"

"Where are the gods when you need them," Caratacus said in an exasperated voice. "Are they in league with the Romans? Now that Tog is dead, I'm even more determined to stop the Romans and drive them back to Gaul!"

* * *

Despite his grief, Caratacus did not despair. The following morning, he received news that the rest of his chieftains were rallying to his cause, and thousands of warriors were making way to his camp. By the end of the week, his army would be nearly as large as it was before the invasion. He would crush the Romans. Avenge his brother's death!

He carved the vow on his heart.

CHAPTER 4

Caratacus studied the goat-skin map as Clud, Fergus ap Roycal, and four clan chieftains surrounded him. The flaps of the command tent were up on all sides but gave little respite from the stifling afternoon heat, which sucked Caratacus's breath away. Sweat poured down his face and back. Hearing the sound of approaching horses, he looked beyond the tent opening and spotted Rhian a short distance away riding towards the command post with an escort of ten women riders. Dust kicked up by the horse caked Rhian's skin and those of her companions, no doubt choking their parched throats.

She slid off the big Cobb gelding and tossed the reins to a groom, who came running from in front of Caratacus's quarters. Rhian ordered Fiona, her second-in-command, and the rest of her women to dismount. She yelled at a servant to bring her riders water as she walked by the twelve warriors guarding the perimeter around the command. The women led their horses to the nearby shade trees.

"Gods curse this forsaken place!" Rhian swore while swatting another mosquito from her grimy face. She passed the two guards immediately outside the front entrance.

They eyed her, as did Caratacus and his commanders. Caratacus gestured to his leaders. "Leave me for now, my friends. I will speak to my wife alone."

They departed and nodded to Rhian as they walked by her. From past experience, Caratacus found it was best to speak to Rhian privately when she appeared to be upset.

"Bring my wife water at once," Caratacus ordered a servant.

The servant handed Rhian a full gourd. She gulped down the water. Handing the melon-shaped bowl back to the attendant, she stepped over to where Caratacus now sat and plopped down on a three-legged stool beside him. "I know you said this was the best place to fight the Romans, but the mosquitoes may eat us alive first." She sighed and wiped the dust from her face with a sweaty hand and rubbed it along the side of her knee-length kilt.

Caratacus followed her eyes as they moved from the fortified embankment to the ramparts and wooden palisade on the River Medway's north side. His warriors had built a defensive ditch halfway up the river's slope, where they believed the Romans would cross, and far along each side to where the area turned into marshland.

"I know this is a miserable place," he said, "but it is the best place to defend this ford."

Rhian huffed and nodded. "I know, I just wished it wasn't so hot." She straightened her tunic-skirt.

"So do I, but we will adjust, mosquitoes and all." His eyes twinkled and then turned serious. "Our discomforts are nothing if we don't throw the Romans back into the sea."

"Still, there is no guarantee the Romans will cross here," Rhian said and sighed.

Caratacus gestured toward the defenses. "True, but it is here they are most likely to cross."

"The Romans aren't stupid." Rhian shook her head. "Won't they be searching for shallow crossings up and down the river to attack us from behind?"

"My scouts are patrolling both sides and will send news if they discover the Romans sneaking around our back."

"Don't forget what happened to Tog." Her aqua eyes peered through his as if he wasn't there.

Caratacus's muscles tightened, his stomach knotted. He glared at Rhian. "How can I? The memory of his death haunts me in a way you can't imagine. Tog was my best friend. I'll never be free of the agony left in my heart, no matter how long I live."

Rhian blushed and pressed her bowed lips together. She reached over and touched his forearm. "I know, and I'm so sorry, my heart aches, too. But he lost his life because his scouts missed the Romans of the Second Legion—killed by their soldiers."

Rhian scanned the bivouac area next to the cattle pens and the main encampment then returned her gaze to Caratacus. "I understand why we must be here," she continued, "but there are times when I wished we were home. Six months is a long time to be away."

"How many times have I asked you to return home even if just for a little while? Dana would welcome your company. She's due to deliver our child in only a few weeks."

"I know, I should be with her. It's my own fault." Rhian's expression returned to her usual determined look. "But I won't leave the women or you."

I could order her to leave, but that would only worsen matters. He jabbed a finger toward her. "That's part of the problem, you need to return home. You are tired—no, exhausted. I can tell by just looking at your face—it's so drawn."

"Is it so obvious? I've seen the dark rings around my eyes. But the others mustn't know about my fatigue. That is between the two of us."

"How can you keep the truth from them? You're pale and need rest."

Rhian glared at him. "All right, I'm deceiving no one. And worse, I've treated everyone around me with a harshness they don't deserve. Including you, my love."

"Don't be so rough on yourself," he said, laying an arm across her shoulder, pulling her closer.

She gave him a halfhearted smile and fanned herself with her palm. "My gods, is that my stench?"

"Probably both of us." He laughed and withdrew his arm.

She twisted her lips into a frown. "Our losses to the Romans still torment me," Rhian confessed. "I know we're supposed to be strong and believe they're in paradise. Yet I feel numb, and I grieve. Maybe I shouldn't be the leader of the women riders. Maybe I shouldn't be a warrior."

He put a dirty finger to his mouth. "Rubbish! All the women look up to you."

"Still, we lost so many," Rhian wiped away a tear.

"That's not your fault, they fought like demons." He was tempted to say the Romans were far superior but didn't.

Rhian exhaled and, for a second, looked away. "You're right, I'll have to make do with those I have left."

A few weeks ago when the Romans first landed, they'd encountered the advanced cohort. Rhian's women had been deployed as cavalry skirmishers against their flanks. Nearly half of her five hundred riders were slaughtered, no match for Romans.

Caratacus motioned for the servant, who had been hovering in the shadows at the back of the tent, to refill Rhian's bowl.

After draining the cup, Rhian closed her eyes.

Opening her eyes, Rhian said, "I realize the battle coming with the Romans will be crucial—we must crush them! You lead the biggest army in the memory of Britannia. I know you will not be defeated." She placed her fingers on his chapped lips. "Then we can go home once and for all, and the Roman survivors will make excellent slaves." She pulled her hand away.

"Yes, they will."

"And when we return to Caleva, Dana will be waiting." Rhian paused and stared at Caratacus. "Sometimes, I wish I were as contented as she."

The king shook his head. "But that is not your way—I love you for who you are."

She smiled. "I could never be like my sister-wife. I love to weave, but the other household chores are so tedious. Leave them to Dana, I prefer being in the field with you even from the first sign of invasion."

Caratacus wouldn't deny that he missed Dana. He still remembered how beautiful she looked the morning the army left for the east coast. Although with child, she still wore the low cut, perhaps a little too low cut, earth-hued, silk dress he had given to her. Sometimes he wondered what Rhian thought of Dana. The battlefield was no place for a woman like Dana, who was better suited for domestic surroundings and the niceties of the court.

He thanked the gods that Rhian and she get along so well. If anything happened to Rhian, Dana would be with him. He believed Rhian liked Dana more than she was willing to admit. In any event, he needed Dana to stay in Caleva since she would soon deliver their baby. He prayed to the gods it would be born alive and healthy. When his armies defeated the Romans, he and Rhian would return home and finally bury their dead.

"You realize something must be done about camp security," Rhian said, pulling Caratacus from his thoughts. "With the exception of the fortifications facing the river, there is no order to this camp."

"I am aware of that, and it will be addressed."

"I hope so. Earlier today I rode through the camp—there must be sixty thousand in a haphazard sprawl along the north side of the Medway at the foot of Strood Hill."

"You don't need to describe it to me," Caratacus said, his voice full of annoyance, "I'm well aware of our position."

Nestled within the temporary base perimeter were hundreds of booths, thrown up along rough–hewn, dirt streets. Merchants sold food and drink at inflated prices and generally cheated and lied about the quality of their other wares. Bards, jugglers, prostitutes, and gamblers made the rounds, plying their trades, gathering many coins from the bored warriors. Every afternoon chariots raced on a small, dirt track at one end of the camp, the betting heavy. *No doubt the Romans have spies among this lot, learning whatever they can about the deployment of my warriors.*

"I am still concerned," Rhian said. "Adjacent to the forest, the camp is vulnerable from the rear. This carnival atmosphere may be customary in any big warrior encampment, but shouldn't you set out a picket of sentries to guard the area? The density of those woods won't stop the Romans should they strike from that direction—they'll find a way."

"We burnt the only bridge across the Medway," Caratacus said. "Besides the palisade and defensive ditch, I've set my warriors to planting the shallow river fords up and down the river from their camp with thousands of hardwood defensive stakes, visible only at low tide. They've scattered the muddy bottoms with three-pronged, iron caltrops to puncture the feet of enemy soldiers and cavalry horses alike should they cross. This will slow down if not halt the most determined Roman advance while our warriors hurl volleys of arrows and slingstones on the

46

fording troops." After Tog's death, Caratacus had wisely withdrawn his quarters from the river's edge to a rise with trenches and palisades thrown up around its mini-encampment.

"I pray the defensive measures will be enough," Rhian said.

"They will," Caratacus said. "I've posted warriors up and downstream to give advance warning."

"Will that be enough? I have heard the Romans are adept at river crossings, no matter the obstacles."

"They will need many hours to cross, allowing ample time for our warriors to counterattack."

"May you be right, Husband, but I believe we are in for a long fight."

CHAPTER 5

Porcius's heart pounded. He gulped one lungful of air after another, attempting to ignore the aching muscles of his flabby legs. He, his small entourage of clerks, and his freedman, Cyrus, trekked up the low-lying hill to General Plautius's headquarters tent. He wiped his sweaty, balding forehead with a silk handkerchief and then tucked it inside the bottom of his muscled cuirass. The summons by the general puzzled him. *Had this anything to do with the slow progress made by the army against Caratacus? If so, what does it have to do with me?*

Despite the destruction of several supply columns by Caratacus's troops, Porcius reflected, the Roman Army had made steady progress. Legions Ninth Hispana and Fourteenth Gemina had advanced along the road to Durovernum, while Legion Second Augusta moved along the southern flank and Legion Twentieth Valeria brought up the rear.

He recalled General Plautius's annoyance with his legion commanders, especially, Vespasian and Geta, who said the army's progress was too slow. He had ordered them to hold their tongues unless they wanted to explain to the emperor, in person, why they had been relieved of their commands.

Porcius stopped to catch his breath half way up the slope. *I'm getting too old and too fat to do this.* A few minutes later, he continued his journey.

After the death of Caratacus's brother, Tog, and the destruction of his forces, there had been no further opposition on the road to Durovernum. Porcius, who had accompanied the general, found the town deserted. However, the small hill fort was well suited as a staging point for future campaigning in the west and as a provincial capital. Plautius had brought along Caratacus's older brother, Adminios, to use his knowledge of the area and people to his advantage. *As provincial ruler, he will make an excellent lackey,* Porcius thought, *albeit a drunkard and dim-witted. Despite the tribal penalty of exile for treason, Adminios is still fortunate Caratacus hasn't killed him.*

The army's halt provided the opportunity for General Plautius to consolidate the legions' positions before moving on. He placed a reinforced cohort of one thousand legionaries on the high ground, beyond the River Stour, and established a fortified control point at Regulbium in the east and by occupation of Dubris in the west. The latter two posts would be the responsibility of the navy.

He had to give the general credit, Porcius thought, he knew how to lead an army.

Porcius waddled into the general's tent, wearing the military garb of an officer entitled him by rank. A too-short, triple-layered, white corselet trimmed in gold fringe covered the ill-fitting, red tunic, and a short, muscled cuirass, encircled by a white and gold sash knotted in front. Sweat poured profusely from beneath the gilded, red-plumed helmet. Many years had passed since Porcius had worn a uniform, but General Plautius insisted that he do so now if he were to remain with his entourage. *Had I more time, I would have had a new uniform made for myself. Curse the luck.*

Upon Porcius's entry, the general's clerk stood. "I will inform General Plautius that you are here, sir." He stepped to the commander's office a few paces away. Moments later, he returned. "He will see you shortly, sir."

"Indeed? He said he wanted me to report immediately."

"Begging your pardon, sir, that is what he said."

I'm sure he is going out of his way to annoy me. He took a seat on a three-legged stool.

Five minutes later, General Plautius's personal slave stepped out of his office and motioned to Porcius. "The general will see you now, sir."

Upon his entry, Porcius said, "I am not accustomed to being kept waiting."

Plautius looked up from where he sat behind his portable desk where a series of scrolls lay in a neat stack next to his wax tablet, stylus, and inkwell. "You just arrived, Senator, I didn't keep you waiting that long!" he snapped. "And even if you were, military affairs take priority over all matters, including political pomp. That is the way it'll be while I'm imperial governor."

Porcius scowled, his forehead creasing into three lines resembling tiny valleys. "You must realize I shall report such shabby treatment to the emperor when he arrives next month."

With the wave of a hand, Plautius dismissed his slave. "Senator, I know you send regular dispatches to the emperor. No doubt you've already reported my treatment as you call it."

Glancing about, Porcius searched the tent for anyone else's presence. Outside the pavilion's open sides lurked the general's guards, posted at a discreet distance. The sounds of camp activity seeped into the room. Centurions barked orders at troops. Braying mules pulling wagons rolled by, the sounds of crushing gravel under their wheels. The bleating of sacrificial goats kept in a nearby pen carried on the mild breeze.

"And you're not concerned?" Porcius asked.

"Why?" Plautius asked. "He knows how *you've* conducted yourself through *my* dispatches."

The general stared long and hard at Porcius as if peering through him. Despite the noonday heat, a chill shot down Porcius's back.

"Emperor Claudius has placed me in a position of grave responsibility," Plautius continued, "which is to *lead* the army in the conquest of Britannia."

Porcius pointed a finger toward the general. "The emperor will be displeased." He dropped his hand to his side.

Plautius gestured as if obvious. "He would be more displeased if I wasted time sopping the puffed vanity of every high-ranking courier."

"Courier!" Porcius protested, bile rising in his throat.

The commander snorted. "If I offend, dear Senator, please forgive me. If our beloved emperor agrees with you, then he can replace me, and place you in charge when he arrives. Until then, I will continue to run this campaign as I see fit, and you will not interfere, is that clear?"

"I—"

He waved away Porcius's protest. "Senator, or rather, Legate, by your military uniform, understand one thing clearly: if I fail, I forfeit my life. Even a legate can be sent home in disgrace."

Porcius wasn't in any position to argue. As military governor and general of the army, Plautius's word was law during the campaign. No one would ride easily over him.

"Very well, General, we will discuss this further when the emperor arrives," Porcius said, "But why did you summon me?"

"It's about that young centurion, Bassus. He may be of some use after all." The general motioned Porcius to a seat.

The senator sat across the desk from Plautius. "For once, we agree."

Porcius had received copies of reports that scouts from Legion Fourteenth Gemina had come upon the putrefying bodies of their comrades that evening after the ambush described by Bassus. As the young centurion had related, the troops found a pile of rotting, bloated corpses, still lying where Bassus had stood his ground. Nearly five hundred dead Romans carpeted an area of less than one acre.

"Grill him on Britannia and see what he really knows," General Plautius said, pulling Porcius from his thoughts.

"That's been done, and he seems very knowledgeable," Porcius answered. "He pointed out landmarks, which only one who had traveled the land, or a native would have known."

The general leaned forward. "Good. Test him to see if he could negotiate with the barbarians. What he doesn't know, teach him."

"Now, that's a challenge, given the fact he witnessed the slaughter of so many of his comrades." A wry grin formed on Porcius's bloated face. For a moment, he cupped his double-chin with a pudgy hand. "But I can overcome that. He's a tough soldier."

"Excellent. Meanwhile, he's to be assigned as senior centurion, Fourth Cohort, in Legion Twentieth Valeria. He's earned it." Both knew the lower the cohort number the better the troops.

"Since you're going to be his mentor, you can give him the good news," Plautius said.

Porcius grinned. "Of course, and I'll begin his education immediately."

"That must wait a few more days, we march tonight."

* * *

"King Caratacus, the revered Havgan is here," the tall guard said. "He says he must see you—it's "urgent".

Caratacus awakened from a deep sleep, his swollen eyes attempting to adjust to the flickering light coming from the lamp carried by the warrior. It was at least two hours before dawn. "It must be *urgent* to wake me this damn early." He motioned to the guard to place the lamp on the floor. "Tell him to wait in the headquarters area."

Caratacus rubbed his eyes and shook his head. Quickly, he rose from his bed pallet, dressed, and trudged out front to the section partitioned from the tent's sleeping cubicle. Havgan waited near the open front door flap that allowed in a feeble cool breeze, on what had been an otherwise muggy night. Purple-black circles surrounded his deep-set eyes, the thinning beard, covering the Druid's gaunt face, failed to conceal pale, sickly skin. The king motioned to one of two stools by a couple of smoky olive oil lamps set in metal tripods. "Sit down." He took a seat across from the Druid.

"The guard said you needed to see me, Havgan." Caratacus yawned.

The arch-Druid nodded and sat. "Forgive the intrusion, Lord Caratacus, I would not have awakened you if it were not so important."

Caratacus rubbed his eyes again. "I'm awake now. What is this urgent news?"

Havgan tightened his reed-thin lips and breathed loudly through his nostrils. "I had a vision last evening and then a terrible premonition came to me early this morning. It startled me so much that it pulled me out of a deep sleep."

Caratacus frowned and shook his head. "I, too, was in a deep sleep," he growled. "This better be good. It is because you are my arch-Druid that I will listen."

Havgan lifted both hands, palms outward, before he dropped them back into his lap. "Great King, if it had only been the vision, I would have waited until later this morning, but not the premonition that drove me out of my slumber. I promise you won't regret this."

"Get on with it," Caratacus said.

"First, I must tell of the premonition. It was very powerful, and I beg you will act quickly."

"As king, that is for me to decide."

Havgan glanced to the headquarters entrance and back to Caratacus. "In military affairs this is your right, but hear me out. The Roman Army is on the march even as I speak. Please, send your scouts to confirm this."

Caratacus snorted. "You want me to send out my men based on a feeling?"

"It is real, lord. Soon dawn will be upon us, we already know the Romans will move at anytime. It should not be much of an effort to send your men out now. Don't you remember I told you about my dream, of the Romans crossing the channel, on the day we spotted their invasion fleet from the cliffs?"

You could have made that up when we first spotted them. Caratacus decided not to mention his doubts. "All right, I'll send out the men."

Caratacus summoned one of his retainers. He ordered him to arouse the captain of scouts. "Tell him to send out his warriors immediately. See if the Romans are on the march. If so, how many and in what direction. There is no time to waste!"

When the guard departed he turned to Havgan. "Now, tell me this vision yours."

For the length of half a dozen heart beats, Havgan closed his eyes and took a deep breath. He opened his eyes and peered into Caratacus's as if he were not there. "If I have not been deceived by the gods ... if I have not been deceived, we shall be victorious when we fight the Romans."

"Is there any doubt?"

The Druid shrugged his narrow shoulders. "Life is full of doubts. Although I am confident we shall defeat the Romans, I needed a sign from the gods. Until yesterday, they had been silent, and so I decided to take a risk even at the cost of my life."

Caratacus shivered, quill bumps raised on his arms and down his back. He crossed his arms, hands gripping opposite elbows, and then released them. "Are you mad, as my arch-Druid, I can't afford to lose you."

Havgan raised his thin eyebrows. "If we are to survive as a free people, I believed it was necessary."

"What kind of madness did you commit?"

"I drank a potion containing mistletoe to help me commune with the gods."

Caratacus stomped his foot on the hard-packed, earthen floor. "By everything sacred, you could have died."

A smirk crossed his lips. "As you can see, I survived."

Caratacus gestured with his hand, his impatience growing. "All right, enough, what did you see?"

Havgan nodded. "It was yesterday afternoon when I led my entourage of lesser Druids and acolytes to the grove of beech trees by the little spring near our encampment." Havgan explained that he would have preferred the usual half circle of oaks, the sacred trees of the Druids, but the beeches served the purpose. "It was obvious that it had been used by the local peasants, and I noticed many little wooden statues of the harvest goddess and crude copper torcs dangling from branches that overlooked the spring," he said. "Although close to the great marsh, the water was clean and running free of mosquitoes.

"We built a fire in a shallow pit and a broth of mistletoe and heated water in a small iron cauldron."

Caratacus noticed that Havgan wore a pure-white, linen robe. Around his long, thin neck hung a heavy, gold chain, in the form of a triskele, symbol of his authority as arch-Druid. "The clothing you are wearing, was it the same as you wore during the ceremony?"

"Yes, lord," the Druid answered.

"Continue," Caratacus said with a nod.

"Once the water was heated, I knelt by the scorched cauldron and raised my eyes to the late afternoon sky, an orange-red light filtered through the heavy branches. The hot sun and leaf shadows danced like a mystery of cold and fire across my face. I lowered my head and gazed down into the dark simmering liquid, savored its rising heat, and inhaled its bitter fragrance. Several smoky pitch torches burned around the altar to ward off the vermin. Clouds of gnats and pests swirled drunkenly, no doubt having gorged earlier upon the Romans."

"No doubt," Caratacus said. "Go on."

"I dipped a forefinger into the cooking broth, and instantly withdrew it," he said. "I turned to my followers of lesser Druids and acolytes and proclaimed, 'The gods are pleased. Bring forth the cup.' I beckoned to my assistant Druid, Owen, and he poured the dark contents into a small golden chalice. He placed it into my hands. I stood and carried the cup to a little wooden altar beneath the branches of a tall beech tree. In the table's center rested a carved, wooden head of Andraste. On each side of the wooden idol sat a bleached human skull.

"As I knelt before the statue, my movements were followed by Owen, the junior Druids, and my solemn acolytes. I viewed the cup and felt the warmth emanating through its sides. Then I recited, 'Great Goddess of Victory, whose name I dare not mention, is there anything I should fear in drinking this potion to your glory?'

"'There is nothing to fear so long as the sky never falls and the sea burst not its bounds,' my followers answered in a ritual chant.

"I hesitated for another moment and prayed that I had mixed the right amount of mistletoe."

"Apparently you did, thank the gods," Caratacus said.

"Indeed. I gazed upon the statue and prayed out loud, 'Oh Great Goddess of Victory, I drink this mistletoe in your honor ... to your glory ... to your truth. Through it may you show me this great battle to come, that I may know the victor and the vanquished. And may I use this given knowledge wisely, that others may know your might ... and fear you.'"

Havgan said he took a sip from the goblet, the bitter-tasting liquid burned its way down his throat. He waited another moment for the potion to cool and then forced a long drink. After a few moments, his stomach churned, and the image of Andraste twisted, its full mouth stretching four different ways, its slanted eyes whirling in opposite directions while the statue's carved hair raised above its head. "I struggled to keep the contents of my stomach down and prayed. I am sorry to say my voice faltered.

"'Give ... me ... the vision ... Great Goddess,' I said. 'Which skull shall I choose? The Skull of Victory or Defeat?'"

The Druid explained the muscles in his shoulders and back knotted, his insides screamed of death. A sharp pain raked his stomach. Havgan dropped the goblet and collapsed. He thought he had made a fatal mistake and screamed within, in belief that he had mixed a lethal concoction. But the momentary panic passed as fast as it had appeared. His muscles loosened, and he controlled his nausea. He pulled himself up, waving off assistance and, turning slowly with shaking hands, grabbed the skull on the left.

"I heard a murmur of, 'victory!' from the priests," Havgan continued.

"But I shivered and drew the word, 'I seeee ... I see thousands fighting ... wolves and eagles of prey ... many ... many deaths. Standards and flags trampled. The wolves are in packs. They chase flying and swooping hunting eagles just out of grasp. But as the wolves attack, one flight of eagles and then another swoop in from the rear and slash heads and backs with talons sharp as swords. My eyes followed the turmoil of battle raging in the sky. My finger pointed upward, and I glared in stark marvel.

"'Look! Many eagles are caught and slain!' I shouted. 'Yet, ours is victory. For the Romans the bird is a noble symbol, but for us it is a killer from which we must defend ourselves with all our powers. We will crush the Romans!'"

Caratacus grinned and nodded. "And we shall."

"I fell silent," Havgan continued, "and saw wolves surrounding a giant fallen eagle, wearing golden armor. The wings were crushed, and it struggled to limp from the snarling jaws of the wolf pack.

"'A great Roman leader will be captured and sacrificed to the Great Goddess,' I said.'"

Caratacus raised his eyebrows. "Who, Plautius?"

"I could not tell, except it was a Roman general—it had to be! Again, I grew dizzy, and the images faded. Just before I lost consciousness, I remember saying, 'Praise to you, Great Andraste, Goddess of Victory.' Darkness crossed her eyes, and I feinted."

"How long were you unconscious?" Caratacus asked.

"I slept like a dead man until the premonition jolted me awake early this morning. I was blinded for the length of a few heartbeats as my eyes adjusted to the dim light of an oil lamp next to my bed-pallet. I was alone, my head throbbing as it always did after drinking mistletoe, and my tongue tasted like the plague. I called for a servant to bring water. A dark figure silently entered and knelt, reverently offering an earthen cup of water. Owen.

"Greedily, I drained its contents. Owen asked me how I felt."

"When I finished drinking, I said, 'I must tell the king of my vision last night and the premonition that awoke me. I will go alone. I have a terrible feeling the Romans were on the march.'"

Clud stormed into the room. "King Caratacus. The Romans. They're here!"

"Impossible! They weren't expected for at least another day."

"My scouts came flying across the river with the news," Clud said. "No telling how many, but we knew yesterday that at least two, maybe three legions and the same number of auxiliaries were moving this way. No reason to believe any different now."

Caratacus turned to Havgan. "Your premonition was right."

"I regret that I wasn't wrong. I will leave you now to attend matters of war." He departed.

"Have you heard from the other scouts searching up and down the river?" he asked Clud.

"Not yet."

"Send out more," Caratacus commanded.

Clud glanced toward the entrance. "They're already on their way."

"Good man. But if the Romans are advancing that quickly, they'll be soon crossing the river in front of us.

We'll have a big surprise waiting for them." He grinned, thinking about the defenses.

"The Romans could cross somewhere else."

"We haven't heard from the outlying scouts. That's why you're sending out more. When you've finished that, go roust the chieftains and captains, I want them here immediately!"

Within fifteen minutes Caratacus's leaders, including Fergus ap Roycal, had assembled outside headquarters by a large, flaming bonfire. He issued orders. "The main army stays in place until we have more information on the Roman movements. I'm certain they will cross here on the river plain." He ordered one captain to take the chariots and half of the cavalry eastward and work their way to the river's mouth. "They may cross there with the help of their navy. I want you," he said, nodding to a Trinovantian chieftain, "to take half of the remaining cavalry upstream. In either situation, if you make contact, you are to halt the Romans at all costs and send for reinforcements."

He gave further instructions to the rest of his men. When finished, Fergus ap Roycal asked that since the defenses had been built along the river, why he was taking such precautions? Caratacus explained not all the legions had been accounted for. "They're the ones I'm concerned about. If one legion breaks through, the rest will follow. That's why I plan to keep part of our forces in reserve," Caratacus said. "The Romans expect us to throw our entire army at them in one single thrust. They are in for a surprise."

Fergus and the rest of his men grinned and voiced agreement.

Dawn crept upon the stirring camp as the leaders left Caratacus's tent. He strode outside a short distance behind them. As he scanned the moonlit area, his eyes focused on the barren ridge of the hill to the west. He spotted the dark silhouette of a huge wolf howling and peering eastward across the river toward the invisible Roman camp.

Where was its mate? Caratacus wondered. *Judging by its size, it has to be the pack leader.* "We've invaded your territory," he said to himself. "We've displaced you as the Romans have displaced us, brave one. Is that why you look to the east? We have a common bond you and me, the return of what belongs to us."

A thought flashed through his mind. *Of course, that's it!*

Caratacus caught up to his chieftains. "There you have it, my lords!" Caratacus bellowed, pointing to the hill. "An omen! The lone wolf. Don't you see? He's pointing the way to the Romans, to destroy them."

A long, high-pitched howl echoed across the hill. Moments later, the animal was gone.

CHAPTER 6

Twilight chased the stars westward over the purple horizon as Caratacus boarded his chariot. The little horses nickered as the driver, a young warrior recommended by Havgan, tightened the reins before they could prematurely move away. The heavenly bodies were like the Romans, advancing as surely as the tide, a tide he must stop for his people, or die trying. He had worked too hard in uniting the southern tribes. Now he had a duty to unite all the peoples of Britannia and crush the invaders.

Caratacus expected a sticky heat to rise soon from the marsh. He threw aside his mantle and nodded to the driver. With a flick of the guidelines, the ponies jolted forward. Accompanied by Clud and Fergus ap Roycal, he set out to inspect the tribal armies. A retinue of warriors and shield bearers flanked both sides of Caratacus in chariots that kicked up clouds of dust.

Earlier that morning, the king's combined tribal forces of thousands of warriors had scrambled to take up defensive positions on top of the palisade wall built above and along the bank of the River Medway. *A Roman attack is inevitable.* Caratacus puzzled over whether this would be the place of the real assault or a feint? He gripped the hilt of his sword and spread his legs to keep his balance in the jolting car, wheels thudding over the rut-filled path. As his entourage approached the Medway, he shaded his eyes from the glaring sun and viewed the chalky, high ground across the river. The Romans would not throw pontoons across the river at this point, Caratacus thought, the tidal movements were too fast and extreme, going from a shallow ford to three times the height of a man in a couple hours. They might attempt to ford the river when it was low, but their timing had to be perfect and would be slowed by the deadly spikes embedded in the floor along with three-pronged caltrops. Being out in the open would leave the Romans vulnerable to a murderous assault by his warriors' arrows and slingstones from the stockade.

"Do you see them?" Clud asked, pulling Caratacus out of his thoughts as he rode alongside him.

"It must be their whole army," Caratacus answered.

Caratacus exhaled and prayed it wasn't so. He didn't believe the entire invasion force of forty thousand Roman troops had mustered across the river opposite them. Despite the reports from dozens of scouts, his warriors had probably missed a number of vexillations deployed by the legions. *They could be anyplace.* Although impossible to cover the entire river length, he had deliberately left one shallow ford unguarded. *No doubt the Romans will discover it and cross, believing they have out-maneuvered my forces.*

The king surveyed the teeming Roman camp. Even at two hundred yards, he heard the barking orders by Roman centurions.

While the high king watched, his warriors left their posts, poured out of the garrison, and gathered along the river's edge. Before long, thousands wearing an array of tartans, striped tunics, and breeches, or homespun clothing crowded the river bank, gaping at the size of the opposing army. Sunlight glinted from armor and shields. One vast, human quilt of scarlet, gold, blue, and green snaked along the shoreline for half a mile, scanning the enemy's activities. They hooted and jeered at the Romans across the way.

Caratacus could have easily ordered them back behind the barricades but decided to let the Romans believe all his warriors were here.

"All we have to do is wait for them to cross," Clud said.

"*If* they cross," Caratacus replied. He summoned and dispatched a messenger with an order to recall his chariot companies from upstream.

Fergus ap Roycal stood in a chariot to the other side of Caratacus. "Is that wise? You're not going to bring all your forces to this location?"

Caratacus motioned towards the river. "Over there are at least twenty thousand Romans. They aren't stupid. I'm certain they didn't concentrate all their forces here." He gestured towards the Romans. "This could be a diversion." He turned about in the car, facing in the opposite direction. "I suspect they'll attack us from behind. We'll keep enough warriors here to draw the Romans' attention. I will send the chariots and a force of infantry to counter any strike at our back."

Sweat poured from Fergus's craggy face as he motioned wildly with his hand. "But we number over sixty thousand —no one can stop us. Your brother's death has stiffened the resolve of our men to fight."

"They'll keep enough troops here believing they can pin us down, while their main assault comes from our rear," Caratacus said. "I've kept the reserves in the forest behind the fortress. They're in position to reinforce the men here, or, if need be, I can send them to fight the Romans to our rear."

"Are you going to recall the other cavalry forces downstream?" Clud asked.

"No, the Roman Navy could land troops there, probably the Ninth Legion. My spies have learned that General Plautius used them in several such landings on the Danubus River at the far end of their empire."

Clud nodded. "At least the cavalry left before dawn."

"Still, it will take hours to move several thousands of our men," Fergus said.

"The Romans have the same problem," Caratacus said.

Moments before leaving the river's edge, a courier reined in his horse before Caratacus's escorting shield bearers. The captain of the escort approached the king on foot with the bare-chested rider, his lathered pony in tow.

"High King, this man has urgent news."

"Speak up," Caratacus ordered. "What is it?"

"The Romans have crossed the river in force downstream, High King," the dusty messenger said.

Clud and Fergus glanced toward one another but remained silent.

"Where?" Caratacus demanded. "At the open ford?"

The spiked-hair rider shook his head. "No, sire, by the great bend near the river mouth."

Caratacus's lips tightened over clenched teeth. "Impossible! Too deep!"

Fergus motioned toward the Medway. "Since when do Romans ride in rivers?"

"Aye, never heard of such a thing," Clud added.

"They're German cavalry, Batavian bastards," the courier said. "They swam across in full gear, somewhere near three-four thousand of them."

"Why didn't our men repel them? We sent cavalry and chariots to the north early this morning," Caratacus demanded, his face flushed.

The messenger gulped and bowed his head. "They tried, High King, but they ... they were wiped out."

Rage stormed through Caratacus's body, his every muscle tightened. He restrained himself from grabbing the rider by the throat. *This isn't the man's fault.* He hissed. "No one wipes out four thousand of my best horsemen!"

"They slaughtered the horses first and then butchered our men escaping on foot. Then, for some reason, they turned inland," the young warrior said.

"Clud," Caratacus said in a calmer tone, "send all our remaining cavalry, including Lady Rhian's company, and ten thousand Catuvellaunian and Trinovantian infantry. Pursue those shit-eaters. No one slaughters our horses and lives!"

The messenger pulled back as if afraid to speak. His mouth quivered. "High King, they're not headed this way, they're riding north towards the Tamesis bridge."

Clud looked northward. "They've reached the bridge by now. Should we send so many reinforcements?" For a split second he paused and huffed. "We've already burnt the bridge, it won't matter. Even if the cavalry can probably be there in an hour or two, it will take at least twice as long to mobilize and march that many infantry to the location."

Caratacus shook his head. "I'm concerned about the mud flats. We must keep them open in case we have to retreat." *My warriors must have an escape route if, gods forbid, that came to pass.*

Caratacus was familiar with the area. Colonized by thick vegetation, the exposed flats created a natural bridge. Its floor was a silting valley laced with stream channels and rivulets flowing between densely thicketed river shrub, negotiable in summer only by those who knew the tides, shallow places, and pathways through the undergrowth. "We can cross only at low tide," Caratacus continued, "that's why we must keep the area clear of Romans."

He had just dismissed the first messenger when another arrived with news that General Vespasian and Legion Second Augusta were approaching from the west, marching at double-time.

"So, that's it, very clever indeed," Caratacus said evenly.

He turned to Clud and then to Fergus. "The Romans plan to hem us in. They already occupy the south side of the River Medway in order to hold down our troops. Their accursed Navy blockades the channel to the east. The Germans are cutting the northern route. Now Vespasian moves from the west. He must have found the shallow ford upstream and circled about."

"Just as you suspected they would," Clud said.

"How many troops?" Caratacus asked the new courier.

"About ten-thousand, including their Gallic and Spanish auxiliaries," the rider answered.

"Which direction are they heading?"

"Toward the North Downs, sire."

Caratacus dismissed the courier. He turned to Clud and Fergus as he shook his head. "I underestimated the Romans' strength."

"We've killed thousands and destroyed a dozen supply trains," Fergus said.

"Not enough to halt their flow of reinforcements from Gaul. How else could they have deployed as they have? The blame is all mine." Caratacus frowned, wiping sweat from his forehead with the back of his hand.

"Don't be too hard on yourself, High King," Clud said.

"I'm responsible." Caratacus gripped the hilt of his sword. "Thank the gods the Romans crossed at the ford I deliberately left vulnerable." As was customary before battle, he took a javelin out of a socket within the chariot and staked the weapon to the chalky ground. "We'll crush them on the plains!"

* * *

West of the marshland, not more than two miles from Caratacus's encampment, a stretch of flatland lay at the foot of the North Downs. He expected Vespasian's attack to come from that direction and was in place, ready for the Romans. He left a contingent of over thirty thousand warriors along the Medway. With him were a like number, whom he rushed to the area, more than enough to overwhelm a legion of five thousand and its auxiliaries. His warriors reached it by early afternoon. The mobilizing of so many men took longer than he expected; even though they didn't have supply wagons to slow them down, they still had to carry water and enough spare weapons to see the fight to the finish.

As he stood in his chariot on a low-lying hill overlooking the plain, Caratacus received news from returning scouts that the Romans were marching up the trackway to the North Downs.

"We attacked them from both sides of the road where the hills slope down. We struck hard and then fled back into the woods," the scar-faced scout said, panting for breath.

"How many did you kill?" Caratacus inquired. He glanced to Clud and Fergus.

"At least a couple hundred."

Caratacus sucked in his breath. "Not many but enough to hurt them. How many did we lose?" Caratacus asked.

"Maybe five or six," the warrior answered.

"Even better. Where are the men now?" Caratacus asked.

"On their way back," the rider replied. "They'll be here soon, but so will the Romans."

From his chariot alongside Caratacus, Clud said, "We've dug defensive ditches along the bottom of the slope leading up to our positions and more across the plain, that'll bog down the Romans."

"Aye, make the fucking Romans come to us," Fergus added, his car next to them.

"They will," Caratacus said. He motioned the courier to leave.

Fergus narrowed his eyes. "This better work, sire, otherwise the men will have wasted a lot of time and effort in building the defenses."

"We have the high ground," Caratacus said, "and the Romans have to clear or bridge the ditches before they can cross. Our sling and bowmen will make them pay for their efforts. By the time they cross, they'll have suffered heavy losses, and our warriors can finish them off."

Clud snorted and shook his head. "I still think our efforts would've been better spent defending the river crossings where they are a lot more vulnerable. It's a fair distance across. Even if the men didn't kill 'em, a sudden swift tide coming in would have drowned 'em."

"Our warriors will destroy them soon enough," Caratacus said. "My fifty thousand will overwhelm them."

CHAPTER 7

On a rise above the plain, Caratacus stood before the host in his chariot surrounded by shield bearers. Clud and Fergus accompanied him in adjoining chariots. Behind them followed Havgan, Caratacus's arch-Druid, in his own car. Unconsciously, Caratacus wiped his sweaty hands along the side of his plaid breeches. Warriors crowded together in one boiling mass of noise, shields, and swords and swarmed around them to hear their words. Thousands gathered into loosely formed companies, their multicolored banners streaming and new trophies, human heads, sticking from the end of bloodied pikes and from the sides of chariots. The sight of these brave warriors made Caratacus proud to be their king.

Earlier, he had designated a captain from each clan or company to pass back the words of his speech and that of the Druid to the groups behind them until it reached to the last clan, so all could hear. He raised his hands, and a hush swept through the host. Caratacus motioned for Havgan to come forward.

The priest stopped in front of Caratacus, who gave him a slight bow. Stepping from the chariot, Havgan carried a ceremonial sword in a white, doe-skin-leather sheath strapped to his waist. Dressed in a long, white robe girdled with a copper belt and draped with sashes of the finest linen, he walked barefooted before the host. Pulling the weapon from his scabbard, Havgan raised it above his head.

"Mighty warriors of Britannia," he shouted, "I foresee a great victory against the Roman invaders. For those who live, there will be many heads as trophies. But fear not those of you who fall. Paradise is assured to you as heroes in the world to come. In generations to follow, your souls shall return in earthly form to live as warriors once again."

67

The commanders repeated the words to the groups behind them. Seconds later, an uproarious cry of approval met his words.

"That is not all," Havgan continued.

The army fell silent.

"I see a great Roman leader wearing golden armor, like the golden eagle, the symbol of Rome. He, too, is a bird of prey, as is Rome, the same Rome that would crush you. This will not happen. I foresee he will be captured and sacrificed to the great Andraste, goddess of victory. Praise to you, great Andraste!"

The warriors roared their approval and pounded swords against shields, the noise echoed across the plain.

Havgan raised his hands for silence and closed with a prayer before quietly returning to his chariot. Customarily, a Druid priest walked ahead of the army and symbolically led them into battle. Being a Druid, neither side would dare harm him. Caratacus had refused Havgan's request when he earlier tried imposing this right as chief priest, knowing the Romans hated the Druids and would slaughter him.

Caratacus drove forward and slowly scanned the gathering mass. Havgan's prediction of victory pleased him. It would strengthen the men's resolve to fight.

"Out there," he cried, pointing to the west in the direction the Romans were expected to appear, "are twenty thousand Roman heads for your taking!"

As they did for the Druid, the commanders passed back the words of Caratacus to the rear ranks.

"Their heads will give you spiritual power, the likes of which none of your ancestors has known," Caratacus said, "and bravery, which only the gods have seen. Bravery and power that ballads will be sung about and women will part their legs for!"

He paused a moment for effect. "But you can have this power only if you stop the Roman devils. If you fail, they will rape our women and overrun our lands for a thousand years. Is that what you want?"

Again, his words went through the ranks.

"No!" they roared, again thrusting swords and javelins upwards.

"If you fail to crush the Romans, they will enslave our people, put our sons in foreign armies, and burn our villages. Is that what you want?"

"No! Kill the Roman dogs! Kill! Kill! Kill!"

The frenzied response pleased Caratacus. He gestured for silence, and gradually, the roar of voices faded away. "No man," he called out, "no warrior will tolerate Roman dogs on our lands. It's not enough to kill Romans. They must be purged from our kingdom forever!"

In the distance came the loud chinking sound of metal on metal, a methodical cadence growing louder with every passing moment. There was no other sound like it in the world, and Caratacus knew its origin. "Chieftains! Captains! Warriors!" he barked. "Form your companies!"

He saw the approaching Roman Army, their articulated, armored vests and iron helmets glinting in the sunlight. The long, pulsating formation weaved like a giant centipede, snaking out of the forest, then forming into tightly disciplined ranks in line across the field. They formed into eight cohorts of approximately 450-480 men each and a double cohort of more than 900 men, which guarded their commanding general at the back. Four of the cohorts separated and moved forward from the rest, marching in ranks six deep—six centuries, eighty men each. The troops halted, and at a signal from a trumpet, the three rear lines stood fast, acting as relief units while the first three ranks moved out in the direction of Caratacus's warriors. Three other cohorts marched to the rear of the first four, covering the gaps left between the formations of the front cohorts. The double cohort and the other unit held back in reserve.

The Romans stood in an opening, surrounded on three sides by trees and underbrush covering the low-lying hills of the North Downs. A thick forest provided protection for their rear. The Britons milled about in the open, eager for the taste of blood. The size of the Roman forces was smaller than Caratacus had been led to believe, perhaps ten thousand. His warriors outnumbered them four to one. He realized what the Romans were doing and was determined to wait them out.

Caratacus's warriors jumped, banged swords against their shields, taunted, and cursed the legionaries. The Romans stayed absolutely quiet. To his men, the Romans' protective formations of interlocking shields, bristling with javelins, was for cowards. They were warriors. Yet, the Romans remained silent and unmoving.

"Why don't our cries terrify the Romans?" Clud shouted to Caratacus above the frenzied din.

"They aren't like our other enemies. They're demons!" Fergus said.

Caratacus sent messengers to all his chieftains and captains ordering his men to stand fast. For a while they did. But his warriors grew impatient. Dozens moved forward and then pulled back on orders by their captains. And still the Romans remained silent. How strange that this quiet resolve was more unsettling than if they bellowed and cursed back.

Trumpets sounded from behind the Roman ranks.

"Look!" Clud shouted, "they're moving out!"

The legionaries began a slow methodical march in tight formations, javelins jutting out like arrow points all along the front line. Scarlet rectangular shields, fronts painted with golden thunderbolts, formed nearly an impenetrable wall. Syrian archers and Belaeric sling men waited in formations to their rear. Behind the sling men stood the looser-knit formations of blue-tunic-clad, chain-mailed, Gallic and Spanish auxiliary infantry. On the wings appeared the *Alae*, Spanish and Thracian cavalry, their dragon-headed standards and streamers at the front held by the lead riders.

As the legionaries moved forward, they stumbled upon the covered ditches. Screams erupted as dozens of Romans fell to their deaths, impaled on pointed, hardwood stakes. The Romans halted immediately, reorganizing their ranks.

Caratacus gave the signal. Out of the woods on both sides of the plain sprang hundreds of bow and sling men, who sent a volley of murderous arrows and stones showering down upon the hapless Romans. Dozens more legionaries went down before the centurions ordered their columns to form the turtle formations of shields raised above the men's heads and around their sides.

The Romans retaliated. Hundreds of chain-mailed, allied Sarmatian archers returned fire, downing an equal number of Celts and kept up the barrage of arrows being steadily supplied from the rear.

Within a quarter of an hour, the Celtic bowmen who had survived ran out of arrows and hastily retreated to the woods while the Sarmatians continued their onslaught.

The king watched as Roman engineers, protected by the infantry, holding shields to the front and above their heads, moved forward with dozens of wooden planks and spanned the ditches.

Despite the murderous fire of arrows and slingstones, the legionaries crossed the deadly ditches. The initial trickle of soldiers turned into an unstoppable tide of legionaries and auxiliaries, who quickly reformed into close ranks once across and halted.

Appalled, Caratacus could not believe his eyes. His archers and sling men had killed dozens of Romans during the crossing, but on they came—their numbers still many.

Cries for Roman blood rumbled through the ranks.

Then it happened.

Warriors broke ranks despite threats and thrashings from company captains. First a dribble, then a stream, finally a torrent of thousands poured towards the Roman ranks. They streamed down onto the plain. The Romans closed shields together with a thunderous bang and a single guttural roar, raised javelins, and waited.

As Caratacus watched, a surge of excitement rushed through his body. "Nothing can stop our men—nothing!"

When the Britons were within fifty paces of the Romans, Sarmatian archers, who had regrouped, unleashed from behind the legionaries a shower of arrows swarming up and slamming down into the warrior host. Hundreds of Britons fell dying to the white, chalky ground, blood-spattered, writhing, their screams lost in the frenzy. Undeterred, thousands more plunged forward, trampling the wounded, wading into an ever-growing, tightening mass. Then in unison, the Romans' first three ranks hurled hundreds of javelins; nearly all finding victims, followed by a volley of a thousand leadened stones from the sling men. The first three lines of Romans opened their ranks to let the rear three through to the front as they stepped back. They released another volley of javelins that found living targets, and hundreds more screaming warriors fell.

A loud hiss echoed down the Roman line as they in unison drew their *gladius* short swords from their scabbards. The legionaries held them to the side, jutting through narrow openings between their shields, pointing outward, waiting patiently for the onrushing Celts.

And onward the battle-maddened British rushed, hurling themselves against the shield wall of legionaries with a thud that echoed across the field. For a moment, the wall wavered, but the iron-disciplined Romans instantly recovered, holding fast. Behind a swath of jutting short swords and boss-smashing shields, the Romans proceeded to ply their deadly trade. Smash, jab, parry, and thrust as wave upon innumerable wave of raging barbarians threw themselves upon the Roman ranks and were slaughtered. The place was a littered nightmare of disemboweled and beheaded corpses, mixed with the odors of salty blood and the sickening smell of feces and urine. The agonizing screams of the maimed—armless and legless wounded— resounded the length of the crimson, mud-laden field.

"Are the Romans possessed?" Clud shouted over the chaos as he and Caratacus watched from a rise above the warriors. "Why aren't they falling? Why aren't they crumbling before us?"

"Our warriors had no room to maneuver—we are hemmed in by the defensive ditches. Why do you think I ordered the army to stand fast?" Caratacus answered. "There is no way our men can outflank them. Even if I slay half my warriors now, they wouldn't stop!"

Caratacus controlled his own increasing urge to join in the foray. He wanted to slaughter the Romans as much as his warriors, to drive those devils across the channel all by himself! As his excitement grew, he gripped the semicircular sides of the chariot, restraining himself.

"I must be down there with my warriors, I can't stay here. They have to know that I'm with them, and this fight is as much mine as theirs. Advance!" His chariot lurched ahead, followed by Clud and Fergus, as he rode back and forth behind his warriors in the choking dust kicked up by the commotion of battle. He shouted encouragement and searched for weaknesses in the Roman lines, but found few.

The legionaries slowly pressed inexorably forward through dirt, muddied by pools of blood. The auxiliary infantry, which had been kept in reserve, double-timed from the rear on both flanks, hacking and slashing with longswords and smashing their way into the exhausted Britons, who slowly withdrew, their fury spent.

"Why won't the Romans' center charge?" Fergus shouted. "They have the momentum."

"They're containing our men," Caratacus yelled back over the noise. "They know we still outnumber them. They fear being surrounded."

"But how long can they last?" Clud asked.

"I don't know," Caratacus answered. "They've lost many, but they keep fighting as if it were nothing. Thousands of ours died hurling themselves at the Romans, and although there are sporadic breaks in the ranks, the Roman lines are almost as tight as before the battle."

Caratacus gripped the hilt of his sword. "Break them!"

CHAPTER 8

From their mounts on a low hill above the field of carnage, Porcius, General Vespasian, and his second-in-command, Senior Tribune Marcus Severus, watched the troops of the Second Legion stonewall the Britons' mindless onslaught. Before the legionaries, bloody piles of bodies littered the ground, the odor of feces and urine, the coppery smell of blood, and screams of the maimed and dying drifted on the hot breeze. Undeterred, the warriors climbed over their dead comrades and kept slamming into the Roman columns of shields and thrusting short swords.

Porcius wondered how much longer the legion could plug their defenses without Caratacus's warriors breaking through. Despite the deployment of Legion Twentieth Valeria, which had been hiding in the forest and now supported the Second Legion, there were still too many gaps between cohorts and centuries. *Surely, the Britons will take advantage of the situation.*

A ring of Praetorian Guardsmen formed a protective circle around Vespasian's entourage, which included his staff of junior tribunes, couriers, clerical support staff, and the officers' personal attendants. To their rear a small tent had been temporarily set up, with pennants and streamers on long poles planted in the ground, announcing it was the Second Legion's headquarters.

The day before, Porcius had been ordered by General Plautius to report to General Vespasian, commander of the Second Augustan Legion. Since Caratacus was expected to engage his forces, Vespasian needed Porcius to identify the leader of the Britons. He realized Porcius was the only Roman who could accurately identify Caratacus.

General Plautius neither trusted Adminios, Caratacus's exiled brother, nor King Verica to point him out. Besides, the general could not chance either would be killed in battle, as he needed to use both as puppet rulers once the Romans conquered the British lands.

Porcius had been reluctant to report to General Vespasian because of his harrowing experience at the Battle of Bagshot Heath years before. Despite everything that had occurred since that time, he hoped that Caratacus would survive this war. Porcius had been saved by the king. After all, he had pointed out the Celtic ruler as soon as the battle started.

Tribune Severus turned toward the battlefield. "Look!"

As if reading Porcius's thoughts, clusters of British warriors spotted openings in the Roman ranks. Like a flooding stream, they rushed around the legionaries. Porcius watched the Fourth Cohort, commanded by Centurion Bassus and the Eighth just below him at the foot of the hill where they were held in reserve.

Porcius realized the two cohorts wouldn't remain out of the battle for long. The legions were taking a beating; their lines fragmenting and falling apart. Where was their discipline?

A trumpet sounded, jolting him from his thoughts. The Fourth and Eighth Cohorts moved forward to plug gaps in the line. The legions desperately regrouped.

A courier riding a lathered horse pulled up before General Vespasian and saluted. "Sir, the two middle cohorts of the Second Legion have lost over three hundred legionaries, and more are being hacked apart."

"I can see that even from here," the general snapped. His large, peasant eyes narrowed, and he appeared to be studying the situation.

"I see a weakness," Vespasian said a few seconds later. He turned to Tribune Severus and then Porcius. "Once they get through the gaps, the Britons scatter or cluster in little groups as they fight. We can isolate them." He turned to a trumpeter who sat on a nearby mount. "Sound the command for the Fourth and Eighth Cohort to move forward—they know what to do."

The trumpeter, using a straight-belled *tubicen,* blared a signal. Bassus and the centuries of the Fourth Cohort formed a line eighty across the front and six ranks deep. To the clanking of shields and rattling of swords and armor, the soldiers of the Eighth Cohort followed suit. Another signal and the legionaries gave a resounding battle cry and surged ahead at double-time.

The Fourth Cohort rushed forward to fill a huge break in the legion's center as the Eighth headed towards the right flank, where the Britons poured between the exposed areas left open by the Romans. The rear centuries of the Second Legion's Ninth and Tenth Cohorts struggled to close ranks.

Bassus's unit was less than twenty-five paces away, and Porcius knew that was close enough for the young centurion to see the enemy's screaming faces and fury in their eyes. Again, the trumpet sounded, and the cohort suddenly halted. As one, the first two ranks raised and hurled the first of the two javelins each man carried.

Wide-eyed and in apparent shock, hundreds of Britons fell screaming to the chalky ground. Others stopped to remove the collapsing spear shafts from wicker shields. As they struggled with the embedded weapons, they were struck by another clattering volley that killed and wounded hundreds more. Again, blades hissed as the legionaries drew their swords in unison from their scabbards.

Undeterred, the yelling, cursing barbarians rushed onward, jumping over dead comrades, slamming into the line of Bassus's cohort, but his men held, and the carnage began anew—metal clashing upon metal, striking bones and flesh. The cries of the wounded and dying resounded across the battlefield, as if all the dead had returned from the bowels of Hades searching for more victims to join them.

Knowing the Britons as he did, Porcius was not surprised by their fanatical onslaught.

Despite the deafening noise of battle that sliced through the fighting chaos like a thunderbolt from Jupiter, Porcius spotted Bassus in the roiling mass of slaughter and carnage. The young centurion's shield and armor were drenched with blood as he sliced heads and hacked limbs off one fanatical Briton after another. Bodies piled up in front of the cohort ranks slowing down the barbarian advance, the ground turning to a slippery chalkish pink.

Bassus roved up and down the front line, urging, cursing, bullying his new unit to keep fighting. At several spots, where a Briton slipped through, he smashed them back with his shield. He ducked beneath the enemy's upraised shield and shoved his sword deep into his rib cage. Time and again he personally filled the void and shoved his men together. Then came the sound of a distant trumpet. Bassus turned, as did Porcius, and watched as the rest of Legion Twentieth Valeria finally turned the enemy's flank, linking with Legion Second Augusta.

Thank you, Father Jupiter. Porcius breathed.

Bassus's men held. The junior centurion turned along with Porcius to the loud tramping of hob-nailed, sandled boots mixed with the jolting, metallic sounds of arms and armor. An auxiliary cohort of Asturians, wearing blue tunics and breeches covered by chain mail, moved in to relieve his beleaguered troops. Bassus's cohort alternately opened and closed ranks with split-second precision, until the Asturian reliefs, equipped with longswords and protective oval shields, filled all gaps in the line. The exhausted legionaries quickly fell back until they were out of immediate danger.

The centurion led the cohort to a rise behind the auxiliaries. They sat on the trampled ground while he poured a goatskin of water over his head.

"He is probably too tired to care that his armor will rust, or his muscles ache," Porcius mumbled under his breath.

Bassus ran a sweaty hand through oily hair and shook it like a wet animal. He hailed a passing *medicus* and pointed to a thinly sliced wound on his arm.

A quarter of an hour later, Bassus and his men were ready to return to the fray. He got to his feet and looked down the rise, apparently seeing General Geta and his troop of escorting Praetorians riding behind the Third Cohort near the edge of the flank.

Porcius noticed that the Second Cohort had just been relieved, and watched as Bassus waved to its cohort commander, Centurion Lucius Flaccus. Too far away for Porcius to understand, they shouted something to one another. Flaccus bellowed a reply and pointed in the direction of General Geta, commander of the Twentieth Legion.

At that moment, a horde of four thousand screaming Britons swarmed past the edge of the flanking cohort.

Bassus quickly gestured a centurion to his side and gave an order. He then motioned to Flaccus, turned back, and barked a command to his men. The legionaries, with Bassus leading the way, sprang to their feet and moved out at a near run.

* * *

On the low hill above the plain, at the opposite end of the field from the Second Legion's headquarters, Caratacus and his companions watched from their chariots as his warriors fell mindlessly upon the Romans. Appalled by his army's losses, the sickening, sweet smell of thousands of dead bodies singed Caratacus's nostrils.

Clud motioned to the Romans. "I must try to kill him, High King. Look! It's the omen! It's the great, gold eagle of the prophecy!"

Caratacus knew by the gold cuirass, purple cloak, and red-plumed helmet that the officer was a general, riding a dark bay gelding. An escort of scarlet-clad Praetorian Guardsman surrounded him.

"You know the odds of getting through are against you?" Caratacus said.

"Wasn't it foretold that we'd capture the great eagle? One must never defy a prophecy."

Caratacus exhaled. He loathed the thought of sending Clud to an almost certain death, but knew he must. His close friend would be insulted if he refused him this opportunity for glory. "Very well, my friend, go. If anyone can break through, it is you." He clasped the old iron maker's wrists tightly. "Take whatever men you need and may Teutates be with you!"

Clud barked commands to his men to follow him and rode into the fray.

At fifty-one, Clud was one of the old ones. He still possessed great strength and power. What he lacked in speed, he made up in cunning. If the gods willed it would be his time to die, so be it. Caratacus had to stay out of the fighting; he must survive to lead the people. But Clud was a warrior and expected to live and die like one.

The king watched from a distance as Clud jumped from his chariot and waded through the frenzied mob of Britons to the Roman line, hacking their way through the hundreds of Praetorian defenders, whose clumsy fighting ability astonished Caratacus. He had heard the soft-living Praetorians didn't have the iron will of the legionaries. The rumors were right—many fell. A few moments later the Britons surrounded the officer and his Praetorians. The general was within their grasp.

* * *

Porcius watched as Bassus's and Flaccus's cohorts raced for the general's standard as the barbarians engulfed General Geta's position, the fighters yelling, weapons clashing, shields banging. Bassus bellowed to Flaccus and pointed to the general's wavering standard. Then he brandished his weapon in a circle above his head. Porcius thought he heard him shout, "Form the turtle!" Bassus pointed to a centurion with his weapon and the First Century moved to the front.

The troops' outer ranks formed an oval wall of shields, and the inner ones placed shields above their heads. It became an impenetrable barrier, bristling with swords like the needles of a porcupine. They knifed through the swirling barbarian host like wolfhounds attacking a wild boar, goring the enemy with smashing iron-bossed shields and body-gutting short swords. The two cohorts sent the Britons reeling as they reached the general's standards and redeployed.

Porcius eyed the thick forest of warriors and marveled at the gashed roadway they'd just cut, now paved with writhing bodies. Bassus approached a blood-drenched centurion after he had positioned the last of his men on the perimeter into a protective circle. He shook the other officer's hand and appeared to compliment him.

Although there was a lull in the fighting, in the distance Porcius watched as the Britons slowly regrouped.

At that moment, he heard Bassus shout an order to another junior centurion to reform the ranks of the cohort, but to leave behind one century to form a defensive perimeter around the commander's headquarters.

Bassus and the other centurion approached General Geta, saluted, and spoke to him. They appeared to be asking questions to which the general nodded. Geta turned to Bassus and said something that brought a grin to both centurions' faces, perhaps a compliment. The two saluted and quickly departed.

Porcius scanned the western area of the battlefield and understood why they had left in a hurry. The Britons were about to launch another attack.

Now we will break Caratacus once and for all!

CHAPTER 9

As the relieving cohorts surrounded the general, Caratacus watched from the rise above the battle. Clud raced toward General Geta. He hurtled over dead bodies and hacked his way through the Roman line. As he closed in on the Roman commander, Caratacus spotted the centurion he remembered. Bassus. Unlike the first day of invasion when Caratacus had spared the Roman's life, he knew his friend was determined that Bassus wouldn't live to see the end of this one.

Clud sliced his way to Bassus's position.

Even in the noisy chaos of battle, Caratacus swore he heard Clud shout something in guttural Latin that sounded like, "Bassus! Bassus!"

The centurion turned as they squared off. Clud swung his longsword at Bassus's head. The weapon caught the top of Bassus's shield and was parried away. Clud deftly jumped aside, eluding Bassus's deadly jab to the stomach. The old warrior made a thrust for the centurion's face and again was blocked by the shield. The Roman's sword jabbed along the side of Clud's waist drawing fresh blood on its blade. Clud's oval shield blocked another flashing thrust of Bassus's weapon and deflected it aside. Three more times they traded blow for violent blow, each caught by one another's shields. Clud's weapon slid past Bassus's shield, lancing the left side of the jaw. In an instant, the iron boss of the centurion's shield smashed into Clud's chest, sending him staggering backwards. Another blow by the shield battered his face. Blood flowed from his mouth and nose. Before he could counterstrike, the centurion slipped his weapon below and past Clud's shield and pierced the Briton's abdomen. Blood spurted from his mouth. Caratacus realized Clud was choking and gasping, fighting for breath, his windpipe flooded with blood. Clud crumpled to his knees, too weak to block the crashing sword that split his skull.

Caratacus clenched the pommel of his sword tightly as his stomach churned. Even though he had been resigned to the fact that Clud would probably die in battle, he stood aghast at the sight of his friend's death. But this was not the time or place to mourn the loss of his good friend. Outwardly, he had to remain calm.

Clud's attack had failed. The general's standards had wavered but never faltered, and General Geta lived. Now both legions moved forward at a run, and a cry ran through Caratacus's warrior host.

"The eagle lives! The priest lied!"

"He's a sorcerer!" another warrior cried.

It was as if that accusation against the prophecy by the Druid, Havgan, had squeezed the last breath out his warriors' attack. The men turned and fled, jumped, and tripped over and around corpses, shattered armor, and weapons. At first a trickle, then a stream, and finally a flood as company after company of warriors waded through the pink-chaulkish mud, the result of the river of blood that poured from the wounded and dead. They headed up the hill through trees and brush, north for the River Tamesis, the noise from their footfalls deafening.

Within minutes, five of Caratacus's chieftains, led by Fergus ap Roycal, crossed the field and reined their chariots before him, their haggard, sunburned faces full of concern.

"High King, they've had enough!" Fergus turned toward the fleeing host. "Despite threats and executing cowards, our warriors still flee!"

"It's the prophecy," Caratacus spat in disgust. "They had more faith in the words of one man than in themselves!"

Fergus gestured with his big hands as if it were obvious. "Whatever the reason, there's no turning them around. What now, Great King?"

Caratacus looked from one leader to another. "We retreat—across the Tamesis—and regroup. Now!"

"What about our dead?" a chieftain asked. "We can't leave them for the Romans—they'll desecrate their souls by leaving them to rot or burn them."

"We have no choice," Caratacus said. "There are too many dead. The Romans will slaughter what's left of our forces if we stop to collect the bodies." He turned his chariot and hurtled ahead as his shield bearers and chieftains scurried to keep pace.

The Romans kept up the pressure, nipping at their heels.

Five miles away, they crossed the broad, mosquito-infested marshlands of the Tamesis. The honeycomb of dense briar thickets, bogs, and quicksand rivulets swallowed men and beasts alike without a trace. Knowing the area well, Caratacus and his warriors crossed with little difficulty. Near nightfall, before the swift incoming tides filled the silting mouth of the Tamesis, all his surviving warriors had crossed the treacherous marshes. His expected victory lay in shambles. Gone were fifteen to twenty thousand warriors. And in the process, he had lost another of his best friends, Clud.

* * *

Now that Porcius had identified Caratacus in battle, General Vespasian had no further use for him, and he was sent back to the headquarters of General Plautius. Only the day before, Plautius had crossed the River Medway. Secretly, Porcius was glad that Caratacus had escaped. He had offered to negotiate the surrender of Caratacus, but Vespasian would not hear of it. If truth be known, Porcius believed Caratacus would not have accepted anything less than complete withdrawal from Britannia by the Romans.

If General Plautius was to conquer the Britons, he would still need Porcius's knowledge, plus that of Caratacus's older brother, Adminios, and that of King Verica.

"I don't trust either one of those barbarians," Plautius said to Porcius. They sat facing each other across the general's portable desk in the headquarters tent. It was almost noon, the sun broiling them. The side flaps to the tent were opened to allow in the little breeze that drifted in from the nearby River Medway. "You know this land almost as well as they do. Despite our differences, I trust your judgment in this matter. That's why I ordered Vespasian to send you back."

"I was puzzled as to why I was recalled," Porcius said.

General Plautius snorted. He grabbed the cloth sitting on the desk, wiped his forehead, and sat it down. "Vespasian is a good general, but outside of killing the Britons, he is not one for negotiating with them. On the other hand, I wouldn't trust either Verica or Adminios to deal with the other British kings who could become our allies. If what you told me earlier is true, the Iceni and Brigantes hate both of them."

"Trust me, General, they do," Porcius said, his eyes narrowing.

Porcius had learned from the general that Legion Fourteenth Gemina, and elements of the commander's beloved Ninth Hispana, had crossed the River Medway north of Caratacus's main camp. The Romans completely surprised the Britons Caratacus had left behind when he went to intercept Vespasian's forces. The enemy made one futile counterattack and, like Caratacus's defeated army, fled north to the River Tamesis. However, the Medway victory had not been as easy as anticipated. Of twenty thousand troops, more than one thousand legionaries died, losses Plautius could not afford. However, thousands of barbarian warriors had been captured.

Auxiliary German cavalry units serving the Roman Army, the Batavians, had failed to find a shallow ford and swam across. Yet, he had received word Geta's legion had crossed a bridge discovered upstream that afternoon.

Porcius had also learned the Batavians had been bogged down on the north side of the Tamesis. They had lost more in the marshes than from the enemy, but Plautius had ordered the Ninth Legion's commander to advance his remaining five cohorts across the Tamesis and join Geta's legion at once.

"I have received word that the bulk of Caratacus's cavalry has been surrounded—trapped," General Plautius said. "I am determined to see they don't escape. I will join the Ninth Legion, which is in route to the area where they were last seen. In the meantime, Legate Porcius, I am ordering you to stay behind."

* * *

Though late, Porcius was completing another secret report to the emperor. As he stamped the imprint of his signet ring on the hot, wax seal of the finished document, a commotion outside caught his attention. Horses trotted by his quarters and someone shouted.

"Barbarian women in camp!"

Porcius looked up from his desk and towards the opening to his large tent. He knew that would bring out the troops and slavers alike. So far, the only women rounded up since the invasion began had been disease-ridden, squat, camp followers and ugly, poxed village peasants. Then he heard another shout.

"They're Amazons!"

If they were warrior women, perhaps one of the captives was Caratacus's wife. When Porcius had fled from Britannia after Caratacus had driven out Adminios and Verica, the Roman knew Caratacus's wife was commander of his female cavalry unit. No doubt she was still their leader. He hoped that she, like Caratacus, had escaped. Nonetheless, his curiosity wouldn't be satisfied until he investigated the disturbance. To Porcius, or any Roman, women who fought as warriors were considered Amazons.

Porcius stood, his joints aching more all the time, and stepped to the entryway. He trudged out into the humid night and watched the torch-lit procession pass by. A stern-faced General Plautius led the escort of mounted Praetorians and a cohort of legionaries. He spotted fifteen women being carried on stretchers near the end of the column. In the torchlight he saw their battered, black and purple faces and bloodied bodies. Porcius gasped as he felt the pain rise in his arthritic hands. He never liked the idea of using women in combat, and this confirmed his reasons. Then he was astounded to see a line of Batavian German troopers, hands chained and necks linked by rope.

"What in the name of Jove happened to these poor creatures?" Porcius called to an accompanying medicus.

"They got caught toying with these wenches, and—"

"Not them, I mean the women, and you'd best watch your tongue!"

"Raped and gutted by the Batavians," he answered in a civil tone.

"Why are they being brought here?"

"General's orders, sir."

Porcius halted the litter carriers and motioned to a passing torchbearer to bring the light over to the Britons. He bent for a closer examination and, to his consternation, recognized Rhian's battered face.

"I know this woman. I will see the general at once." He turned to the medicus. "You are to take exceptional care of her. Is that clear? She is the wife of a king!"

The Roman caught up to Plautius as he was entering his quarters accompanied by a young tribune and a couple of slaves. "General, a word with you. It's most urgent."

"Senator, I have no time for imperial chitchat."

"General, do you realize who those women are?" Porcius motioned to the passing stretchers. "And one in particular? The tall blond is the warrior-wife of Caratacus."

Plautius handed his helmet to his servant and slowly turned to Porcius. "Are you certain?"

Porcius narrowed his eyes. "I've known her since she was a child. There's no doubt in my mind."

"Interesting." Plautius sat on a small stool as a slave poured him a cup of vinegary wine. He took a long swill and continued, "That presents many possibilities if she lives. I admit when we caught the Batavians torturing those women, I was enraged. I immediately ordered the arrest of the Batavians. There was one woman I examined that was tall for a Briton. Despite her swollen face and bloody mouth, I found her striking, if not beautiful. She couldn't have been much more than thirty. Is she the one you say is Caratacus's wife?"

"The same," Porcius replied.

Plautius pounded the desk with the palm of his hand. "Killing those Amazons in battle was one matter, but staking them out like animals and then gutting them like cattle is beyond human decency. Sell them into slavery, yes. But not this!" He lowered his hand to his thigh as he shook his head. "I saw many women lying dead or badly wounded. All had similar wounds."

"What are you going to do with the Batavians?" Porcius motioned in the direction of the chained prisoners who were being herded to a temporary detention area. "What they did was utterly barbaric."

The general glared right through him as if he weren't there. "What I do with them is a military matter, not yours."

"The men deserve execution for their crimes," Porcius said. "The knifing must be some sort of German blood ritual. It is the only logical explanation for their barbaric behavior."

"I know about many German rituals," General Plautius said, "but this is the first time I had witnessed anything like this. Up to now, the Batavians have been good soldiers. On the other hand, why should I be concerned?"

"Concerned?" Porcius said, aghast by the general's answer. "This goes beyond anything I have seen or heard of. Are they not trained to obey orders? By disobeying your orders, they deserve death."

"That remains for me to decide," General Plautius said in a wooden voice.

"My dear General, the emperor shall read of this military matter within a few weeks of this night's dispatch!"

Plautius's face flushed scarlet. He waved the small entourage, who had followed him into his tent, outside. "Senator, you and I must discuss this matter further. Alone!"

* * *

It was dawn, but Porcius had not slept upon returning to his quarters. For some time he pondered the information he received from Plautius during their private meeting. The general told him he had quietly given the order for the execution of the Batavians at first light. Porcius then rewrote a secret dispatch to Emperor Claudius including that information. Caratacus would soon know about his wife's death. During the middle of the night, she had been stabbed to death by a scalpel through her chest. Only minutes earlier he had learned that Rhian had been killed by one of her own female riders. Porcius snorted. He didn't expect Plautius's men to catch the frightened, half-clothed girl who had escaped from the medicus tent. That would be too much to ask of the world's finest troops!

He feared a renewed savagery in Britannia's will to resist. The end result would be the same. Defeat. Now, many more of his men would die.

General Plautius had ordered the other captured Briton women to be freed. They would be told fully what had occurred and would witness the executions, then allowed to transport the queen's body to their homeland.

* * *

The following day, Porcius, riding with the other troops in General Plautius's entourage, halted on the general's orders. They set up camp where they would wait until the arrival of Emperor Claudius. The general could have pursued and destroyed Caratacus after crossing the Tamesis, but he had been ordered to wait for the Emperor's arrival before assaulting Camulodunum. Porcius saw the fury in his flushed face. The time lost would be immeasurable. Complete victory had been in Plautius's grasp, and now it was gone. Caratacus had escaped. This gave him the opportunity to regroup his forces. He could counterattack while the Romans waited for the delayed arrival of the half-senile Emperor Claudius, whose arrival was a politically contrived move. The emperor needed a military victory and a triumph to strengthen his position with the Senate—at Plautius's expense!

Porcius had no doubt Caratacus was carefully planning the defense of Camulodunum. How many Romans would die in taking Caratacus's seat of power?

Chapter 10

The Romans had crossed the River Medway and Caratacus's army retreated to the small village, Chelmsford, eighteen miles north of the Tamesis on the edge of a great forest. He commandeered the fortified homestead of the village chieftain for his quarters. Two days had passed since his warriors fled across the River Tamesis. He'd not heard from Rhian, nor could his scouts locate her position. *Surely, I would have heard something by now. I pray Teutates she is still alive.*

The following evening Caratacus met in the new headquarters, a large circular hut, with Fergus ap Roycal and his other chieftains. They stood beyond the pulsating light of the fire in front of a goat hide stretched between two poles, on which was drawn a map of southeastern Britannia. As the leaders discussed their next move against the Romans, they heard steps behind them and turned. A warrior emerged from the shadows and approached the gathering.

"What is it?" Caratacus asked.

The long-haired fighter gestured toward the open flap at the entryway. "High King, there is a small, dirty woman outside who claims to be a companion of Queen Rhian. She says she has news about your wife."

Caratacus jolted, his chest and arms tightened. *By Teutates, I pray she is not injured.* The chieftain's eyes were upon him. He managed to regain control of himself. "My wife? Bring her in." As the warrior turned, Caratacus said as an afterthought, "Who is this woman?"

The man stopped. "Says her name is Fiona, sire."

"I know Fiona," Caratacus said. "Well, don't stand there, send her in." He remembered that ever since Fiona had discovered and reported the treasonous sorcery performed by the Druid, Ibor, she had been one of Rhian's cavalry companions. *That was six years ago. She must be twenty or twenty-one by now.*

"I pray that your wife is alive and not in the hands of the Romans," Fergus said, pulling Caratacus out of his thoughts. "We've had no news since before the battle." He shook his balding head.

Little Fiona, face drawn, clothed in a ragged, dirty tunic, staggered into the presence of the tribal leaders. Caratacus pressed his lips together. Her appearance bode ill for what might have happened to Rhian and the rest of her women cavalry.

"Where is my wife? Where are the others, Fiona?" Caratacus asked.

Fiona's full mouth quivered, her eyes darted about like that of a hunted animal. She brushed back her matted, chestnut hair. "I am alone, High King."

"I can see that," Caratacus said, an edge of impatience creeping into his voice. "How did you find us?"

The young woman's close-set, dark eyes peered into his. "I followed the wide trail left by your retreating warriors, High King."

Caratacus kept a sober face, but inside, his mind reeled, knowing his army had been defeated. No matter, they would fight the Romans again. "I was told you had news of Queen Rhian and the others."

She lowered her head. "I ... that is ..."

Seeing her distress, he gently said, "Go on Fiona, no one will hurt you. Tell me what happened—everything."

"Your ... your wife is dead," she answered in voice barely more than a whisper.

Caratacus flinched. "Dead? How?" He inhaled deeply. *No, not Rhian.* He balled up a fist, finger nails digging into his palm.

"Please forgive me, lord," Fiona said, "but she ... she begged me to kill her."

"You killed her?" A deafening roar filled his ears like huge waves from a storm crashing onto the beach.

"Please, let me explain," Fiona said. "So much happened to us, to your wife—my friend."

The sounds in his ears faded. He exhaled and nodded to Fiona. "Go on, I grieve for my wife, but I see this is just as painful for you. Tell me the details—leave nothing out." She sighed. "Yes, lord. It happened two days ago. We were trapped, and dusk was falling." Fiona reminded Caratacus that earlier that day he had ordered the cavalry, including Rhian's women, to support the Trinovantian infantry heading for the Tamesis River. Their orders were to halt the German cavalry, who the Romans called Batavians, before they could cross a shallow ford and attack Caratacus's army from the rear.

"I knew the men wanted revenge for the deaths of our tribesmen," Fiona said. "But the Batavians surprised us, and we were crushed. Not only did we fight the Germans, but part of a Roman legion. Only Rhian and fifteen women, including me, escaped. We were chased across the north side of the Tamesis Marshes."

"The marshes," Caratacus said. "You know them better than the Romans. Why didn't you escape?"

Fiona shook her head. "We knew the marshes, but the swampland still bogged us down. It should have slowed the Batavians, but it didn't." Fiona said that the Germans overtook and surrounded the women. She and the others hurled their remaining javelins at them, and a couple of careless troopers paid with their lives, but they moved closer and fended off the women's sword blows. It was as if they were playing with them. Rhian, Fiona, and the rest of the women were overwhelmed and dragged from their horses.

"Even as I was grabbed by a filthy German," Fiona said, "I saw Rhian pounding the face and chest of another brute." Fiona hesitated.

"Don't stop now," Caratacus said.

"Yes, lord." Fiona cleared her throat. "The animal held her in a bear grip and grinned through his broken teeth. Then he struck her face with a huge fist. He hit the queen so hard it knocked her unconscious." Fiona glanced from side to side, to the chieftains and Caratacus.

Although grim-faced, Fergus ap Roycal and the other chieftains held their silence.

Caratacus bit his lip, the coppery taste of blood in his mouth. For a split second, he turned away fighting back the tears. *No, not now!*

The king gestured to Fiona. "Go on, I am listening."

"I tried to resist the one who grabbed me, but he beat me, too. He raped me." Tears flooded her eyes, running down the sides of her mottled face, and she sniffled.

Caratacus motioned to a servant nearby, who stepped forward and handed Fiona a cloth.

She wiped her eyes and blew her nose. After the servant retrieved the rag, Fiona appeared calmer, brushing back strands of hair from her face.

"Do you remember what happened later?" Caratacus asked.

Fiona nodded. "When I regained consciousness. It was dark, the moon overhead. I was naked, my hands and feet tied, staked to the hard, rocky ground. I couldn't move my body or legs. My arms were pulled above my head and legs drawn apart, my insides burned. Still, I managed to turn my head and saw Rhian, a little ways from me, tied the same way. Then I saw him."

"Who?" Caratacus asked, already suspecting the answer.

"The one ... the one who raped her. He was just getting off the top of her."

Caratacus shook his head. "Animal!" He vowed to butcher him, slice his manhood with a dull blade, and tear him into a thousand pieces.

Fiona cringed. "I'm sorry, lord."

"Is this pig still alive?" he asked, barely containing the rage in his voice.

She shook her head. "No, lord, he was executed after the Romans found us, but that was later."

"What else?"

"Both of us were raped again, lord, by other Germans." She choked on her words and wrung her soiled hands. "The other women suffered like us, I heard their screams. There was no escape. I thought we would die. As one German finished with me, I turned my head to the side and heard another scream near me. Then I saw a blade flashing from a dagger. Rhian was stabbed in the groin by a filthy German. She screamed again."

"No!" Caratacus cried out before he could control himself. His stomach contracted into a tight ball. He paused before motioning her to continue.

Trembling, Fiona nodded. "I wish it were not so. The one who had been down on me was about to do the same thing when I heard the sounds of approaching horses, the ugly brute bolted and raced into the night. The laughter ceased, and someone shouted, 'Seize them!' It was in Latin, but I knew what it meant."

"The Romans came," Caratacus said in flat tone, barely able to maintain control of himself. "What did they do?"

"They surrounded us, but instead of abusing us like the Germans, they placed us on stretchers. That's when I passed out." Fiona explained that the next thing she remembered was waking up in a tent with the other survivors.

One of the Roman healers examined their wounds. He even cleaned and sewed them up and said soothing words she could not understand. A soldier acting as an interpreter said Fiona would live with good care and would be sold as a slave when fully recovered. The medicine man made her drink a bad tasting liquid, and soon she fell asleep.

"Before that happened," Fiona said, "I twisted my head toward where Rhian lay and saw the healer examining her. He said something in Latin to the soldier who had talked to me. The healer shook his head. I'm certain he said she was dying."

"You said my wife ordered you to kill her. When did that happen?" Caratacus asked.

"It was later, Lord Caratacus, sometime after midnight," Fiona answered. She explained the dim light radiating from a miserable little oil lamp was the only illumination within the gloomy medical tent. "It was after the Romans had retreated to their drinking. One of the soldiers brought in a small jug and waved to the healer to join him outside. "My hands were bound in front of me," she said. "Like me, Rhian was still in the tunic that had been ripped by the Batavians. Her face was swollen badly from her beatings.

"When they left, I slipped my hands through the cowhide bonds that the Romans had tied me with and crept through the tent, keeping to the shadows."

Caratacus noticed the scrapes on Fiona's narrow wrists and small hands.

"In the twilight of the sputtering lamp," Fiona continued, "I found pincers, strange looking knives, and clamps on a table by the goat-skinned wall. I grabbed a thin knife. I knew I had to escape and find you, Great King. Yet I couldn't leave my queen to die a Roman captive. Her soul would wander forever."

"When did you take the queen's life?"

A visible lump rose in Fiona's throat. "I returned to Rhian's stretcher and quickly sliced away her bonds. I woke her up and told her I was taking her out of the camp."

"And she refused?" Caratacus asked.

"Yes, lord," she answered, her voice etched in sorrow. "She told me in a slurred voice that she couldn't escape, her arm was broken, smashed by one of the Germans. Then her body shook, and she moaned and complained about bleeding inside. Her nose was broken, too."

Caratacus's body tightened as if a closed fist squeezed his heart. It was all he could do to contain his anger. "Go on."

"I told her that I couldn't leave her, she had to escape." Fiona wrung her hands again. "The queen refused, saying she wouldn't survive. I was to go alone." Fiona hesitated.

Caratacus nodded.

"My queen struggled to speak." For a split second, Fiona turned away. Caratacus thought she was about to weep. She faced him again, only now did he notice the dark shadows around her eyes. "The queen said I was to tell you that all the women were courageous—they died a warrior's death. Then with her good hand, she weakly grabbed my wrist and struggled to raise her head. She looked at me in the dim light. Her next words I remember clearly. 'You must not let them have my soul—take my life. I will bless your name to Teutates and Andraste as I go beneath the earth.' She released my arm and dropped her head back on the cot."

"Was it at that point you took her life?" Caratacus asked in a rasping voice.

"No, lord, I told her I couldn't kill her. That's when the queen struggled to say these words, 'Lord Caratacus would want it so. He will understand and bless you for it. Tell him to take care of Dana and the new baby when it is born. Now, help me die.'"

"Did you?"

Fiona nodded. "I tried holding back my tears. My body shook. What she commanded me to do was the truth and the only choice. I managed to pick up the strange tool I had stolen earlier and held it aloft. That's when the queen said the gods would bless me. Her last command was that I was to tell you everything. The queen closed her eyes." Fiona paused. "I carried out her command. Then I escaped from that place of death, slipped into the darkness, and vanished."

Caratacus turned away, the terrible news striking him like a hammer blow. Once again, his chest tightened, his heart seemed to shrivel. He inhaled several deep breaths. Soon his muscles had relaxed enough for him to get a grip on his feelings. He twisted his body back toward Fiona.

"Please forgive me for carrying out your wife's last request, lord," Fiona asked.

"You had little choice in the matter, you had to obey her command," Caratacus said. "It was the right command, Fiona, and you honored us both."

She went down on her knees to thank him.

And for a fleeting instant, Caratacus hated her.

* * *

A day after Fiona had arrived with the devastating news, the king gathered his surviving chieftains for council in the little house. During the council a messenger entered with news that Rhian's body had arrived.

Caratacus would never forget that humid morning when her body, covered in a purple linen cloth, was returned to his headquarters in Chelmsford in a rickety wagon with an escort of freed prisoners.

As he approached the wagon where Rhian lay, he suddenly felt the urge to flee. Caratacus had seen thousands of bodies, but now he wanted only to escape.

This wasn't just another corpse, it was his wife. He dreaded what he would find. For a moment, Caratacus stopped in the dusty compound and looked around, seeing chickens and pigs running about. They seemed oblivious to the chieftains and warriors milling in little clusters, all at this moment watching him. There was the smell of breakfast fires and the aroma of porridge and fresh baked bread on the warm breeze. Distant laughter drifted on the wind. He took a deep breath of these ordinary smells and walked quickly to the wagon.

Caratacus pulled the sheet gently from her gray, pallored face. For a split second, he closed his eyes. He opened them to see the purple, swollen lips and bruises around Rhian's eyes and on her jaw. One broken arm was splinted, yet still twisted at an odd angle. In the heat, her body was already beginning to putrefy. The sickening smell invaded his nostrils. Yet, all he could think of at that moment was how anyone could do this to Rhian, to his wife! He couldn't help himself, he had to know it all, and drew the cover off her naked body.

He mastered the sudden urge to cry, to rage at the heavens, to bellow like a wounded animal. Caratacus slammed one fist into the wagon's splintery side and barely noticed the pain or the rapid swell of the knuckles. Desperately, he struggled to contain his grief. His love for Rhian had possessed him, but it took her death for him to realize how deeply it ran. He had been blind. But this was not the time for recriminations. Now she was with Teutates. Still, he cursed the gods for not waiting. He stared at her mutilated form, even after the women came to re-cover her.

His thoughts rambled. He hated all that was Roman, no matter that the Batavians alone were to blame. *They never would have committed this outrage if the Romans had not invaded our lands. May Taranis hurl an army of thunderbolts upon their accursed legions!* It didn't matter that the Roman dog executed her butchers or that the general had returned her body. By whatever method, whatever the cost, he was determined to destroy all Romans to avenge Rhian and all his people.

* * *

The following morning the women braided and perfumed her hair and crowned her head with a golden Greek diadem. The servants applied white powder makeup to her face, and she was dressed in her finest clothing. They laid her upon a ceremonial cart detached from the wheels of a chariot. Fiona and another survivor warrior reverently covered her in a gold-stitched, leather sheet, fastening it tenderly to the sides of the bier. She and the rest of her jewelry, weapons, and food for her journey to the underworld were lowered into the grave next to the detached chariot wheels. A great, silver cauldron, engraved with the pictures of shielded infantry warriors and cavalrymen, was the last item placed in her grave. They buried Rhian outside the village.

Rhian's burial gifts seemed incomplete. Caratacus realized she required a sword. His sword. Clud's masterpiece that had saved her and served her so well against the assassin so long ago.

"Halt! She must take this along." The grave diggers waited. Caratacus unsheathed his sword and ordered it placed beside her.

Even as the dirt filled the grave, Caratacus held his grief. This was not the time. He still had to fight.

He knew only that he loved her still. The form below him was truly a warrior, but now he could only remember her beauty. Her softness. Her gentle embrace, and the passion in their love making.

I will avenge her!

CHAPTER II

Despite Caratacus's grief over the loss of Rhian, he had to concentrate his mind and all his efforts in defeating the invading Romans. After retreating under Caratacus's counterattack, the Romans had dug in along the north bank of the River Tamesis and waited for the arrival of the Emperor Claudius. Caratacus received daily reports of the Romans' aggressive patrol movements. They were pushing inland again along the north bank of the Tamesis, until reaching its mouth two weeks after Rhian's death. Now they controlled access to and from the river.

Caratacus's depleted forces had withdrawn to the meandering River Chelmer and were scattered from north to south along its shoreline, where it bordered a scraggly, pine forest. Warrior tents and shelters clustered in a haphazard fashion among the trees, bushes, and by the river bank. Smoke from hundreds of cooking fires drifted upward creating a brown haze over the area. The king's warriors constructed temporary corrals from tree branches for the surviving horses and cattle they had managed to confiscate and bring along for food. Men and beasts drank at the river's edge, the same area where they eliminated their waste. Soon the stream became a churning mud hole, the current not moving quick enough to remove the filth. Sounds of hacking coughs mixed with the murmur of warrior voices, and baying of cattle and horses whinnying carried across the river and echoed through the forest.

That evening while Caratacus waited for the rest of his army to arrive, he, Fergus, and Venutios sat on stools by a campfire. He heard approaching footsteps and turned to see a bare-chested warrior jogging towards them. The sweating man stopped before Caratacus, swatted the drifting smoke from around his face, and saluted. "I have good news, sire."

Caratacus sat straighter, alert. "That's something I could use."

The runner grinned. "You have a healthy, new-born daughter. Congratulations, sire."

Speechless, Caratacus heart shot into his throat, but quickly he relaxed and a smile crossed his lips. After three still-born children by Rhian and the miscarriage that Dana experienced two years ago, finally, a child born alive. The gods be praised.

"Healthy and alive?" Caratacus asked. "Are you sure?"

The warrior bobbed his head. "Yes, my lord, the midwife told me that your daughter and Queen Dana are doing well."

Caratacus clapped his hands once. "Wonderful news." He turned to Venutios on his left and Fergus on his right. "I have a child. She may be a girl, but one day she will rule after me." First, he must drive the Romans from our lands.

"Congratulations, sire," Venutios said.

"Aye, congratulations," Fergus said. "May she grow up wise and beautiful."

Caratacus turned to the messenger. "What is my daughter's name?"

"Macha, sire."

The king arched his eyebrows. "A goddess of war? I think not, although I will train her to fight. A plain woman, no, that can't be—not my daughter."

"The goddess is also associated with being queen and ruling tribes, lord," Venutios said.

Caratacus raised his hand curling it into a fist. "Yes, that's it. Dana knows that one day our daughter will be queen."

The messenger stood taller.

"Was there anything else, man," Caratacus asked the messenger.

"The queen said she looks forward to your return so you can hold your new daughter."

The king huffed. "Unfortunately, that may be awhile. In the meantime ..." He turned to a passing retainer, flagged him down, and nodded to the courier. "Take this man to the nearest cooking fire and see that he is fed. He deserves a good meal."

The guard motioned to the messenger to follow him and departed.

Fergus shook Caratacus's hand. "May the queen bear you more children, sire."

Venutios did the same. "That she may."

Caratacus grinned. "Thank you, my friends."

As eager as he was to see Dana and baby Macha, Caratacus still had to deal with the invading Romans. He must stop them. Now!

* * *

The morning after the last of Caratacus's surviving forces had arrived, the king summoned the clan chieftains, including Fergus ap Roycal and his cousin, Venutios, who had arrived the day before with a contingent of five thousand warriors. Cartimandua, Venutios's wife and queen of the Brigantes, refused to support Caratacus in his fight against the Romans. Venutios had defied her by bringing his own loyal followers to Caratacus's aid.

Included among the leaders was Caratacus's new arch-Druid, Owen. He replaced Havgan, whose prophecy over the Romans proved to be false. Havgan had fled in disgrace to the Sacred Isle of Mona, on Britannia's west coast, to be dealt with by his superiors. Slight of build, horse-face Owen wore a long, white tunic. A gold chain containing a disk resembling a half-moon hung around his long neck.

It was almost noon before all the leaders had gathered in his headquarters tent, identified by multicolored streamers limping from wooden poles and a bronze wolf looking fiercely from the top of a standard. The place was on a clear rise above the river. During the summer months, mornings warmed quickly in southern Britannia. Sweat rolled down the side of Caratacus's weather-beaten face and neck, disappearing inside his green and gold, tartan tunic.

The king and his men gathered inside near the goat-hide map marked with Roman positions. Tent flaps opened on the sides to allow in sunlight and what little breeze that drifted in from the British Channel. Fergus ap Roycal and Owen stood to his right, Venutios on his left, and the rest of the leaders stood to the king's front.

For a second, Caratacus remained quiet as he wiped the sweat from his face and then the side of his breeches with his hand. Grim faced, he studied each leader and hardened himself. "I have decided to regroup and withdraw our forces north to Great Dumnow."

Venutios, in his late twenties and clothed in a scarlet and white tunic with matching breeches, gestured toward Caratacus with a calloused hand. "I don't understand—you've kept the Romans in check."

Fergus ap Roycal and the other perspiring clan leaders who surrounded Caratacus murmured in agreement.

"Have I, Cousin?" Caratacus said. He gestured toward the entrance. "I've received reports that even as we stand here, the Ninth and Fourteenth Legions are moving through the Great Forest north of Durolitum. It's their intention to outflank us, turn west, and march straight for Camulodunum."

There was a stir and murmuring from within the group of chieftains at this revelation.

Venutios's deep-set eyes focused on Caratacus. "Why don't we fall back to Camulodunum? We still have more than enough warriors to stop them."

"Think of this," Caratacus said. "We've lost nearly all our cavalry forces." He glanced beyond the opened side of the tent. "We don't have enough companies to guard our coast and river defenses from attack. If we made our stand there, we'd be trapped like rats in a ship's hold."

Fergus ap Roycal, the tall, mustached giant of a chieftain, lowered his balding head. His raven eyes locked onto those of Caratacus. "Then where exactly do you plan to fight them?"

Caratacus glared back, holding his ground. "We move to the forest near the road to Camulodunum." He broke eye contact, turned to the other leaders, and explained the army would be close enough to defend the fortress without being trapped inside.

"Yet," he continued, "we're close enough that if General Plautius attempts a landing from the sea, we can meet them on the beaches and throw them back before they gain a foothold. Of course, many of the merchants there would welcome a peaceful entrance to Camulodunum by the Roman dogs."

The slit eyes in Fergus's leathery face narrowed. He spat on the chalky ground. "I'd rather see the stronghold destroyed than see those fat, fucking merchants living off Roman gold."

"I agree," Caratacus said, "but too many poor people depend on the merchants for their existence—they'd never survive as peasant farmers or fishermen. I won't tolerate any more unnecessary loss of life, nor the destruction of a prosperous town. If we fail, we resort to other means of fighting Rome. We're still raiding their supply columns, destroying hordes of food and equipment—we're far from finished! But should we be defeated, we will take to the hills and forests. The bastards will never know peace."

* * *

Two mornings later, a battle raged along the narrow, muddy banks of the Chelmer. The Romans broke through the British lines. Caratacus ordered a retreat when their resistance began to crumble. Taking Owen, Fergus ap Roycal, and Venutios with him, Caratacus withdrew the army northward, circling west behind the Roman forces. Once in the clear, he halted his armies near the great marshes of the Fens. Those wounded wrapped their injuries in whatever cloths available, while warriors with minor wounds used thick cobwebs to absorb the blood. Sounds of the dying echoed through the scattered ranks. Although their comrades tended to them as best they could, many men died from their wounds as they lay among the bushes on the chalky ground.

The night after his forces had withdrawn from the Fens, Caratacus gathered his chieftains and Owen for another war council. They stood in the shadowy light around the small bonfire outside the king's tent. A few of the chieftains, including Fergus ap Roycal, had rags covering cuts and slashes to their arms and shoulders.

"After we bury our dead, I'm going to disband the army, except for a select group of warriors," Caratacus announced.

A gasp went through the men.

"But why, Cousin?" Venutios asked.

"We will no longer fight the enemy on their terms. They've slaughtered too many of us. We can fight the Romans more effectively by using harassment and hit and run warfare."

"Is this wise, Great King?" Owen asked.

"What about the rest of the army?" Fergus ap Roycal questioned. He glanced back to his retainers who hovered outside the circle of leaders.

"It's too big for what I have in mind," Caratacus answered.

"They would rather fight and die in the open," Venutios said.

"It is the honorable thing to do," Owen added.

"That's exactly what the Romans want," Caratacus said. "There is no honor in that. It is a waste of good men. Britannia cannot afford the deaths of thirty thousand more warriors."

"If you scatter the army, how can we stop the Romans?" Fergus questioned.

"With a select group of no more than one or two thousand of our best fighters, I can attack where they least expect," Caratacus said. "We'll raise chaos with their supply lines and couriers. They're going to have to spread their men very thin to protect their gains. It'll keep them from taking any more of our territory."

"Aye, they'll be too busy chasing ghosts," Fergus ap Roycal added.

Venutios spat. "Better a few loyal followers than an army of traitors."

"Then we are in agreement?" Caratacus said. He eyed Owen, who frowned but nodded.

"Aye!" the chieftains exclaimed.

"Each of you will select your most loyal men," he said to the chieftains. "Disperse the rest to their villages. If we have a need to recall them, we'll meet in Caleva. We'll return there now to plan our next move. Something tells me we're to have an early fall and winter. Send them home to bring in the harvest while they can, we'll need it."

* * *

Ten days later, Caratacus returned to Caleva. It was late afternoon with the sun sliding behind the trees in the forest beyond the hillfort. He and his retinue pulled up their horses before his home within the moated compound. Dana held baby Macha swaddled in a fur blanket. Three servants, who stood behind her, waited on the covered porch at the front of their large, whitewashed wattle and daub house. An ankle-length, emerald and yellow, tartan skirt covered her willowy figure. Small looped earrings, glistening in the afternoon sun, hung from thin earlobes from beneath the close-knit, wiry, auburn hair that crowned her head. Silver armlets in the shape of mythical dragons, clasped above the elbows, circled her slender arms. A smile radiated from her delicate face.

Caratacus dismounted and tossed the reins of his mount to an awaiting groom. He stepped toward Dana, hugged her, and then looked at baby Macha's tiny face, wide, alert eyes and thick hair, bright as the rays of the rising sun. "She's beautiful."

Dana's smiled. "She is."

Caratacus looked away, noise as loud as a roaring avalanche filled his ears. His vision became fuzzy. Shaking his head vigorously, he attempted to clear his sight and hearing before facing Dana.

Dana's smile disappeared. She stared at Caratacus, and then her eyes searched the members of his party. "Where is Rhian?"

Caratacus shook his head and stepped towards her. "I have bad news, Dana. Our beloved Rhian is dead."

She gasped. "Dead?"

"Killed in battle," he answered in a voice little more than a whisper. "Let's go inside, and I will explain everything."

Dana turned to a servant behind her, nodded the young woman forward, and placed Macha in her hands. "Take good care of my little one." Tears welled within Dana's eyelids and placed a hand to her face. She turned and darted into their house, her servants following her.

The king dismissed his entourage and entered his home. Inside the warm circular room the smell of baked bread permeated the air. Flames from the center hearth glowed brightly while strands of smoke drifted to the ceiling and escaped outside through the straw-packed roof. He motioned for the serving women to leave.

Dana ran to Caratacus, and he held her close, smelling the scent of lavender on her body. Shaking, she no longer held back, but wept.

A few minutes passed before she regained control, and after wiping her tears she said, "Rhian and I became very close in the last few months before you and she went off to war."

"So I noticed," Caratacus said. "You two always seemed to be working together on one task or another."

"Yes, we did."

Rhian had undertaken to teach Dana to be a better horse rider. The thought brought a smile to Caratacus's face. In turn, Dana taught her how and where to look for plants and herbs used for medicinal purposes. This had been something Dana had been learning from the aging woman known as Crone, the tribal healer. As a result, Dana's riding improved, and Rhian learned the rudiments of healing.

But now his beloved Rhian was under the ground with the gods.

"Tell me, how did she die?" Dana asked, which pulled Caratacus out of his thoughts.

"Let's sit down first."

"No. I want to know now." In a softer voice she said, "Please hold me, don't let me go."

Caratacus explained at length the circumstances of Rhian's death.

"I didn't realize how much I had grown to love her," Dana said when Caratacus had finished. "Those men deserved to die."

"They deserved worse, but at least the Roman general, Plautius, was decent enough to execute them."

Dana sniffled. "She was like the good sister I never had."

Caratacus frowned. "I know. Cartimandua wasn't a sister to anyone."

"Cartimandua is evil. She only looks out for herself. Now I have no sister with Rhian gone."

"Considering the fact she had threatened to murder you before I took you as my consort, that's not surprising." He gripped tightly the hilt of his sword. "You may not have heard, but she refused to send warriors to fight the Romans. Perhaps if she had, Rhian would be alive today. Damn the traitorous bitch!"

* * *

"Wake up, Caratacus! Wake up!" Dana shook the thick ball of furs where they slept.

"What ...," he answered groggily.

"You were groaning. Another nightmare?"

Caratacus pushed away the wolf skins, dropping them off the clay-built sleeping ledge onto the hard-packed dirt floor. Thick tanned cowhides walled the area from the rest of the home. He wiped the sweat from his forehead and chest and sat upright, drawing his knees to his chin. He exhaled deeply, frustrated by the grotesque images. "It was the same dream," he mumbled, rubbing his face with both hands.

Outside, a steady drizzle had been falling all night. The faint smell of smoke drifting from the low-burning embers in the great hearth seeped through the cracks beneath the leather walls. Caratacus looked about the dark room, fearful that he might see evidence that his dream was real. It was February, and for the last six months the same dream had tormented him every night. The nightmares first began when he'd returned to Caleva after the fall of Camulodunum. The image of a bloody corpse with three heads: Clud, Tog, and Rhian. But tonight he had hoped the soothing sounds of rain would lull him into a dreamless sleep.

"I know. I prayed the gods would take it away. It's a curse," Dana replied after a moment of silence. She slipped an arm protectively about his shoulders, soft and warm to the touch.

He nodded and leaned his head upon her breast. "I wish to the gods I knew what it meant. Not even the priests can give me a logical explanation."

"They're afraid of telling you the real answer," Dana replied.

"And what is the *real answer*?"

"Owen and the other priests are afraid to say the gods blame you for the death of Rhian, of all three of them. That's why they think you're haunted with the dream."

Caratacus stared into the chamber's darkness, searching for her invisible eyes. For a moment he silently listened to the muffled tapping of the rain. "Do you believe that's true?"

"No ... no, I don't. They knew the risks of battle. That's not the answer at all," Dana answered. "The priests are like old women blaming everything bad on the gods. If they were truly wise, they should have seen the omens the gods provided."

"But they didn't," he growled.

For several moments they snuggled together, listening to the patter of rain playing upon the thatched roof. He thought she had dozed off again when he softly asked, "What do you think it means?"

"It means," she answered with a sigh, "... that you blame yourself for their deaths. As leader, that seems the natural thing to feel."

He pulled away from her arm. "Woman, you're mad!"

"Am I? The great wolf within you is howling its sorrow, and you won't let it out, except through your awful dreams."

Caratacus turned back toward Dana even though he could barely see her. "Speak plainly, Dana. You sound like a crone soothsayer from the Isle of Mona."

"You dearly loved all three of them, Caratacus, and now you're hurting. But you won't allow anyone to help. You won't even allow me to share in your sorrow."

He wiped his clammy hands on the bedding and closed his eyes, struggling to understand the feelings that fought to overwhelm him. His moods and depressions, tears always threatening. And the way he'd treated Dana, rebuffing her offers of love and comfort, such he had for three weeks after he had returned to Caleva.

It was late October, the weather growing cold. Once again, rain and fog had become the norm, and soon winter would be at hand. The wheat fields had been harvested.

During the evening meal, Caratacus barely touched his food. Now he sat in front of the hearth staring into the glowing embers, oblivious to the heat on his face. Still depressed about losing Rhian, Tog, and Clud, he couldn't get their deaths out of his mind. He had grown listless and irritable. Dana, who sat nearby, moved towards him, but he waved her away. It seemed only in the presence of baby Macha did he find consolation. He turned to Dana, seeing the downcast look on her pale face.

"Bring me little Macha," he said.

Dana smiled, stood, went to Macha's crib, lifted and brought her over, and handed her, bundled in furs, to Caratacus. A dimpled smile appeared on Macha's little face. He touched her tiny hand with a finger. She grabbed and had a surprisingly strong hold, which pleased him. Caratacus turned away from Dana, keeping his eyes fixed on Macha so she couldn't see tears welling in his eyes.

Later, on that cold night, Caratacus lay in bed, tossing and turning, unable to sleep. He sighed loudly, waking Dana.

"What's wrong?" she asked.

"You should know by now." He turned away from her.

"Isn't there anything I can do, my love? I want to help."

"No one can help me."

Dana snuggled next to him and kissed his shoulder. "Maybe I can take your mind away from your troubles, even if for a little while." She reached down and with her hand grabbed his flaccid member and stroked it.

Instead of arousing him, he became annoyed and pushed her hand from him. "Leave me alone!"

"Oh, Caratacus, how can you be so cruel," she said in a soft voice and slid away from him.

* * *

Only now did Caratacus realize, as he lay next to Dana, that she, too, had struggled with his dream and knew she was interpreting his negative acts as rejection.

"Dana ...," he whispered her name, "you have helped by being here. You understand my feelings better than I do," he said softly.

"Do I? You've kept your grief within, my Husband." Her hand reached over and gently stroked the side of his stubbled face.

"But I'm ..."

"Let me finish," she whispered, pulling her hand away. "I love you, you are my dear one. I willingly shared you with Rhian. And now she's gone." She motioned with her head toward the small bundle of furs near their bed-pallet. "But you still have Macha and me. You can share your grief with me as you can with no other."

"I'm not a weakling, Dana."

"Of course you're not, the gods know and so do I. You're a great leader, but you're a man, and not a beast."

"I know I'm a man," he answered in a sardonic voice.

"What I'm trying to say is, you can weep. No one will know except me. Women cry and afterward feel better. It's how we release the hurt and the pain. You hurt very much, I know it. It's in your face and in your voice. At night, before the dream wakes you, tears fall from your eyes."

"Rubbish!"

"Is it? It's obvious to many, and behind your back the chieftains are beginning to question your abilities as king. I've heard the whispers of the servants and wives of the other chieftains. I wouldn't bring it up if I didn't think it was serious."

For the span of a dozen heartbeats, Caratacus lay motionless struggling to comprehend the impact of Dana's words. *What she says is true.*

Dana's hand lightly brushed the hair on his arm against the grain then smoothed them gently.

"Caratacus, release that great wolf inside you. Release him before he destroys you! And us!" In a softer tone she added, "For their sake: Tog, Clud, and ... Rhian's."

"I can't ...," he answered quietly, "I must control it!"

"I know the reason you've refused to love me since ... it's because you're afraid to show me your true emotions, your sadness. Let go my love, please, for me, for them ... for our people." She embraced him, drawing the furs over them as they lay together. "My love, if there was a poison inside you, the healers would bleed away the sick blood with a knife, and you would submit to it. Tears are the knives to bleed away a wound to the heart. I can't cry for you, and you must, for the good of our people. Until you vent your grief, you will never master yourself."

He bent toward her breast as he tried desperately to divert his emotions to lovemaking. But it was no use. He couldn't, not yet. He turned away, and the muscles in his face, the back of his shoulders, and arms tightened. Caratacus took a few deep breaths hoping that would relax them, but they didn't. He shook. Something was happening inside him, something that he couldn't describe except that he felt pain, terrible pain, pain in every muscle and crevice of his body. A soft, low howl erupted from his mouth, and tears poured forth in a torrent. He did not care if the servants outside of their room heard him.

Through the tears that followed, anger, guilt, hate, and pain tumbled out like a rampaging flood breaking the wall of a dam. He had been foolish to have waited so long. He blamed himself for their deaths and the deaths of all his warriors; a terrible burden. But it was his alone. No one could share this with him. They had achieved what all warriors pursued, the glorious death of battle. What absurdity! It was waste. All waste.

He felt dishonored. A weakling. It was a miracle that anyone followed him. Yet, thousands did. They couldn't all be fools. Did they really believe he was their only hope? He thanked the gods they couldn't see him now. He felt ashamed that he couldn't contain himself like a man.

And yet, it was true; he felt a sense of relief. As the weeping subsided, so did the pain and anger. Perhaps there was something to what Dana said.

Her hand stroked his wet face once again, snuggling next to his side.

"The wolf is at peace," Dana said. "He no longer cries. Sleep well my husband."

The rains continued heavily through the night and indeed lulled him into a peaceful, dreamless sleep, while Dana lay awake, holding him close.

The rain stopped, and the first rays of dawn entered their skin-covered door. Caratacus's thoughts returned to Dana as they lay in quiet embrace. She slept serenely as he quietly stared at the reed-matted ceiling. He breathed in a voice just above a whisper, "Dana, there won't be any more nightmares."

CHAPTER 12

In the Great Hall, Caratacus's chieftains and Owen took their seats at long tables and haggled over the next step to take against the Romans and their Briton lackeys. The Cantiaci and the northern Dobunni, who had once been Caratacus's allies, had turned against him when the Romans promised their lands would be left alone.

Caratacus had wisely moved to Caleva. The Great Fortress at Camulodunum was too vulnerable to Roman attack and had been overrun two weeks after the Battle of the River Medway. Yet, if need be, he could move swiftly from his new capital to meet any enemy attack. His realm still encompassed the old territories of the Dobunni and Atrebates, reaching to the lands of the Catuvellaunii in the east and north, and southward to the borders of the Regni, now in the hands of his old enemy, Verica.

For a few seconds, Caratacus studied each man, including Fergus ap Roycal, Venutios, Owen, and the rest in an effort to gauge their responses to what he was about to say. "The time has come to strike a major blow at the Romans before they launch their next offensive."

"We've harassed them all winter, Great King," Fergus said. He gestured toward the other leaders. "They'll be expecting us."

"That's true, but we have the advantage," Caratacus said. "They'll never know when or where the wolf pack will pounce."

Fergus shook his head. "If we move too many warriors, blood-sucking spies will report it to the Romans."

"That's right," Caratacus said. "But consider this, our raids have confined themselves to the southeastern coast."

Venutios raised a hand as if it were obvious. "They've built auxiliary forts every twenty miles to protect their arses. It's tied down their army."

"Not for long. They'll be on the move soon enough," Caratacus said. "In the meantime, we gather strength and allies in the west and north."

The king paused and looked about. The hall was quiet, all eyes were on him.

"We'll stir up rebellion," Caratacus said, "among their allies, the Iceni and Coritani. The Durotrigians are now with us, so we can still drive the Romans from our lands."

Caratacus had heard from his spies that the Romans halted their advance on the borders of the Trinovantes, Catuvellaunii, Cantiaci to the west, and the Regni to the south. They'd established a series of small, wooden fortresses along the frontier, positioned at strategic locations, such as fords and trackways. They were manned by the Romans' mercenary auxiliaries while the legions were being billeted in Camulodunum and Durovernum for the winter.

"What means will you use?" Venutios asked.

"Frontal attack is out of the question," Caratacus answered, "but there are other ways. In any event, we'll strike at the heart of their allies. We will strike where the Romans least expect."

"Which fucking traitor will we hit first?" Fergus ap Roycal asked.

"None other than my old enemy, Verica," Caratacus replied. "I'll never forget that it was he who invited the Romans to invade our lands. May the gods forever curse his seed!"

"The Romans allowed that cursed piece of shit to raise a small army," Venutios said. "The traitor has trained his warriors like Romans to use against his own people."

"If the gods truly have a victory in store for us, then we'll see how well his Romanized warriors fight," Caratacus said.

He turned to Owen. "Arch-Druid Owen, take your followers to the Sacred Grove and sacrifice for our success.

Owen nodded and left.

Caratacus faced his chieftains. "Now, here is my plan."

* * *

Five days later Caratacus and a band of one hundred hand-picked warriors were on the move. They kept to the impenetrable forests of firs and pines, avoiding spies and Roman sympathizers. Not only had Caratacus chosen his fighters for their loyalty and bravery, but for common sense and specialized fighting skills. He dared not use more than that number lest they be detected before reaching their destination.

Although all were noted for their stealth, thirty were chosen for their unique fighting abilities. Ten were particularly adept at creeping up on an unsuspecting enemy, slitting throats and just as quickly disappearing without leaving a trace. An equal number were skilled in close-in fighting with daggers alone, and the last group excelled in burning buildings and ships. Yet, the entire group would act as one when Caratacus gave the command.

Using Sidhe, the dark, little people of the woods, as guides, Caratacus's raiding party traversed many isolated valleys, impassable forests, and icy-clear streams. The twisting network of trails stretched to Noviomagnus and the sea. The band skirted the ancient Great Stone Circle on Salisbury Plain, reaching the chalky, bow-headed South Downs. They followed its whale-bone spine southeastward, dropping to the rich farmland north of the Regni capital. The Downs was crisscrossed by time-worn trackways reaching to the remotest parts of Britannia. The thick forest grew within a mile of Verica's re-occupied stronghold, the scent of pine heavy and foreboding.

The seaport of Noviomagnus sat aloof at the end of the easternmost of four channels that comprised the great harbor. The narrow inlet to Noviomagnus harbor curved like a cricked skeletal finger, its tip extending to the foot of the hillfort.

* * *

"Your warriors wait here 'til dark," jabbered the head Sidhe guide to Caratacus. The dark figure squatted barefoot and peered through the heavy underbrush located at the forest's edge. He stabbed a finger towards the valley. "Cannot cross the plain in daylight, it be too dangerous."

The little scavenger patiently repeated his words until they were understood. Caratacus knew that the man considered them giant dullards and slow of wit.

"Yes, I know," Caratacus answered, as he viewed the newly-planted wheat fields. Tiny green shoots timidly pushed through the cold, chalky ground. He squinted in the cool afternoon light, seeing the twelve-foot-high stone walls of Noviomagnus, less than a mile away.

"It doesn't matter," he said, turning to the little man, "we would have waited until nightfall anyway."

"Aye, be end of celebrations this night," the guide said. "Everybody be drunk."

It was late April, and the Spring Festival of Beltaine was nearly over. Many peasants, wearing their best rags, had journeyed to the flourishing seaport for the celebration before dawn. *For whatever reason, the Romans have not bothered to enslave them,* Caratacus thought, *apparently, Verica persuaded his new masters they were needed to till and harvest the land.*

"Then you keep promises to Sidhe folk?" the young, scraggly-bearded guide asked. His youthful assistant stood near with the same questioning look on his child-like face.

"I keep my word. Your people will be freed."

"Good." The Sidhe guide pulled a small, bronze dagger from inside his smelly, fox-skin cloak and deftly fingered its sharp edges. "My father say you be honorable man. We kill many tall folk tonight," he said with a missing-tooth grin. The smiling, younger man nodded in agreement.

Before the march, when Caratacus had contacted the Sidhe leader for guides, he was reminded that he had promised to pay back their favor. When Verica returned to Britannia and again became king under the Romans, he enslaved the Sidhe once again. The little people had originally been freed years ago by Caratacus's uncle, Epaticcos. The Sidhe kept long memories.

Caratacus turned to his warriors. "All right, spread out and rest until nightfall. No fires, and above all, silence."

Not everyone rested. Caratacus sent a small advance party that Venutios insisted on leading. Disguised as farmers, they set out to Noviomagnus to gather information about the size of the garrison and their positions. Caratacus was determined to prove a point. The Romans must know that he could strike anywhere at any time. No place was free from his havoc, and Verica must be the first to know.

* * *

The full moon was high, and the air was chilly when the advanced party returned. "What news do you bring, Venutios?" Caratacus asked.

"The feasting and drinking are over. Only young people are out—rutting in the fields."

"Ah, youth," Caratacus said with a grin. The Beltaine celebration had began early that morning with the solemn passage of cattle between purifying bonfires and continued with a big country fair and games. It was an evening of joyful feasting and drinking, ending with lovemaking in the fields, the symbolic planting of seed by young people.

"What about the guards?" Caratacus asked. "Did you see any?"

"If dogs can be called such," Venutios snorted. "They're Regni tribesmen. Most of them were celebrating with the people. I didn't see one that wasn't drunk."

"Ha! If their Roman masters could see them. Were there any Romans in the city?"

"None."

"And the docks?"

"Two merchantmen moored next to the warehouses. The crews are drinking and whoring. No guards about."

"Did you see any Sidhe slaves?"

"No, probably chained in the barracks for the holiday."

"Is Verica there?"

"Aye, his standard is planted in front of the Great Hall —in the Roman fashion."

"Good. His humiliation will be all the greater when we destroy his port and disappear like ghosts into the mist."

Caratacus's men smeared their faces and bodies with mud from a nearby stream and covered their weapons with chalk dust to keep their iron blades from glistening in the moonlight. The warriors left their hiding place in the forest.

As the band drew near the village at the fortress's edge, they heard the last remnants of laughing and singing. Beltaine was drawing to a close. The light of a full moon guided Caratacus's men as they quietly circled the many couples celebrating Beltaine's fertility rites in the newly planted fields. In the distance Caratacus heard the mournful cry of a wolf. It was as if it were howling over the loss of its mate. *How well I know the feeling.* But he didn't have time to dwell on that.

When they crossed a dip in the rolling plain, the group stumbled on an amorous couple in one of the deep furrows. The young man's heavy breathing and the woman's groaning had been their salvation. Fortunately for the pair, they were on the brink of ecstasy, oblivious to surroundings. Caratacus's men quietly backed away before the young people came out of their rapture.

Caratacus's men bypassed the dark fortress and its surrounding defensive ditches and parapets. They avoided the road from the garrison to the port. Instead, the warriors skirted numerous small streams and sandbars along the edge of Noviomagnus channel.

The king motioned for a halt on the muddy flats directly east of the port. The fighters crouched as Caratacus searched for signs that they had been observed. Looming as black silhouettes in the moonlight less than five hundred yards away, he saw the docks and warehouses. Countless small fishing boats were beached along the muddy banks. A heavy scent of rotting fish and salt water lingered about the area.

A damp cloudbank of fog squatted just off shore, illuminated by the moonlight. Huddled together like aliens in a foreign land sat five two-story warehouses built in the Roman manner, with wooden walls, double-shuttered doors, and tiled roofs. Gone were the rustic wattle and daub shacks with mildewed, thatched tops, leaving no doubt that Verica was trying to please his Roman masters.

An icy breeze wafted in from the inlet carrying the reeking smell of dumped sewage from ships in the channel, nudging the fog closer. In nearby pens, the fetid smells of sleeping cattle, horses, and sheep added to the foul stench.

"Look," whispered Venutios, "there's a warship."

"That changes things a bit," Caratacus said in a flat voice. He eyed three ships moored dockside gently rocking on the current. Two merchantmen and one they hadn't expected—a Roman trireme. The galley was ablaze with lamplights fore and aft. He could see the triple-banked set of gunnels that lined the side of the wooden hull and protective, overlapping shields straddling the length of the timbered deck. An iron ram, fixed to the red painted bow, protruded just above the water line. A limp streamer hung from the lone center mast.

"It's part of the channel fleet," Caratacus said a moment later.

"And fighting sailors," Venutios said. "They're reputed to be as fierce as the legionaries. If my sources are right, there are thirty marines and one hundred seventy oarsmen aboard."

Caratacus knew that most Roman marines and sailors were Egyptian, Greek, and Syrian.

Venutios gestured. "There's the watch—one sailor and one marine."

Caratacus gazed toward the ship and spotted both men standing next to the gangway. He looked back toward the hill fortress. "Most likely the rest are in town celebrating."

"May the whole lot be infected by the local whores," Venutios growled.

Caratacus grinned. "Aye, it would ease our task. But don't underestimate those remaining. Be prepared to fight."

Torches lit the muddy street fronting the warehouses, illuminating the Regni sentries assigned to guard the five buildings.

"Humph, ten Regni dogs to do one man's work," Venutios said.

Instead of patrolling the area, the guards warmed themselves around a small fire at the end of the westernmost building. A long-stemmed amphora wine jug was passed among them. Caratacus understood. *Was this not Beltaine, a night for celebration?*

Caratacus turned about and peered into the darkness hiding his men. "If we reach the road without being sighted, we'll attack before they can sound the alarm."

"May the guards stay around the fire and get drunk," Venutios said. "There's nothing between us and them but the flats."

"Aye, but silence is a must. Pass the word. I will slay any man who gives away our position." Caratacus tightly gripped the hilt of his sword.

117

After what seemed an agonizingly long time, no more than an hour by the moon, the band reached the bank of the road. Suddenly, they heard a loud bellowing. Caratacus and his men froze.

Out of the darkness a sailor appeared, staggering toward one of the merchantmen. He was singing at the top of his lungs a drunken ditty about the captain's unchaste daughter. Then the seaman halted, stopped singing, and looked about.

He rubbed his eyes, shook his head, and stumbled along again, shouting in a raspy voice something about seeing barbarian warriors. The Regni guards and Roman watch ignored him, but he kept complaining.

"Shut up, you bloody drunk! Go sleep it off!" yelled the sailor on watch.

"But I swear by the gods, I saw 'em," the drunk said.

"Aye, you and Bacchus both!" the marine barked. "Get out of here!"

"It's true! They're warriors—got shields and swords—on the flats!"

"What goes here?" called the triarch, the commander of the ship, as he poked his bearded face through the hatchway of the small, stern cabin.

The seaman on watch explained.

"Send him to my quarters for questioning," ordered the triarch, "no sense taking any chances."

Moments later the commander reappeared. "Wake the crew and arm yourselves. This man speaks true."

Within minutes, seventy chain-mailed marines and sailors clambered topside, armed with short swords. On the triarch's command, they grabbed shields hooked to the deck railing and double-timed down the gangplank to shore.

Caratacus passed the word to prepare for battle. As the Romans deployed in three columns in front of the main warehouse, Caratacus gave his men the command to attack.

They stormed out of the darkness, their fury and momentum catching the Romans before they could lock their shields into a defensive wall. The Britons hacked and chopped through their ranks with lightning speed. The

Romans fought bravely, never giving a foot. But they were no match for Caratacus's select band of fighters and died fighting where they stood.

"Look, the Regni guards are running away!" Venutios shouted.

"Take your men and hunt them down," Caratacus ordered. "The cowards mustn't warn the garrison."

Within minutes, after the last Roman was slain and the warehouses torched, Caratacus's warriors set the ships ablaze. Moments later, storage bins of wheat and ship stores of cut wood, pinetar, pitch, and resin lit the late-night sky like a hail of exploding meteorites.

A detail of men scattered livestock from the pens. Next to the warehouses sat the slave barracks—a dirty, vermin-infested quarter. The warriors then freed sixty Sidhe slaves, including six women used as kitchen help and whores. The Sidhe guides jabbered for them to do as they were told.

"Once we reach woods," the older guide said, "we remove your slave collars, and you be free to go where you want." The little people shouted for joy, hugged one another, and began dancing and singing.

The moon was setting when Venutios and his men returned from the chase. "We got all but one," he reported to Caratacus.

"By now they've seen the fires from the fortress, and the guards will be alerted." Caratacus looked about and surveyed the destruction. The burning ships were sinking, and the warehouses had collapsed in the flaming inferno. He looked to the sky. *These drunken sots must think they've been overrun by a hoard of barbarians—we've caused enough chaos for it.*

"Perhaps Taranis, the thunder god, will be kind. Look Venutios." Caratacus pointed to the black clouds, silver-rimmed by the moon it now cloaked, drifting across harbor. "I may be wrong, but even in the fading moonlight those look like rain clouds."

"That's what I pray they are," Venutios said. "May it come soon and slow down the enemy."

The fogbank rolled in over the harbor, masking their escape. Caratacus looked back. The burning ships and warehouses were engulfed in a glowing halo of orange fog, which muffled distant shouts.

The scent of rain tickled Caratacus's nose, and he knew they must race onward, hoping to stay just ahead of the rain now pelting the flames.

"Round up the men. Let's go home!"

Less than a half hour later, a torrential rainstorm poured across the coast and Noviomagnus. The hungover Regni garrison was seriously bogged down by heavy mud, and Caratacus's men made good their escape.

Even as he and his men made their way back to their holdings, Caratacus knew he must keep the pressure on the Romans. *It's time to trap and destroy another Roman cohort.*

CHAPTER 13

ROME - JULY. AD 47

Porcius shook his head when recalling how quickly the last three years had flown since returning from Britannia to Rome. He paced impatiently about the colonnaded garden of Plautius's mansion awaiting the general's appearance. He occasionally paused to examine one of the costly, flesh-colored, marble busts lining the outside corridor. The general's ancestors were a grim-faced lot. Porcius took a two-handled, silver cup of expensive Alexandrian Mareotian wine from a passing slave and swilled its contents.

He wiped his hands on a corner of his toga and admired the grounds, leaving purple-red stains. Gilded, lion-head chairs lined the green, marble floor, and intricate frescoes covered the upper half of the adjoining walls. Every doorway was framed with curtains woven in silk and gold, and pillars carved from pink, striated Numidian marble lined the corridor. Scrolled, marble columns guarded the giant courtyard seemingly bearing the weight of a brilliant, blue sky. The fragrance of red, violet, and yellow flowers filled the huge garden in the center of the court. Nearby dwelled a tranquil pond stocked with exotic oriental fish and tamed fresh-water eels.

Rome was a stifling place on a hot afternoon in July. *Why couldn't Plautius be like other decent aristocrats and buy a villa on the coast at Antium where the shoreline basked in soothing winds?* Porcius thought. *The crafty veteran soldier probably loved the excitement of the ancient city, stench and heat notwithstanding.*

Porcius had read the reports. At the end of three years, Caratacus was still waging a murderous guerrilla campaign. Rome had lost thousands of troops. He had raided the Port of Noviomagnus, taking Verica by complete surprise, and burned every warehouse and ship dockside. In another raid, he destroyed an entire cohort from Legion Twentieth Velaria, five hundred brave Romans. Porcius shook his head. The Britons swarmed like clouds of gnats. A person could clap hands and kill hundreds, but the cloud never seemed to thin. Warriors flocked to Caratacus's standards from as far away as Germania and Scandia. General Vespasian, leading Legion Second Augusta, may have conquered much of western Britannia, but only because Caratacus was more interested in harassing Plautius's forces along the northwestern frontier.

In the last year, Plautius had been recalled to Rome after three years of campaigning and given an honorary triumph. His replacement was Publius Ostorius Scapula, a competent general, but known for his impatience and ill temper.

If Scapula expects to capture the Briton leader, he will have to fight Caratacus on his terms.

Porcius had developed a grudging respect for General Plautius. Although he knew little about Scapula, what he had heard he didn't like.

"Ah, Porcius my friend, welcome!" came a familiar voice.

Startled, he turned to see a grinning Plautius standing at the edge of the pond. Attired in the same fashion as Porcius, the stout, balding general wore a flowing white toga with wide, purple trim denoting the rank of senator. Porcius quickly regained his wits, but was puzzled. Never had the general greeted him in such a comradely fashion.

"I'm flattered that you invited me to your home, General," Porcius said.

"Another diplomatic lie—no matter—I don't take offense."

"None intended, I assure you."

"I'd wager you're wondering why I've asked you here."

"I am curious, yes."

"Let's be honest, we've never been real friends. You sent secret letters to the emperor, which I hated. There were other differences, but despite all of that, I respect you. Do you know why?"

"No, not really."

He gestured toward Porcius. "It's your ability to manipulate the Britons. Since returning to Rome, I have realized the wisdom in trying to get them to ally with us."

Porcius nodded, feeling a little smug, but still wondered why the general invited him.

"I never told you, but my reports to the emperor described the brilliant way you and Centurion Bassus persuaded the eleven petty kings to swear allegiance to Claudius. Damndest thing I've ever seen." The general seemed sincere.

"I appreciate your confidence."

Plautius looked about and then motioned to him. "Let's walk through the garden." After a few moments, they halted near the center. The general kneeled to examine one of the purple violets.

"The insects ate this one," he said in a loud voice. "My gardener has to take better care of them if he doesn't want a flogging." He slowly stood, favoring a knee, and whispered, "That was for the benefit of my nosy slaves. I didn't ask you to my house to smell the flowers."

"I didn't think so, but they are lovely. I must make time to work in my own garden. Believe it or not, I enjoy working with the soil."

The general's alert, green eyes flicked to the surrounding shrubs and bushes and back to Porcius. "Do you have any plans to return to Britannia?" he asked, his voice low.

"Not at this time, although I admit I still have a great fondness for the wretched land."

"Then find some reason to return—anything."

Sensing his concern, Porcius searched the old general's eyes. "Why? Obviously, I'm missing something."

"In a word, Agrippina." There was a long pause. "Isn't that reason enough?"

Agrippina, Claudius's niece and fourth wife, had married the aging emperor less than a year before. He executed his libertine wife, Messalina, for treason after she and her latest lover, Gaius Silius, made an ill-fated attempt to take the throne.

"But why are you warning me?" Porcius asked. "Wouldn't it be in your interests to see me dead?"

General Plautius shook his balding head. "No, it would not. Despite our differences, you and I have two important things in common. Loyalty to the emperor and the best interests of Rome, which Agrippina lacks."

As the men strolled leisurely through rows of blooming roses, Porcius looked about the grounds. He eyed the curtained doors of the hallways, which surrounded three sides of the garden, and viewed the frescoed wall at the end. No one was about.

"Now do you understand?" Plautius inquired, his firm mouth set below his wide nose, as if challenging Porcius. "Agrippina will have your head if you don't leave."

"Exactly why would she want my head?"

Plautius halted and faced Porcius. "For opposing the succession of her son, Nero, when Claudius dies."

"But his son Britannicus is the true successor to the purple." Porcius fiddled with the sleeve of his toga.

"Agreed. He's the far better choice for Rome." The two resumed their stroll. "Britannicus, however, doesn't have a vile and domineering mother to back him. He's just a boy, not even ten. He'll never live to see his first toga at fourteen. And there is one other reason Agrippina wants you dead."

Porcius shuddered. *This isn't the first time someone in the imperial household has been after my head. That monster, Caligula, wanted it, too.* "What else?"

The old general tightened his lips into a thin line and nodded. "Remember the great feast we attended last week in honor of the emperor's favorite gladiator, Lucanus?"

"Jupiter, yes. An insufferable lout."

"Do you recall what you said in confidence to Senator Maximinus?"

Porcius stared at Plautius dumbfounded. "How did you—"

"The pillars have ears." The general's weathered face scanned the garden. "One of Agrippina's slaves overheard you calling her an incestuous slut."

Plautius waved away the expected denial. "And the slut told Claudius and demanded your head. Fortunately, our mutual friend, the emperor's freedman secretary,

Narcissus, was present. He managed to convince the emperor that the slave was lying and had his tongue split like a serpent's."

"Thank the Lucky Twins for Narcissus," Porcius said. He wiped his sweating hands down the side of his toga.

The general's forehead creased into three crooked lines as he searched Porcius's eyes. "Of course, he will demand a gift for his favor."

"Anything. I'll even give him one of my prized boys."

Plautius snorted. "Fine for him. But that won't deter Agrippina."

Porcius's heart pounded, and his mouth went dry. *How could anyone have heard my conversation with Maximinus? It was barely a whisper.*

"On second thought," Porcius said, clearing his throat, "I'm sure that I can find business requiring my immediate attention in Rome's newest province."

"I don't envy your journey," Plautius said. He looked away then back to Porcius. "At least you'll be away from her prying eyes."

"Perhaps if I had been awarded a triumph like you and acclaimed a hero of the Roman people, Agrippina wouldn't be so quick to move."

"As politicians, we both know better than that," Plautius reminded Porcius. "It wouldn't stop her."

Porcius tightened his lips and nodded. "Of course, you're right, I'm deluding myself."

"My friend, I have never considered myself a hero," the general said.

Porcius stopped and faced the general. "But you are." He met and held Plautius's eyes. *The man is genuinely modest.*

A caustic laugh escaped Plautius's lips. "Am I? For three years Caratacus made an arse of me and my generals. He knew my troops were spread too thin. I needed Vespasian's Second Legion to secure the northern channel to the west. So Caratacus took full advantage, breaching the holes in the frontier. Hero indeed!" His voice took on new strength reliving his recent command.

"You secured the eastern flanks and the west. A splendid accomplishment," Porcius said.

Plautius's eyes blankly stared beyond Porcius's sagging shoulders. "Aye, but I failed to destroy that shit-eating savage. A full triumph would have been mine instead of a lowly *honorium.*"

"There will be other campaigns and victories." Porcius gestured widely. "You have many years of imperial service ahead of you."

The general snorted. "If it's the emperor's will and not Agrippina's."

"It's just as well I'm returning to Britannia," Porcius said.

"I've never understood what you see in that freezing wasteland."

"Sometimes I've wondered, too. But all I have to do is observe the changes here, and Britannia isn't as unhealthy or barbaric as we might think."

"Now that Agrippina is Claudius's wife, I fear the emperor will soon be among the gods," Plautius added in a sad voice. They walked a few paces in silence until the old soldier stooped and picked up a discarded flower. He brushed away the trace of soil and placed the small violet in his toga's inside pouch without comment. Porcius decided to believe his warnings because of the general's compassion for a simple flower.

"On occasion, I've hidden my fears well. I've never been a brave man," Porcius reflected, "but I must be now. I'm in your debt."

"Thank you, my friend," Plautius answered as he clasped Porcius's right hand and wrist. "Farewell, and may Fortuna smile upon you."

CHAPTER 14

Porcius reached Camulodunum in late August. He wasn't greeted at the docks, and that was fine with him. He had quietly left Rome, not sending word ahead of his arrival, knowing well that word would precede him.

Finding his small villa outside of town in a state of neglect, Porcius spent the next month hiring a new overseer, buying slaves, and seeing his home restored to order. After settling in, he planned to see the new imperial governor, Publius Ostorius Scapula.

The day before Porcius's intended ride to Camulodunum, he paced about the grounds in front of his repainted villa, giving Cyrus, his Persian freedman and steward, orders on its maintenance. Hearing whinnies, jingling pendants, and rumbling hooves of what had to be many horses, he turned and squinted into the midmorning sunlight. A *turma* of at least thirty cavalrymen, drawn up in columns of two, churned up a cloud of chalky dust as they cantered along the elm-lined roadway.

"Roman cavalry," Cyrus said. "Why are they coming here?"

A chill went up Porcius's back, and his knees nearly buckled. "I don't know." *Jupiter, are they here to arrest me? Agrippina must have persuaded the emperor to have my head after all.* Porcius looked about. He could flee, but they would catch him soon enough. Even if he did manage to escape, where would he go? The army would hunt him down like a common slave or thief. Porcius stood as straight as his rotund body would allow and planted his sandaled feet squarely on the ground, mustering all his dignity. No, he had to stay where he was and try to meet his fate like a true Roman—he hoped!

Porcius motioned to Cyrus. "Stay here, we'll see what they want."

As the riders drew closer, he noticed they weren't the usual chain-mailed, blue tunic, and breech-clothed auxiliaries like Gauls or Thracians. Instead, they wore segmented armor over burnt-red tunics and knee-length trousers. *Legionaries! I'm going to be arrested for sure. Scapula wouldn't send them if the matter wasn't serious.* At once he recognized the leader and confident demeanor. *Bassus! Of all people, why did they send him? Was it because we worked together in dealing with the barbarians?*

Centurion Bassus barked a command, and the squadron slowed their foamed-mouth horses to a walk and then halted as the sounds of squeaking leather and jangling pendants faded away.

"Greetings, Centurion Bassus," Porcius said in a flat tone.

"The same to you, Lord Porcius." The centurion grinned, his lower teeth slightly crooked. He nodded to Cyrus.

The Persian motioned to a groom, who raced forward and grabbed the reins from Bassus as he climbed out of the saddle.

Bassus swatted the dust off his segmented armor and tunic before removing the transverse, crested helmet covering his head. He ran a calloused hand through his close-cropped hair before approaching Porcius.

"What brings you to my home?" Porcius asked. *As if I didn't know.*

For a split second, Bassus halted and studied Porcius. He stepped closer, the smell of horse sweat on his armor and clothing. "I brought a detachment to escort you to Camulodunum to see General Scapula."

Cyrus raised a shaggy eyebrow.

"Why the escort?" Porcius asked.

Bassus gestured back toward his men. "As senator and legate, you are entitled to the army's protection."

"I thought this area had pacified," Porcius said.

"The savages still raid us occasionally. General Scapula feels responsible for your safety. It'd be his head if anything happened to you."

It might still be my head if Agrippina has her way.

The Roman scrutinized the centurion's face. "Why does General Scapula want to see me?"

"He has need of your knowledge on British matters."

"What sort of *matters?*"

"To negotiate with Queen Cartimandua."

"Is that all?"

Bassus regarded him with a puzzling look. "What else did you expect?"

Relieved that he wasn't going to be arrested, Porcius sighed, the tension throughout his body vanished in an instant. He cleared his throat. "Why, nothing. Before we leave, why don't you stand down your men for a while? They must be hungry and thirsty. I will have my slaves bring them food and drink—that goes for their mounts." He nodded to Cyrus who bowed and hurried toward the house. "In the meantime, Bassus, come along and join me in some refreshment."

The centurion turned and barked an order to his men to dismount and stand at ease.

Porcius nodded to the groom, who led Bassus's horse away. He motioned toward his house. "I just received a new stock of wine from Germania."

The centurion raised his eyebrows. "German wine?"

"Made by Romans," Porcius answered as they strolled along the graveled walkway, pebbles crunching under their sandals. "Our colonists planted the first grapes less than ten years ago in the Rhenus River Valley. It's not bad, and it's cheap."

Porcius led him through a shaded, ivy-draped archway to a marble bench near his newly planted roses, imported from Italy.

After their drinks were poured and the slave departed, they sat quietly in the newly painted fresco atrium. "I realize this isn't a social visit," Porcius said a few minutes later, "but, nonetheless, I am pleased to see you."

Bassus nodded and touched the hilt of his sword. "The same here, sir. Too bad it had to be on official business. As I said earlier, General Scapula needs your talents."

Porcius jabbed a finger at the centurion. "He should include yours, too. You have a natural gift for diplomacy, my lad."

Bassus shrugged.

"Come now, you were an enormous help in getting those eleven petty kings to surrender."

A wicked smile creased the centurion's mouth. "I appealed to their greed. The bloody barbarians like Roman gold."

Porcius grinned. "They like any gold. Isn't it wonderful what it does for a man?"

Bassus had promised the kings they could rule their lands unmolested, providing they paid tribute. At first they had balked. But when informed that much of the gold would be returned to their private treasuries, they had a sudden change of heart. Each received the same bargain. Bassus knew the rulers would contact one another and compare. And yet, each was given a special gift to make them feel one-up on their rivals and seal the bargain.

The centurion had taken each tribal monarch aside and told him the others would not back him in a fight against Rome. *Had not Caratacus been defeated, and the Catuvellaunii and Dobunni changed sides?* Porcius thought. *They would discover later that it wasn't true, but by then it would be too late. The doubts were sown and the gold paid. As a Briton and king, a man didn't go back on his word. By the time the kings tested the agreement's mettle, the Roman Army would be entrenched enough to crush any rebellion.* Porcius placed a fore finger and thumb to his double-chin as he thought about the brilliance of the ploy.

"The general didn't say much about this Queen Cartimandua," Bassus said, pulling Porcius from his thoughts. "Who is she?"

"Besides being queen of the Brigantes," Porcius said, "she is the younger sister of Caratacus's wife, Dana. Unlike Dana, who is devoted to her husband, Cartimandua is a dangerous snake who will sleep with anyone she can use." He didn't add she would also castrate those who might cross her.

* * *

An hour later, Bassus and Porcius, who had changed into a plain, woolen, traveling tunic, made the short journey to Camulodunum. Porcius rode in an ornate wagon, covered by a scarlet canopy opened on the sides, and pulled by four matched, red ponies. A slave driver sat on the front bench. The Roman settled into a cushioned back seat while Bassus trotted alongside on his chestnut gelding. In front rode two squads of horse soldiers. The one farthest out scouted both flanks of the road while the closer unit trotted directly ahead of the wagon team. Five slave attendants and clerks on donkeys with Cyrus, in the lead on a mule, followed Porcius. The third squad brought up the back acting as a rear guard. The army had recently built a stone-based, hard-packed, gravel road, replacing the old, rutted trackway. It was harvest time, and farmers along the route were cutting ripening wheat and barley with their bone-handled sickles. The sweet smell of cuttings floated on the early, morning breeze. This was a part of Britannia Porcius truly loved.

"Do you realize," Porcius said to Bassus, as the wagon rattled along, "that Caratacus was a boy of only seven when I first built my villa in Britannia?"

Bassus leaned from his saddle toward Porcius, his square jaw and firm mouth appeared as if carved from a Greek statue. His penetrating eyes studying the Roman. "It's unusual for any Roman, let alone a senator, to live so far from Rome."

"True, but when I first traveled to Britannia I was only a rich merchant—later, I bought my way into the Senate. Now I realize Britannia has become more of a home to me than Rome."

"Doesn't the law require senators to live in Rome unless they get permission from the emperor to leave, especially when traveling overseas?" Bassus asked.

A silver fox darted out of the bushes at the side of the road, crossing in front of the entourage, momentarily spooking Bassus's mount and the horses pulling the wagon. Once the driver and Bassus had calmed their horses, Porcius answered Bassus's question.

"You're quite right, but because of my vast knowledge of Britannia, I had no problem in obtaining Emperor Claudius's consent to return."

"The only reason I can see a man wanting to come to this sodding hole is because he had woman trouble," the centurion blurted.

"All too perceptive, my young centurion." Porcius pulled a silk handkerchief from his tunic pocket and wiped the dust and sweat from his face and forehead.

"In Rome they view Britannia as a place of exile."

A flock of ravens flew overhead squawking a raucous call.

"I never have," Porcius said as he tucked the cloth back into the pocket. "Perhaps that's why my enemies let me be. So far, I've outlived them all. Despite being a Roman, the British people have treated me hospitably. I can always return to Britannia when the political climate in Rome grows too warm."

* * *

As they journeyed to Camulodunum, Bassus filled him in on the local events that had taken place in Britannia during his absence. "King Verica died in a hunting accident of suspicious origin after Caratacus's raid on Noviomagnus."

"That's not surprising," Porcius said. "Who replaced him?"

Bassus drew his mount closer to the wagon and leaned over. "Togidubnus, another Atrebate and Roman lackey."

"Humph," Porcius answered with a sniff. "Almost useless, but he'll do Rome's bidding."

Porcius fell silent. The entourage passed through a narrow, fertile valley with several small farmsteads lining the road. The golden wheat was high, ready to be harvested. He scanned the tree-lined hills. Low ridges covered with oaks bordered both sides of the vale. The autumn leaves fell in an amber-rust carpet below.

Winter will come early this year. I wonder how much longer my enemies, especially Agrippina, will leave me alone? Porcius sadly concluded that if he ever returned to Rome he would never see Britannia again. Agrippina would see to that.

The wagon bounced over a small pile of rubble in the road, jolting Porcius as its wheels slammed down on the other side. Bassus's horse veered away.

"Watch where you are driving, slave, or I will send you to the mines," Porcius said.

The pock-faced driver turned his head toward Porcius, his eyes wide. "Yes, master."

"What other news can you tell me?" Porcius asked Bassus.

"A few weeks later, the Second Augustan Legion, led by General Vespasian, launched a campaign in the southwest and easily destroyed thirty tribal hillforts. He encountered the greatest resistance at Maugh-Dun Castle, capital of the Durotrigian Tribe. He lost two to three hundred legionaries."

"Thank the gods the losses were so low."

Bassus snorted and a wry smile crossed his lips. "The Lucky Twins were with the legion. Had that fool, King Unig, united his forces into one army, we wouldn't have defeated the Durotrigians so easily. He was killed, but remnants of his army escaped and made their way to the great forest north of the mouth of the River Sabrina, Caratacus's new base of operations."

"The land is impenetrable."

Holding the reins of his mount in his left hand, Bassus threw up his right hand as if disgusted. "That's why he chose it. Legions would be swallowed like fish in a shark's belly."

Porcius pursed his mouth. "Go on."

"Vespasian was too busy securing the southwest coast," Bassus continued as he lowered his hand to the hilt of his sword, "and the Sabrina River Valley channel to bother with Caratacus."

"What's the status of the army now that Scapula is in charge?"

"The army is spread too thin," Bassus answered. "To keep the lands the army's conquered, Plautius was forced to build wooden frontier fortresses every twenty miles along a northeast frontier axis, billeting each site with one hundred or more auxiliaries. The Ninth and Twentieth Legions are guarding the northeastern frontier to insure the Icenis and Brigantes remain loyal to Rome. That's left Caratacus free to raid at will."

Porcius winced. "Why hasn't Scapula moved on Caratacus?"

"He was about to," Bassus exhaled, "until the damned northern and western tribes rebelled. Scapula ... I mean ... the general, needed the entire spring and summer to quell the revolts. And then the bloody Dumnonii crashed through the western frontier and raided the area around Isca. He sent Vespasian reinforcements and threw them back. But his plans to fight Caratacus and his allies have been set back at least another year if not more."

"Is that why Scapula wants to negotiate with Cartimandua?"

Bassus pulled the scarf wrapped about his neck and wiped the dust from his face. "Aye, so far the queen has proven her loyalty by holding the northern and eastern tribes at bay. If she continues, the commander would be free to undertake his campaign to get rid of Caratacus once and for all."

Porcius had known Cartimandua, Queen of the Brigantes, and her sister, Dana, since they were children. Cartimandua had been married to Venutios, Caratacus's friend and second-in-command, at the age of fourteen. The union ended in failure, and she had gone through many lovers since leaving him. Her father died when she was twenty. Cartimandua was left in a dangerous position. The throne wasn't hereditary, and she had many enemies. Only the tribal council could elect a new ruler. That didn't stop her from becoming queen. Using beauty and intelligence, bribing some council members and sleeping with others, she was elected to the throne. Since that time, she has ruled with an iron fist.

"And what does Cartimandua expect in return?" Porcius inquired after seeing the puzzled look in Bassus's eyes.

"She demands a great deal for her continued loyalty, far more than Scapula is willing to give."

"As I suspected."

* * *

Porcius's meeting with Scapula confirmed Cartimandua's demands. Scapula looked from Porcius to Bassus, the only two present, and then around the plainly furnished office. His eyes paused at the open door where two sentries stood at a discreet distance, their uniformed bodies and javelins silhouetted as dark shadows in the afternoon sunlight. He turned back to Porcius who sat, along with the centurion, across a plain, wooden table from him.

"The bitch demands control of Iceni and western Brigantian kingdoms!" the general roared, his bull face flushed from too much wine. He slammed his silver cup on the wooden table and yelled, "More!" to a slave standing just outside the entrance. His neck muscles bulged through the top of his gilded cuirass, as if they might explode through the skin's surface.

"Promise the whore anything she wants," Scapula continued, exhaling through quivering lips. "We'll renounce the agreement when it's to our advantage. Then we'll toss her carcass to the troops."

"No woman deserves it more than she," Porcius replied.

Bassus nodded. Porcius knew from military protocol the young centurion could not say a word until Scapula addressed him first. He was fortunate the general had allowed him to sit in his presence and only at Porcius's insistence.

"That's why I requested you for this mission," Scapula said. "Since you are a senator, it is only that, a request. However, I can tell you as imperial governor and fellow senator, it would be in your best interest."

Porcius cupped his chin with his thumb and forefinger. "I knew it would come to this," Porcius said.

"It's common knowledge that you're in Agrippina's disfavor." Scapula jabbed a ham-like hand in Porcius's direction. "But the emperor still holds you in high esteem." He lowered his hand. "I received a message soon after your arrival urging you to take this assignment as a favor to the emperor."

"You mean a command?" It seemed to Porcius the room had grown uncomfortably hot. His toes curled within his dyed, red-leather boots.

"Call it what you wish," Scapula said. "Nonetheless, I suspect it will strengthen your position and diminish Agrippina's if you negotiate a favorable agreement with Cartimandua."

"Very well," Porcius said, "it will be amusing to see her once again." He paused and gave Bassus a knowing grin. "She was a lying strumpet before reaching age twelve, and over the years, she's changed little. She would sell a dozen lovers if it would accomplish her ends."

"Then we are in agreement."

"Definitely."

Scapula turned to Bassus. "Centurion, you are to accompany Senator Porcius and provide security."

"Yes, sir!"

A slave appeared with wine for Scapula and his guests. A crooked frown crossed the general's lips. "It's about time, you waddling fool. What took you so long?"

The slave halted and lowered his head as Scapula snarled, "Never mind! I'll deal with you later. Pour it and get out!"

Porcius and Bassus glanced to one another. The senator observed that even Bassus appeared embarrassed by Scapula's outbursts.

To their surprise, the general composed himself. "You, gentlemen," Scapula said in a calmer tone, "must forgive my rudeness. Britannia has been a very difficult province to govern. I don't mind telling you this Caratacus has the army in turmoil. He instigated the rebellions, you know."

"So we've heard," Porcius replied.

"They've set back my campaigning for at least a year, maybe more," Scapula said. "I promised the emperor I'd take the Silurians within the year, and Caratacus, too. That was a mistake. Claudius doesn't tolerate mistakes or excuses." He took a gulp of wine and continued, "My physician tells me to ease up on the drinking. He's afraid it's going to kill me. But it's me and not him that has to deal with this savage!"

"Knowing Caratacus as I do," Porcius said, "I would say even he can't hold out forever. He's bound to make a serious blunder sooner or later. In the meantime, I'm certain I can negotiate an agreement with Cartimandua that will keep her and the tribes loyal."

Scapula narrowed his smoldering eyes. "For both our sakes, see that you do!"

I shall see to more than that, Porcius thought.

136

CHAPTER 15

OCTOBER, AD 47

Before noon, after a three-day, coastal voyage, Porcius arrived by ship at the port of Eburacum on the Ouse River. Amid the usual noise and clattering activity found at any busy dockside, Porcius, clothed in a white tunic trimmed in scarlet and wearing the red, sandaled boots of a senator, debarked from the naval Liburnian. He was escorted by forty legionaries led by Bassus, clothed in plain tunics concealing weapons. Should anyone ask the senator about the close-shorn, burley men surrounding him, he would answer they were his "retainers," entitled by his rank. No Celt with an ounce of sense would believe him, but as long as their swords were kept out of sight, they were in little danger and among allies. Cyrus and a trusted scribe were the only other civilians who traveled with him.

Porcius hated traveling by sea, but General Scapula gave him no choice. Despite the pacification of the Iceni and other tribes located between Camulodunum, from where he sailed, and Eburacum to the north, the general could not guarantee the senator's safety traveling overland. He refused to allocate the large number of troops needed to protect him. "If you were to die by the hands of those savages while traveling to Eburacum, it would literally be my head," Scapula had told Porcius when he was planning his journey. "The emperor is holding me responsible for your safety. You'll go by sea. Once you reach Eburacum, Queen Cartimandua will see that you come to no harm."

The entourage entered Eburacum on a dusty market day. It was the major crossroads of northern Britannia. Trackways from Caledonia to the north and from the lands of the Silurians and Ordovices in the west led to this

bustling trading center. Cartimandua had been expecting
the Romans and had ordered the guards to pass them
through the city gates. Porcius had visited Eburacum in
the past and knew the way to the Great Hall.

The city was alive with jostling crowds and hawkers.
Tall Brigantians, wearing hooded capes and dressed in
brightly colored, tartan tunics and trousers, mingled with
purple-tattooed Caledonians and Venicones. Among the
crowds, from the mountainous west, roamed short, dark
Silurians and Deceanglians, clothed in wolfskins and deer
hides.

Silence descended on the crowd as Porcius and his
retainers passed. Then someone spotted the green sprigs
on the standard carried before Porcius.

"Look! They come in peace! They come in peace!"

At first there was a murmur and then a din as the
festive mood returned to the crowd. Natives and hawkers
alike approached Porcius's retinue attempting to sell their
wares to him and his escort.

Above the mob's noise Porcius shouted to Bassus, who
hiked alongside the senator. "Their hands are out for our
gold, and they smile. But I see hatred in their eyes! They
know we are Romans."

Nevertheless, the carnival atmosphere amused Porcius.
Hawkers, trading from goatskin-covered stalls, bleated to
the crowds. Bargaining was the amusement of the day as
wares and foods of every description were sold. Brigantian
master craftsmen offered their ornate jewelry of gold and
silver designs. Fishmongers sold fresh and not-so-fresh
shellfish, lampreys, carp, eels, smelt, and cod brought from
the Ouse River or the sea.

A stinking fishmonger slipped between the escorting
retainers, ran to Porcius, and shoved a maggot-ridden eel
into his face. The stench nearly made him tumble from his
seat. "Get away from me, you lout!" he shouted.

"But me lord, I got it just for you. I sell cheap." He
thrust it again towards Porcius's face. Porcius instinctively
grabbed the dead eel by its head and began flogging and
cursing the merchant with it like a whip.

Two husky, white-tunic-clad retainers grabbed the
grimy-faced hawker, lifted, and threw him headfirst into a

deep tub full of live, blue-clawed lobsters. One of the
soldiers quipped, "At least with them lobsters he's got a
chance."

As Porcius wiped the slime of the eel from his hands
onto the sleeves of his tunic, the retinue moved onward,
passing ironworkers, making everything from cauldrons to
daggers and swords, who displayed their wares along a
dusty street set aside especially for them. Roman pottery
was abundantly arrayed and purchased, especially by the
richly dressed Britons. Taverns did a brisk business, and
Porcius noticed flourishing prostitutes. Their red-and-
saffron-colored booths, located near the city gates, had a
steady stream of customers entering and leaving.

The scent of freshly baked flat bread and honeyed
cakes, roasting pork, chickens, and ringed sausages drifted
over the bazaar, mixing with the choking stench of
tanneries, slaughter sheds, and sheep pens. Porcius was at
once hungry and revolted.

Bassus, Porcius, and their retinue made their way to
the Great Hall built of unmortared, close-cut stone in the
fortress center. At a nod from Porcius, Bassus ordered the
detail to halt.

Porcius spoke to the two posted sentries in Cumbric,
the language of the Brigantians. It was obvious by their
startled expressions they weren't expecting a Roman to
speak their dialect. He told the guards the queen was
expecting him.

"The queen has known of your coming for the last
couple of days," the tallest of the two sentries said. "You
are to pass without further delay."

"This is a diplomatic mission, Centurion," Porcius
reminded Bassus. "We shall take no more than ten of your
men as honor guard escorts inside."

"Ten?" Bassus protested, who at once quickly tempered
it. "Yes, sir. I'll keep the rest at the alert."

"They are to keep their weapons hidden," Porcius said.
"I know these people, they'll do nothing unless they are
provoked."

Bassus ground out the words between clenched teeth.
"I'm responsible for your safety. If anything happens to

you, my head will be sticking on a pike." Bassus paused and added, "If I survive."

Porcius shook his head. "Nothing will happen. If they intend to kill us, forty legionaries in plain tunics won't stop them. What I want you to do is what Caesar did in Alexandria."

"You mean go into the market and trade with the natives?" Bassus looked about. "Is that wise?"

"Absolutely. They'll know our intentions are peaceful." Porcius grinned. "If I know Cartimandua, she can't afford to have Roman blood on her hands. Not yet."

The centurion scowled, and a frown crossed his face.

Porcius turned and lightly touched Bassus's shoulder. "I know how you can handle it. Allow half of the troops to go to market place at a time. Give them orders not to drink, and if they have to be recalled, at least they will be mostly sober."

Bassus passed the order to his optio, the second-in-command, then marched into the Great Hall with Porcius and ten retainers armed to the teeth. The outline of their weapons showed from beneath their tunics, much to Porcius's distress and Bassus's glee. Porcius glared at his centurion, his annoyance tempered by the pleasure of the arrogant officer's ingenuity. Bassus held eye contact knowingly, his smile just short of insubordination and one-upmanship.

The senator entered the cool, dry hall. Smoky torches hung in wolf-headed, iron casings along the walls. The noisy crowd of chieftains, noblemen, and warriors grew quiet as Porcius approached in the hazy light. He and the escort slowly and deliberately crossed the Roman-style, mosaic floor. Bassus stayed to Porcius's right and a couple of steps behind.

Porcius took his time admiring the picture created from thousands of tiny pieces of colored stone. It was the story of the British God Lugh, an ancient legend Porcius knew well. Discovered by the three queens of the underworld who came upon him while riding horseback, they awoke Lugh where he slept beneath a tree and made him a god. Porcius found the picture and story an admirable blend of old British legend adapted to modern Roman artistry.

Word had been sent ahead of the senator's pending
arrival, and Cartimandua and her court of chieftains and
Druids were waiting. Beyond the great hearth the queen
and one of her consorts brooded from high-backed chairs
on an ornately carved, wooden dais. Shield bearers lined
the wall behind and at each end of the dais. All, except the
queen, viewed the Romans with suspicion, if not hatred.
Her gaze revealed less than the craftiest chess player from
Persia.

At thirty-one, Cartimandua was a stunning woman,
even for a barbarian, observed Porcius. Her curled hair was
the color of a flaming sunset, tightly woven like a net, and
combed in a wave along the sides. She wore a small, gold
headband with a large, green emerald in the center. Light
freckles covered her full but pleasant face, and her lips
were the color of rowanberries. A bright, purple and white
gown with long sleeves trimmed in gold covered her
voluptuous body. Twin gold, torc collars, the shape of
serpents, surrounded her neck. *Regal in every detail.*

Behind the queen, and to one side, a bard played a soft
ballad on a small Celtic harp, a melody of a lady who lost
her love on a hunt.

Famished from the long journey and the smells of the
marketplace, Porcius was grateful they had arrived at
dinnertime. After the usual greetings and salutations, he
sat on the dais next to the queen in the place of honor.
Bassus took a place between two lesser chieftains, but his
ten men stood along the wall keeping a close eye on their
surroundings.

Accustomed to reclining in the Roman custom, Porcius
found it uncomfortable sitting in a chair while he dined.
Cartimandua was becoming more Romanized, but Romans
hadn't used these kinds of chairs for more than one
hundred years!

Nonetheless, it didn't stop him from greedily munching
on a large piece of venison from a roebuck.

As he ate, Cartimandua inquired, "And how was your
journey, Senator Porcius?"

Porcius turned slowly and looked into her dark, green
eyes. He searched momentarily for weakness, and was
rebuffed by the liquid pools of sensuality. He swallowed his

food and took a long swill of beer before answering. "Quite pleasant, my Queen."

As Porcius stuffed himself, Cartimandua asked, "Who is the handsome, young man with you—the one between the chieftains?"

"Bassus. He's one of our most valiant soldiers," Porcius replied. He motioned with greasy fingers to one of the lower tables in front of them.

"Does ... Bacchus ... Bassus," the queen rolled his name across her tongue like a juicy morsel, "usually send his men to market fully armed?" Obviously enjoying the portly senator's discomfort, she continued, "And are his warriors accustomed to cracking open the wine gourds they buy with the heads of my peace-loving merchants?"

Porcius glanced at Bassus, who busied himself with an invisible spot on his tunic. Unless Cartimandua spoke directly to the centurion, he would be forbidden to answer any comments related to him.

She waved off Porcius's attempt at a reply. "Then I assume he's also slaughtered many of my cousin's people?"

Porcius winced. "It's true that Centurion Bassus has killed many, but only in battle. In fact, he has great respect for the British people, treating the civilian population with kindness and praising the bravery and honor of British warriors in battle."

An approving murmur rippled over the assembly.

She silenced them with an uplifted hand.

"You mean he likes to bed our women," she surmised.

The diners laughed.

A tight smile crossed Porcius's lips as he answered slowly, "Well, I don't know about his private affairs, but Caratacus himself spared his life."

"Is he the one?" She paused, turning to Bassus, her interest apparently inflamed. She studied him. "The same one," she continued, "who killed Caratacus's friend, Clud?"

"The same."

"Hmm, he's desirable in a rough way," she remarked as if thinking aloud. "I want to meet him."

The Roman exchanged questioning glances with Bassus. A dubious expression crossed the centurion's face.

"Of course, my Queen," Porcius said. "When?"

"Later. Alone. In the meantime, we have business to discuss."

"I strongly urge that our discussion be private."

Cartimandua glanced about the hall, "By all means. There are too many among my own who would follow Caratacus given the opportunity. He may be married to my stupid sister, but that doesn't make him less dangerous to me."

"I take it there isn't any love lost between you two?"

"None," she sniffed. "By rights, I should be his wife. Together we would have ruled all Britannia."

"But you were already married to Venutios."

"He was little more than a cub. I would have dropped him at the snap of a whip if Caratacus had chosen me."

Porcius felt as if he were intruding on a family quarrel, and he didn't like it.

"Instead," Cartimandua continued, "he picked my sister, the simpering bitch. Her only ambition is to suckle babies! The wolf is the only man who could have tamed me."

Porcius filed that remark of animosity for future consideration and observed Cartimandua's latest lover, sitting to her left—a husky, scar-faced shield bearer. *The whelp nods approvingly at her every remark.*

Taking another leg of chicken in his greasy hand, Porcius thought about what he knew of the Britons. He doubted she would keep her lover for any length of time before flinging him away for another. Venutios was no longer her husband but still a clan chieftain. The last word Porcius had received said he was in Caratacus's camp. After the raid on Noviomagnus, Venutios returned to Brigantia and led the revolt in the west against the Romans. When it failed and Cartimandua refused to lend her support, he fled just ahead of the Romans, who captured and executed the other ringleaders.

"Well, the emperor is grateful for your loyalty," Porcius commented after a moment of thought.

"And I shall remain loyal ... for a price." Her emerald eyes peered right through Porcius as if he didn't exist. Then a wide smile crossed her ample mouth. "The emperor is most generous with his clients, isn't he?"

Porcius regarded her with cold speculation. "You are very presumptuous about his generosity."

"You haven't come this far just to grace my presence with your company, Senator Porcius," Cartimandua said icily. "The noble Claudius doesn't send an emissary of your status without expecting something in return. Am I not correct?"

"Quite perceptive indeed."

"After dinner we shall retire to my private chambers. My chief Druid shall be present as my advisor." She glanced to the lower table, smiling at Bassus. "And bring your brave centurion."

* * *

After dinner, Porcius and Bassus followed Cartimandua and her chief Druid to her private chambers. In the smoky light of eight Roman olive-oil lamps Porcius looked about Cartimandua's bedchamber. He noted the ornately carved, full-length, polished, bronze mirror hinged to the stone wall. To its side stood a wide, mahogany-framed bed containing a gold and red striped mattress and pillows. Folded into neat squares, woolen blankets of purple and silver lay across its top. Two small, bronze tables with spiral bases were covered with ivory cosmetic jars, dragon-headed gold rings, broaches, and other jewelry. Three oaken cupboards containing latticed doors, unheard of luxuries among the Britons, sat side by side near the chamber entrance. The last item he observed was the green and gold, plaid, silk cloak about her shoulders, fastened at the right side of the neck with a gold, double-headed bird of prey broach. A slave had placed it about her after they had entered the icy room. Her taut nipples traced a sharp, teasing pattern beneath the silk.

The senator and the queen sat in the cold bedchamber on cushioned chairs by the jewel-encrusted, wooden table next to her bed, with the Druid close by. Bassus stayed to the shadows of the room ignored by all of them while they negotiated.

"I will be blunt, Senator Porcius," Cartimandua said, "were it not for me, your army would have been destroyed."

"That's absurd. We smashed the Iceni and western Brigantes." He wouldn't admit to her that the army did have its hands full.

"Barely. Had I thrown my lot in with Caratacus, the Romans would have been slaughtered."

Porcius's mouth hardened in annoyance. "But you didn't, and Rome was victorious. What is your point?"

"I demand the rebel lands as reward for my continued loyalty." Her Druid, old but alert-eyed, concurred.

"What you ask is impossible," Porcius lied. "What guarantee do we have that you won't betray us?"

A wicked smile formed on her lips. "Grant me those lands. If for no other reason, bringing them firmly to heel would keep me occupied for a time. It will be years before the Iceni and the western Brigantes are strong again. They lost thousands."

"Nevertheless, what you ask is out of the question," Porcius said. "Rome has chosen Prasutagus and his wife, Boudicea of the Iceni."

"And they are like all Iceni, horse-thieving slime."

"That may well be true, but on that issue neither the emperor nor General Scapula will budge."

"You have wasted a trip, Senator," Cartimandua finally said.

"I will make you an offer, my Queen. I'm certain I can persuade the emperor to give you the lands of the western Brigantes alone. That is my only offer. And you will be honored by your people."

Cartimandua's Druid bent his head to her ear and whispered.

She nodded and turned to Porcius. "I will accept, providing you add five hundred pounds of gold a year!"

You contemptible bitch. Porcius had no patience for this woman. He decided to take a gamble and prayed to Minerva that Cartimandua wouldn't call his bluff.

He cleared his throat. "My Queen, I will not quibble, you are trying not only my patience, but the patience of Rome. There will be no gold."

"Then Rome shall not have my loyalty."

"No? Then Rome will have your head," Porcius threatened dryly.

She glared. "How dare you show contempt to my person."

"I don't, but Rome does, and I speak in her behalf. It is not a threat, but a statement of fact."

"You know that it is in my power to see that you never leave this place alive?"

Porcius sighed. "That would be a grave mistake. What would you accomplish except incurring the wrath of Caesar, and that would be a pity?" Porcius shook his head. "Rome offers you so much, and I come in peace. Rome would rather see you remain ruler of the Brigantes."

"And so I shall."

"Only if you comply with the emperor's wishes," Porcius said in a hardened voice. "If you don't, the army will march on your capital, seize, and replace you with someone of Rome's choosing. Someone we know who will be as loyal as Togidubnus of the Atrebates. I suggest you think on it, but only for a moment!"

For the space of six heartbeats, Porcius studied her face. *By the gods, she's so incredibly beautiful,* Porcius thought. *I can't understand why Caratacus chose Dana for his wife when he could have taken Cartimandua for his consort.*

"Togidubnus ... that worthless lapdog! My army will meet yours in the field and slaughter it to a man."

"Your army will be crushed with or without the aid of Caratacus," he replied evenly. The certainty of what he spoke was felt by all four.

"If we are defeated, I will flee rather than become a Roman bitch."

Porcius scowled, the ends of his fleshy lips curving downward. "To flee admits loss of everything, including Rome's generosity. I don't envision you leaving the comforts of Eburacum, especially your palace. You don't impress me as one who would live in a mud hut in the wilds of the black Silurian mountains," he said. "No, my Queen, you won't run. You were destined to rule. And rule you shall." Porcius folded his hands across his paunch and waited for her to force the issue. *If necessary, I will grant Cartimandua everything as Scapula suggests, and she won't suspect how we will deal with her in the future.*

146

Cartimandua bit her lip as her face darkened. He had won. She looked to her Druid, who imperceptibly nodded capitulation. She took a deep breath and then, in an apparent effort to compose herself, flashed a big smile. "Very well, I accept the western lands."

"A wise decision," Porcius said smoothly, although trying to mask his astonishment. "I must leave before dawn on the next tide to notify General Scapula." Porcius paused, glanced to the entrance, then to Cartimandua and the Druid. "Oh, one other matter, don't get any ideas about planning my demise before I leave Eburacum. Any accidents I suffer will be interpreted by Rome as an act of war and be met with swift and cruel retaliation."

"You can assure the emperor I will remain loyal to Rome."

Porcius didn't believe her for a moment. *However, when the time is ripe, Rome will invade her kingdom. Then she will be no more than a puppet. If she wishes to survive!*

"You may go, Senator Porcius," Cartimandua commanded soberly, apparently recovering her dignity. She turned and nodded to Bassus, who stepped away from the wall.

"However, you are to stay, Centurion." She smiled, stroking her lower lip with a long fingernail.

* * *

"What did the queen want?" Porcius inquired of Bassus early the following morning as if he didn't already know. They breakfasted alone in a small, dimly lit dining area adjacent to the kitchen, sitting on wooden benches at a splintery table. Covered with straw, the floor reeked of rotten vegetables and rancid meat.

"She wanted me to rut with her," he reported directly, munching on a pear.

"That's wonderful." He studied Bassus's impassive face for a moment. "Well, did you?"

"No. Though I was tempted. She's a beautiful woman."

Porcius nearly choked on the cheap Gallic wine and slammed the bronze cup to the ash wood table. "But why not? It's to our advantage for you to be her consort."

"I won't be entangled in her claws," Bassus said, his face flushed with indignation. "That wasn't part of my orders."

"Orders can be overruled. By your union, she'd believe that she could use you to get what she wants."

"And when she tired of me, I'd be murdered by accident or poison."

Porcius shrugged. "She must have been furious. That explains why we're eating in this abominable place!"

"No sooner had you left when she grabbed my hand and led me to her bed," Bassus said. "The slut ordered me to take off her clothes, but I refused. Instead, she ripped hers off as I stood there. Gods, she was as ripe as a pomegranate."

"And you did nothing?"

Bassus smirked. "I was aroused, but no, I didn't."

"Gods, are you alive?"

Bassus chuckled. "I admit it took all the will power I could muster. I did want her despite it all."

"I can't stand this, what happened next?"

"She groped me and knew I was ready. But I gritted my teeth and turned away. That must have done it. She cursed and screamed and threw a shoe at me and questioned my manhood. Then she ordered me to get out, and I did."

Porcius stabbed a chubby finger in Bassus's direction. "You must go to her again. Ask for her forgiveness. Anything. We need a Roman in her court!"

"No, my lord." The centurion tightened his jaw. "I won't be used by her—or you."

Porcius felt the heat rush to his face. "You know that I can have you broken for refusing to obey the order of a Roman senator, a representative of the Roman people?"

"My lord, with all due respect, you can do anything you want. I'm a soldier. I've never been and never will be a politician," Bassus answered calmly.

Embarrassed, Porcius had never spoken in such pompous tones to Bassus before and had no need of it now. That kind of rhetoric was appropriate for the Senate but had no place here. He felt an almost fatherly affection for the young centurion.

"I know," he said in a conciliatory tone of voice, "and a good one, too. Exceptional. You claim you're not a politician, but remember, you negotiated the surrender of the eleven kings like a veteran of the Senate."

"I'm a Roman soldier first. Marching at the head of my cohort is where I belong."

"So you will when we return south. However, isn't a woman of her beauty worth taking a risk?"

"Why don't you go to her?"

"You know why." Since his wife's death, Porcius had a preference for young boys and men. Although this was tolerated in Roman society, he had always felt uneasy about it. And he was discreet. He respected women and appreciated their charms, but since his short-lived marriage at a young age, they had never been a temptation. "Why do you think I was sent to negotiate with that strumpet?"

Bassus sipped his wine. "I must be mellowing, or maybe it's love. There is a woman in Camulodunum I fancy."

Porcius raised a bushy eyebrow. "You've never mentioned her, and that shouldn't stop you. These native women aren't worth pining over."

He snorted. "She's not a local woman, and I'm not pining."

"Who is she?"

"She's the daughter of Barates, a wealthy Palmyrene merchant."

"Indeed, he's worth millions." A wry smiled crossed Porcius's lips. "Then she is a fine catch. What is her name?"

"Regina."

"That's Roman."

"They're Roman citizens. He holds the franchise to supply weapons and armor to the army in Britannia."

"It will be a good alliance for you, marrying into money."

Bassus looked coldly at Porcius. "I don't want to jeopardize it. She even seems favorably disposed toward me, and our forthcoming marriage is arranged. If word got back to her father that I consorted with this royal slut, the marriage agreement would be canceled."

Porcius squinted. For a moment, he seemed lost in thought. "Now I understand. If only I had known before, I could have seen that you weren't placed in such a precarious position. Barates has made a good choice for his daughter."

Bassus grinned.

"Well, perhaps there was unintended wisdom in your refusal of Cartimandua's bed," Porcius said. "She is used to having her way with all men. But in this case, she can't have you. Perhaps it will cloud her thoughts for a day or two, and buy time for my plans to take root."

* * *

A week later in early October, Caratacus received a verbal message from Cartimandua, given to him by a Druid acolyte. Months before, Caratacus had sent word to the queen in an effort to persuade her to join his forces. He wondered if she now had decided to come to his aid.

"What is your message, acolyte?" Caratacus asked.

"These are my queen's words, High King. 'Although I have given my oath to Rome, it is a sham. It is you whom I support, let there be no doubt. You must understand this to be kept a secret.'" The acolyte paused.

"Don't stop now," Caratacus said. "Continue."

The acolyte briefly bowed his head. "'Tell him the Romans are planning to cross the Sabrina River estuary soon. When the time is ripe, my forces shall join yours.'"

"We will be ready," Caratacus said. "The Silurians are loyal allies, and the mountainous country is well suited for my style of fighting. We will wear the Romans down."

"Yes, High King. The queen concluded her message with this: 'But for now, the wolf must carry on the fight alone.'"

CHAPTER 16

JULY, AD 48

The Romans waited until late the following April and landed where least expected. Instead of invading the Great Forest, the Twentieth Legion and its auxiliaries turned northwest and overran the small but strategically located Hillfort at Llanmelin. Its position on the gentle promontory, lying between the Rivers Usk and Wye, made for a clear view across the Sabrina River Valley to the northeast and the sea to the southwest. Now the Romans controlled access to both land and sea, and nothing moved in or out of the area without their knowledge. Another two weeks elapsed before Scapula's forces invaded the Great Woods.

Caratacus's warriors resisted and inflicted heavy Roman losses. Repelling one sortie after another, his fighters bogged down their advance. Still, the muscles tightened in his powerful shoulders and neck when Caratacus mulled over his failure in driving the Romans back across the river. They had too many soldiers. An endless stream of supplies and reinforcements arrived daily by Roman naval barges at the busy camp established on the river's sprawling bank.

Caratacus's rambling camp lay in a large clearing at the base of a hidden valley. A rushing stream tumbled white from gray sandstone rocks above and mellowed into a clear, tranquil pond stretching nearly three hundred paces downstream.

It was late afternoon when Caratacus and his band of blood-spattered and dirty warriors, dozens of whom were wounded, approached the rocky creek on foot. Despite butchering an entire Roman century earlier that day, Caratacus's forces had suffered their highest losses. Out of

151

nearly two hundred, more than forty died. As they approached the settlement, messengers reported from six other raiding parties, including one led by Venutios, that the Romans had successfully counter-attacked, inflicting heavy casualties. Another raiding group had been led by Fiona, who had developed into a hardened warrior since the death of Rhian and was now one of Caratacus's trusted captains. Soon he would have to decide whether to stay in the secret vale, continue his raids, or withdraw.

As Caratacus waded across the knee-deep stream followed by his men, he spotted four warriors dressed in bloodstained, wolf-skin cloaks and ripped, tartan trousers, armed with longswords and battered, oval shields. Fergus ap Roycal, bigger than the other three, led the group. He wore a tarnished, bronze helmet with simulated, spiked horns.

Fergus shouted a guttural victory cry as he pulled off his helmet and waved it over his bald head. "Good news, High King! We chased the Romans to the river."

"Excellent! That's the best news I've heard all day." Caratacus reached the far bank, his legs numbed from the freezing waters, and approached the sun-darkened warrior.

"We stopped the shit eaters when they sent a rescue column for the survivors—like you said they would," Fergus gesticulated to the east. "They ran for their stinking camp."

"My praise to you and your men's bravery," Caratacus said.

"Many thanks." Fergus wiped the sweat from his forehead with a grimy hand and crammed the helmet back on his head.

"I want you and your men to return to camp, now," Caratacus said.

"Aye, will do," Fergus said. "The men deserve a rest and to take care of their wounds.

Caratacus nodded. "While the men recover, I will hold a meeting with all the chieftains."

Fergus momentarily shaded his eyes, viewed the glaring afternoon sun, and turned to Caratacus. "Sounds urgent."

"It is, but we'll have time to drink our dead to the underworld and eat before the meeting begins," Caratacus said.

Caratacus and Fergus ap Roycal, along with the remaining raiders, many of whom were foreign mercenaries and Roman deserters, entered the encampment. Dirty rags covered the injuries of the many wounded who hobbled along with the assistance of fellow warriors or were carried on makeshift, roped stretchers. The band trudged passed the longhouses scattered among the cedar and oak trees whose branches still dripped from summer rains. Carefully they navigated through the pathway's treacherous, oozing, ankle-deep mud. Dirty-faced women and children, many dressed in mildewed clothing, ran to the sorry collection of rag-tag warriors. The forest resounded with their shrieking and wailing upon hearing of the deaths of their men. More took up the painful chorus after discovering other loved ones among the injured.

One woman ran up to Caratacus and waved a blackened stump of an arm in his face. "How much more do you expect us to endure?" she shouted. "For years my family and I have followed you. When do we stop running, lord? I've lost my husband and a hand fighting for you."

"Get away from him, woman!" Fergus commanded.

Caratacus turned to his left side where Fergus walked. "Leave her be." Caratacus stopped and met her piercing, blue eyes. She was no more than thirty, but wrinkles crawled down the side of her gaunt face and streaks of gray ran through her greasy, fading, red hair.

"We won't run much longer," Caratacus promised. "Soon, we'll stop the Romans."

"With what?" She pointed to Caratacus's rust-covered sword. "These weapons aren't fit to fight pigs."

She was right. No matter how many times Caratacus's warriors cleaned their weapons, within hours they were streaked with rust.

"I have a son who is nearly thirteen," she continued to rant. "He's afraid he won't live to see his manhood."

Caratacus briefly touched her shoulder. "I'm not that desperate, woman," he said in a soothing voice. "He'll live to see Britannia free of the Roman menace."

"When? In a thousand summers?" She turned on her heels and stormed through the broken line of warriors.

"The woman is wiser than she knows," Caratacus remarked to Fergus as they continued moving along the path. Gradually, the wounded fell out of the ragged formation to be cared for by loved ones and friends.

"We can't stay here much longer," Caratacus said. "The Romans' pressure is reducing our people to squalor. Did you see their rags—they're wearing animal skins."

"What did you expect?" Fergus said. "They haven't had decent clothes to wear since we left Caleva more than three summers ago." He glanced about. "The camp is overcrowded—it's become a den of disease and pestilence. Have you seen how many of those poor souls have eye inflammations? How many will go blind because of this damned rain!"

"Too many," Caratacus said. He had seen people suffer from this disease in the marshlands along the coast. The Romans called it ophthalmia, and his people had suffered horribly from its effects.

As they neared the Great Longhouse, Caratacus spotted the medicine woman respectfully known as the Crone, a title given to any woman over fifty years of age and a healer. Following her were several female assistants, including Dana. They were removing two more covered stretchers from the house of healing. Dana, wearing a mud-spattered, long tunic turned and saw Caratacus. Smiling, she darted ahead of the Crone and approached Caratacus. He turned to Fergus and told him to move on with the men. Leaving his warriors behind, he walked toward Dana. They stopped and tightly embraced one another.

"Thanks to the gods you are safe," Dana said as she pulled away a step. Loose strands of her sunrise-colored hair fell down across her forehead and side of her face. The beginnings of crow's feet extended from the edge of her hazel eyes.

Caratacus exhaled. "Unfortunately, many of my men are now with Teutates beneath the earth."

Dana looked past him to the wounded hobbling away with the help of their comrades and relatives.

"How many?" she asked, her eyes fixed on Caratacus.

"Too many." He told her the number.

Dana looked back toward the Crone who had halted with her other women. "We can't afford to lose so many—the losses grow worse every day."

"That's why we must move and soon," Caratacus said. He shook his head and changed the subject. "How is our little girl feeling?"

Dana smiled as she brushed strands away from her face. "Macha is much better, thank Mother Goddess. It was a nasty cold and could have been worse. But she should be well by tomorrow. The Crone gave her a potion that helped her."

"Good. Gods how I regret not being able to spend more time with the both of you. This damned war goes on and on."

"We'll talk more about it later. Here is the Crone."

The older woman, taller than the others assisting her, raised a veiny arm in salutation as she approached Caratacus and Dana.

He gave her a slight nod out of deference to her high status. "What's your news today?"

The woman's tired, but intelligent, cobalt eyes focused upon Dana and then Caratacus from a weather-beaten face. "Six more deaths, lord," the gaunt healer replied. "My best potions and herbs are worthless without cleaner conditions. The garbage pits overflow, and the latrines are near capacity. They breed only more pestilence. I took it upon myself to order new ones dug."

"You made the right decision."

The Crone ran her long fingers through the frizzled, gray hair tied into a single-roped tail running down her back, "Thank you, my lord, but they will fill up fast. Soon there won't be any place left to dig new trenches."

"I agree," Dana said.

He glanced around the area once more, shaking his head. *How do I resolve this dilemma for my people?* He placed a hand on the woman's narrow shoulder. "Put your mind at ease, Old Crone, we shall move before the week is out."

"It is good that we will leave. With your permission, I must see to the other sick ones."

"I will go with her, Husband," Dana said. "Crone needs all the help she can get."

"All right, but I want you at the council meeting tonight. It's important that you know what I plan to tell the chieftains."

"If it is the same one you told me about last night, I pray that your leaders will see the wisdom in it. I will see you later." She kissed him on the cheek and followed after the old healer.

* * *

"We can no longer contain the Romans," Caratacus announced to the gathering of clan chieftains, warriors, including Fiona, the arch-Druid, Owen, and lesser priests in the stifling, low-ceiling longhouse. Dana sat silently at the back with wives of the other counselors. All those present had parked themselves at small tables on the hard-packed, dirt floor, drinking beer and eating venison and fowl.

"I've received word the Twentieth Legion has launched a major offensive," Caratacus continued after readjusting himself on the crude makeshift throne. "Roman troops and their thieving auxiliaries are spreading through the forest."

Fergus ap Roycal, who sat up front along with Venutios and the other leaders, including Fiona, looked about the room. He turned and studied Caratacus's face a moment with his charcoal eyes before speaking. "Are you saying that we cannot halt them in the Great Forest?"

"The Romans aren't after the whole forest—only us. Their plan is to isolate then destroy one band at a time. That's why we must withdraw before we're trapped."

"The forest is too big! We are many and spread like wheat in the field," Fergus said.

"This afternoon I was informed by my messengers that the Romans know our positions," Caratacus said. "They have the resources to isolate our clans from one another and cut our escape routes and supply lines. The Romans need only to destroy major groups such as ours, and the rest they can butcher at their leisure. Let them have the forest. We will continue fighting."

156

There was a murmur among the gathering.

"What about our friends, the Silurians, who live here?" Venutios asked.

Brath, a short, shaggy-haired warrior and leader of the Silurians who sat near the front, said, "This is our homeland, and we won't leave. Stay we will to harass the Romans and protect our land."

Caratacus nodded in approval. "It allows us time to withdraw our warriors and set up fortified positions elsewhere. We will move to the Black Mountains, the Brecon Beacons, and other forests and valleys in the east from which we can fight."

"We won't be alone long," Fiona said. "What about the Ordovices?"

"My plan is to unite with the Ordovices," Caratacus continued, "and persuade my cousin, Queen Cartimandua, and her Brigantes to join our cause. My spies say the Romans will strike Cartimandua when the time is right, but we don't know when. That is why we must unite to defeat them."

Caratacus locked his eyes on the chieftains, then on his advisors and Druids. They nodded. He glanced around the room and shrugged, knowing the chieftains would unite behind him.

"We are in agreement?" Caratacus said.

"Agreed," they said unison.

"It will be a fighting withdrawal," Caratacus said. "I will use our bravest warriors and harass the Romans. Whenever they enter the woods to shit, let their searching comrades find their heads on pikes. Allow them no rest. Deny them sleep. Teach them to fear every shadow of the forest. Exact revenge without pity. Make them pay for every step forward into your lands. Topple trees in their paths and boulders from the hillsides. But deny them your blood and add to their frustrations. By the time we next meet them in battle, they will believe us demons. The rest of us will take everything with us. What we can't remove, we destroy. Leave nothing but bones to the Romans!"

* * *

Upon conclusion of the High Council's meeting, Caratacus and Dana left the Great Hall. He glanced westward across the meandering creek to the jagged-toothed Black Mountains, now covered in purple shadows, as the last rays of sunlight faded in the western sky. The low murmurs of voices from nearby huts echoed off the surrounding pines and firs as people settled in for the night. The smell of smoke from cooking fires drifted on a breeze.

"At least the chieftains agreed to the plan to leave without too much of their usual bickering," Dana said.

"I knew they would see the wisdom in the plan." Caratacus grinned. "Now it's time to see Macha."

Entering their longhouse, they found their five-year-old daughter lying on a bed-pallet near the fire pit snuggled in a heavy fur, asleep. A female servant hovered nearby.

Caratacus motioned to the child. "How is she?"

"Better, lord," the servant said. "The Crone says she be well by tomorrow, and I believe her."

Macha stirred about, opened her aqua eyes, and yawned. She spotted her parents. "Mum, Da," she mumbled.

"Hello, sleepy head," Caratacus said. "We're home."

"How are you feeling, darling?" Dana asked.

"Hungry," Macha answered in a scratchy voice.

Dana nodded to the servant. She stepped to the iron pot hanging by a tripod over the fire pit and ladled out a small bowl of broth, the smell of venison filled the home.

She moved toward the freckle-faced, little girl, whose hair was the color of a sunrise, and was about to stoop down when Caratacus stopped her.

"I'll feed her." The servant bowed as she handed him the wooden bowl and spoon.

Caratacus sat down next to Macha. "Can you sit up?"

"Yes." Slowly, she pulled off the fur, placed her little hands along both sides of her body, pulled back her knees, and pushed herself up into a sitting position.

"Here, try some of this. Open wide." Carefully, he placed the spoon to her lips.

Macha sipped a little, but choked and spat out the liquid. "It's hot."

Caratacus inhaled sharply. "Oh, I'm sorry sweetheart." He scooped another spoonful and grinned. "Now, I want you to blow on it first, real easy, to cool it down. Then just try a little bit."

She did, swallowing the broth.

"Better?" he asked.

"Yes," she said.

"All right," he said gently, "try some more."

Macha ate about half a bowl and said, "I'm full."

Dana stepped closer and smiled. "Good girl."

Caratacus took the bowl from her and handed it to the servant. He turned back to Macha and gave her a hug. "That's my girl."

"I miss you, Da. You not here much."

He nodded and quietly answered. "I know, but tonight I'm here."

"Good. Don't go away—don't die."

Caratacus and Dana looked at one another. "Where did you hear that, Macha?" Caratacus asked.

Macha's face tightened, a thin line crossed her forehead. "My friends tell me."

Dana kneeled, her eyes fixed on her daughter. "When?"

"When I play with them—when they don't help their mums and das."

"Don't believe them," Caratacus said. "They don't know any better."

"But some mums and das died."

"That's true," Dana said, "but your da is alive. He is very careful."

"Good." Macha closed her eyes as she held onto Caratacus and fell asleep.

"For her sake, if for no one else, we must leave this wretched place," Dana said.

"We will, Dana, and I will stop the Romans once and for all."

But how much bloodshed will it cost?

Chapter 17

JULY, AD 50

Stripped to the waist, a sweating Caratacus hiked with Fergus ap Roycal and Venutios along the base of the newly reconstructed defensive wall while the sun beat on their backs. A cloth sweatband covered the king's scarred forehead and was knotted at the back of his shoulder-length, tawny hair. Shieldbearers and grooms leading their snorting horses followed the ruler and two chieftains who stopped every few paces, checking for weaknesses in the roughcut, graystone facing.

A lower rampart crossed a gentle slope below the only access to the hillfort of *Caersws*. In between, Caratacus's warriors had dug a defensive ditch the depth of three tall men and the width of eight. Dark, overhanging cliffs protected the three other sides of the citadel. Below the barrier, at the foot of the grade, a narrow ford crossed the swift, flowing River Sabrina, its rushing water echoing up toward the citadel. Washing clothes, slapping them on small boulders, a cluster of women stooped or kneeled along its edge downstream. Nearby, their children played games and ran about laughing and screaming. A tiny village of herdsmen and shepherds squatted among the worn-down hills beyond the watercourse.

Nearly one year before, after a two month trek northward from the Great Forest, Caratacus and his army had arrived within the protective range of the Berwyn Mountains.

Hidden within its deep recesses, an ancient hillfort loomed above the narrow valley. From Berwyn's jagged heights the land of the Ordovices rolled southward in a succession of towering cliffs, forested uplands, and isolated vales.

Caratacus attempted to slide his dagger blade between two well-placed stones, but the stones didn't budge. He grinned as he rubbed his forefinger along the gritty sides of the wall and shoved the weapon back into its scabbard. "That does it!" he said to Venutios and Fergus ap Roycal, who were also bare-chested like their king. "Teutates himself couldn't have built a better wall."

Thousands of warriors had labored eight months to complete the huge barrier. Almost twelve feet high and more than six feet across, it was reinforced by wooden crossbeams, as thick as temple pillars, laid out in regular intervals and filled with earth and gravel.

Fergus twisted his crooked mouth into a sneer. "Let the shit-eating Romans take us now. Only Teutates could destroy us."

Venutios nodded. "When will the rest of the Ordovician levies arrive?"

"They're still gathering, but they should be here within ten nights," Caratacus replied. He motioned to his groom to bring a Roman-style, wooden canteen filled with water. Caratacus passed it to Venutios and Fergus. When they had taken their fill, he drank from it as well. Although tepid, it was wet and soothed his parched mouth. He returned the flask to the groom, who stepped away at his nod.

Caratacus gazed for a moment down the length of the wall, turned, and peered across the river to the village and the hills beyond. He took a deep breath. "If we don't halt the Romans here, Britannia is lost. But that won't happen. We hold the boar's head. The location is ideal."

Caratacus had selected the sight for a list of reasons. A sheer cliff protected the north side. A gentle gradient reinforced with a stone rampart formed the south end. A huge stone battlement blocked the only approach. At the fort's rear lay the supply and escape route running through the forest and over a pass to the far side of the mountains.

"The Romans will never get over the wall," Caratacus said.

Fergus guffawed. "Aye, if we don't get them first, the floodwaters will."

Caratacus surveyed the area beyond the settlement's sparsely cultivated fields, searching for Roman scouts. None. At least his forces wouldn't be taken by surprise. The natives had told Caratacus that over the years large tracts of hillside land had been cleared by grazing flocks of sheep and herds of cattle. They destroyed the protective ground covering of heather, bilberry, and wild grass, leaving the valley at the mercy of the fickle rains and repeated and disastrous floods. His eyes confirmed the truth. The marshy land about the Sabrina and its sandy banks were strewn with boulders the size of horses, gnarled uprooted trees, wild undergrowth, and other debris.

"The Romans aren't fools," Caratacus cautioned. "Their engineers will spot the flood areas right away. They'll pile timber high and build a brushwood road above the water level. Then they'll throw pontoons across the river."

"Let them," Fergus snarled. "We'll shower spears and slingstones on their pig-sticking heads!"

"Listen to me, if they can't swim it, they'll bridge the river. If they can't bridge it, they'll dam it, or by the gods they'll change its course and walk across dry land. Never underestimate the Romans." Caratacus glanced away.

For a moment they all remained silent. In the distance, the sound of the river resonated along the canyon walls, women chattered while rinsing clothing by the shore. The baying of sheep radiated across the stream.

Venutios wiped the perspiration from his scarred face with a calloused hand and squinted in the glaring sunlight towards the fortress and then Caratacus. "What plans have you made in case we have to retreat?"

"Retreat? Are you mad!" Fergus narrowed his raven eyes and threw up his gigantic hands. "They don't have enough troops. The Silurians are tying down half their army."

"It's the other half that concerns me," Caratacus said. "Venutios is right. We must always prepare for disaster. I've made alternative plans, and you'll know before we fight."

"Don't forget, Fergus," Venutios said, "they have twenty thousand troops to throw at us."

"Regardless, the reports I have received from the Druids say that Roman forces have been thinned out," Caratacus said. "Between our raids and those of the Silurians, the Romans have been forced to build small watch forts every twenty miles within their lines. It has been a drain on their manpower and supplies. But it still leaves about fifteen thousand that we will have to deal with. We wait here. The Romans will come to us."

Venutios's eyes flicked to the river crossing and back to Caratacus. "For once they'll fight on our terms."

Caratacus nodded, pleased that Venutios grasped his plan.

Mounting their horses, the group headed to the fortress.

* * *

As the king and his retinue returned to Caersws, Caratacus reflected on what Fergus had said about Brath, the Silurian king. True, he had kept his promise. The Romans had paid dearly for every step they advanced in the Great Forest. Brath and his men continued to keep the Twentieth Legion at bay, allowing Caratacus to retreat northward after staying the autumn and winter in the Valley of Mwr. Despite Caratacus's ongoing raids against the Romans and the reinforcements he had received from some of the tribes bordering the Ordovices and Silurians, as well as foreign mercenaries, the men available to him had diminished as the number of Romans increased.

And the situation had worsened. Besides the Twentieth Legion, he'd received word General Scapula was leading the Fourteenth Legion Gemina northeastward from its southern base at Isca to attack him and his Ordovician allies. The Romans drew closer every day, and his warriors clashed with their cavalry patrols. Soon he must begin battle or risk being cornered.

* * *

Other problems had to be dealt with before the Romans arrived. They weren't Caratacus's only enemy. His own people presented an even greater problem. Although he had put a score of his men to death for crimes committed in their midst, the hatred and animosity among the allied tribes lay just below the surface.

By moving to the land of the Ordovices, Caratacus stopped the Silurian tribe in the south and the Ordovices to the north from warring against one another. The Ordovician king considered him a hero and invited Caratacus to move his forces to his lands. He became a buffer between the two tribes and joined them with his hodgepodge of the southern and eastern tribes fighting against the Romans—at least for now. He had no illusions. If the Romans were defeated and forced eastward, within a year the tribes would again be at each other's throats.

When Caratacus and his entourage rode up the gentle gradient, they met a hunting party returning from the surrounding hillsides. Feral mountain sheep, their long, spiral horns scraping the rocky ground, hung from forty hardwood poles and were each carried by two struggling warriors. Strings of otters and badgers dangled from saddles, and goatskin bags full of thrushes and redwinged kites were dragged along by the footmen. There would be feasting tonight.

Caratacus signaled for his entourage to halt. "Let them pass," he said. "It's more important to get the game home, cooked, and smoked before it spoils. Especially in this heat." He pointed to the swarm of buzzing flies. "We don't eat rotten meat."

* * *

The king spotted Dana and Macha picking rock flowers near the fort's main gate. He found the broadleaf flowers most unusual. Caratacus hadn't seen them in any other part of Britannia except the Ordovician lands. Dana and Macha waved, and he did the same.

He grinned and turned back to his men. "Go on ahead," Caratacus said, "I'll join you later."

After dismounting, he led his horse by the reins and approached his smiling wife and giggling, freckle-faced daughter. Both wore matching yellow and green plaid, ankle-length tunics girdled at the waist by a scarlet, cloth belt. Like her mother and father, Macha wore a gold torc around her neck and bracelets on her upper arms.

"Look, Da!" Macha exclaimed as she shoved the strawberry-like plant his way. "Smell it."

Caratacus bent forward, carefully wrapping a sun-chapped hand around the long stem. He drew the rose-white flower to his nose and loudly inhaled its sweet fragrance. "Uum, that smells so good!"

Macha giggled again. "Oh, Da. Don't be so noisy," she said in the most dignified voice she could muster. "I'm a big girl now, almost eight. That's for children." The afternoon light burnished her sunset hair as she turned. It glistened as if it were on fire.

Surprised by her remarks, he chuckled, "Of course, my little fox, you're right. You're a big help to Mum. But I thank you all the same." He placed the flower back into her little, soiled hands, stooped, and gave her a peck on the cheek. "You're very thoughtful." A dimpled smile came to Macha's freckled face, and she turned and scurried away to pick more flowers.

"It's nice to see you smiling for once," Dana remarked. "It's been a long time."

"There hasn't been much to smile about lately, but today it is different."

"Then the wall inspection was a success?"

"Aye, it's solid. We'll hold. Tonight we celebrate."

As they approached the fortress gate, a blissful smile returned to Dana's suntanned face. Caratacus took her hand in his.

* * *

On an early afternoon, three days later, Fiona and her contingent of warriors, both men and women, returned from their journey to Eburacum. She had been sent there by Caratacus to again request Queen Cartimandua to send her army to aid in his fight against the Romans. With the addition of those warriors, Caratacus was certain he could halt the Roman advance once and for all.

Fiona was now captain of Caratacus's warrior women contingent and commanded a company of male fighters as well. She had also been placed in charge of a band of archers made up primarily of foreigners from as far away as Germania and Scandia. One would have never guessed that when Fiona was recruited by Rhian for her contingent of warrior women, years before, she had been a shy and timid farm girl. It was only after she had reluctantly slain Rhian, who had been raped and badly wounded by the Batavians, that she had become a hardened veteran. Thereafter, Fiona proved herself worthy in several skirmishes and raids and gained Caratacus's trust.

Caratacus had been informed by a warrior guarding the front entrance to the Great Hall that Fiona had arrived and was waiting outside.

"Tell her to enter and proceed to the dais where my councilors and I await," Caratacus said. He turned and nodded to Fergus ap Roycal, Venutios, and Owen, the Druid who sat to his right. He stood behind and to one side of Caratacus's throne on the dais. Fergus sat to the king's right, while Venutios was to his left.

The king watched as Fiona entered the stifling building, passing dozens of soldiers, whose unwashed bodies filled the interior with a sour smell. Although the side doors and flaps had been opened to allow in the sunlight, it did little to alleviate the heat and stench.

The young woman, wearing a dusty, tartan tunic and trousers, halted before the king and planted her feet on the straw-covered floor. She bowed slightly to Caratacus and his advisors.

While she stood waiting for permission to speak, Caratacus studied Fiona. Besides her clothing, she wore her chestnut hair in a single braid that cascaded down her back between the shoulder blades. A thin scar sliced downward left to right across the forehead of Fiona's sunburnt face to the bridge of her buttoned nose. Numerous thin scars could be seen on the young woman's exposed lower arms. Fiona's small teeth remained a polished white. She used a forearm to wipe the sweat from her face. She carried a longsword held in a baldric that crossed from her right shoulder down to the left side of the waist. A dagger, enclosed in a leather scabbard, hung from a belt at the right side.

Caratacus motioned to Fiona. "Tell us your news, Captain."

"The journey to Eburacum lasted ten days, lord," Fiona said. "Had it not been for the Roman patrols, my warriors and I would have arrived in seven."

"I understand," Caratacus said. "And your audience with the queen?"

She took a deep breath and nodded. "After waiting for many hours in a dingy back room, I was greeted by Queen Cartimandua's arch-Druid who led me into the Great Hall."

Fiona had explained that no others were present except herself, Cartimandua, the Druid, and her shield bearers, who stood at a discreet distance. Her icy-blue eyes silently studied Fiona from where she sat on the shoulder-high throne. Fiona boldly returned her stare, knowing the queen was attempting to make her feel uncomfortable, yet Fiona held her tongue until addressed.

Now Fiona hesitated, but Caratacus gestured with a hand for her to continue.

"She asked me why you, lord, had not sent her word of my pending visit?"

"I wanted to learn what kind of reception you would receive," Caratacus said.

Fiona raised an eyebrow as she stared at Caratacus. She lowered her eyelids. "Pardon me, lord, did you believe I would have been taken captive?"

Caratacus scowled. *You are impertinent, but your question is valid.* "If I had thought that, I would not have sent you. Continue."

"The queen said, 'This is most unexpected.' When she motioned me a few steps closer to her throne, I explained that there were too many Roman spies about the lands, and had the Romans known of my journey, I would have been captured and tortured. The queen replied you could have sent a courier with a secret message. I answered that couriers can be tortured to confess. Even if they had gotten through, a spy in her midst would have learned who I was and where I came from. Naturally, she denied harboring spies."

Caratacus snorted. "Which means she does."

"I said neither you nor I were accusing the queen." Fiona gestured with a hand. "I looked at the queen and suggested there may be one, a trader perhaps, who had used his oily tongue to wriggle his way into her midst."

"The queen probably didn't take kindly to that," Caratacus said. He looked to his chieftains and the Druid. They nodded.

"Cartimandua told me that I should consider myself fortunate that she consented to a private audience on such short notice," Fiona said. "With all the humility I could muster, I said I was very grateful. The queen informed me it was only because I represented you, lord, that she received me. I touched the gold torc wrapped around my neck as in a blessing and answered, 'Teutates forbid that I mean you any harm, I swear on my sacred oath as a captain in Caratacus's army.'"

"You were wise to swear your allegiance to me in front of the queen," Caratacus said.

The council and Owen murmured in affirmation.

"I would have no matter the situation, lord, you are my king." Fiona bowed her head. "But Cartimandua gave me a look that could have scorched meat and said oaths were easily broken. I quickly answered that the queen was a great power in her own right. At first, she didn't respond. She sat there staring at me, and then an evil smile formed on her full lips, and she tossed her head back and laughed."

Caratacus raised an eyebrow. "Laughed?"

For the length of a couple of heartbeats, Fiona swayed on her feet. "Yes, she said, 'Isn't this absurd?'"

Caratacus raised a hand and jabbed it in Fiona's direction. "What was absurd?"

"It was something that alarmed me. She said, 'Do you realize we are the two most powerful women in all Britannia?'"

"She what?" Caratacus shook his head.

"This is a ploy," Venutios said. "I know the scheming bitch all too well. She wants all power to herself. She was saying that to flatter you, Fiona."

Unless we stop the Romans, they will control all of us. He raised his hand toward Venutios and turned to Fiona. "Proceed."

168

"Forgive me, lords, those are her words," Fiona said. "I was shocked to be included. I said, 'Great Queen, I don't understand. I am only a warrior. If there is another powerful woman, it is Dana, wife of Caratacus.'"

Caratacus nodded. "Dana may not agree with you, but she is in her own right. What else did Cartimandua say?"

Fiona wrapped her fingers around the handle of her dagger. "She laughed and said some terrible things about your wife, lord." The young woman hesitated. "I would rather not repeat them. I have heard how much Queen Cartimandua despises Dana, but I was still shocked by her obvious hatred."

Caratacus clenched his teeth. "You don't need to repeat what she said, I can guess." *Am I wrong to think Cartimandua will ever come to our aid? She hasn't so far.* "Continue."

"She said I was a captain and a leader in Caratacus's army. My warriors listened to me, men and women. I explained that I only led the women, and they were few."

"We both know that isn't the truth, you lead many warriors, male and female," Caratacus said.

The chieftains and Owen nodded in agreement.

"Yes, lord, but I didn't want her to know that."

"Wise, indeed. Proceed."

"The queen said I underestimated my abilities. She reminded me of my escape from the Romans and that I had replaced Queen Rhian as a leader. Her sources told her that I had fought bravely since that time. Cartimandua knew about the raids I led."

"The queen is right. You are a much stronger warrior than you may believe."

Fiona shrugged. "I asked her if we should not work together for the good of our people. That was why I came. The queen said she always worked for the welfare of her subjects. Begging your pardon, lord, but I don't believe the queen works for anyone's good except her own."

"You are right, but we still need her alliance if we are to defeat the Romans."

"The queen asked why I was there to see her. Before I could answer, I caught her staring at my breast." Fiona blushed. "I said I brought her a vision, but her gaze made me feel uncomfortable."

"Cartimandua has been known to have female lovers—it's unfortunate you were put in such a position," Caratacus said. "Did you tell her of the false vision?"

Caratacus had contrived the vision to measure the queen's sincerity to aid his cause.

Fiona explained Cartimandua seemed skeptical that Caratacus would send a warrior all the way to Eburacum just to share a vision. The young woman answered that Caratacus trusted no one as much as her, not even a Druid. He had a dream in which he went to see the queen even though he was in danger from her. When Fiona finished, the queen told Fiona she was upset that he believed the danger came from her and surely that Caratacus didn't believe it. Fiona said if that were true, Caratacus would not have sent her on such a far journey.

"She asked how could she know this wasn't a spell—sorcery?" Fiona said. "Why hadn't you sent a Druid to interpret the dream? I explained it wasn't sorcery, and that you, my King, knew how she hated it. I said that you believed yourself in danger."

Fiona said Cartimandua's eyes had narrowed, a sneer formed on her lips, and she demanded proof. Fiona explained that Caratacus asked that the queen use her own Druids to interpret the dream to see if he was telling the truth.

"What was Cartimandua's response?"

"She sat silent as if hesitating before answering, 'If what you say is true, then this is indeed serious.' Cartimandua glanced to the bored, young shield bearer standing closest to her."

Fiona looked at Caratacus. "I must admit, Great King, that I prayed that her chief Druid would believe the vision. I'm sure my lord remembers the report we received about the queen's favorite consort, the shield bearer who had attended the feast for the Roman, Porcius, on his last visit. One day after her Druid foretold that he was in danger, the warrior died. He fell from a horse while hunting and died of a broken neck."

"Did the Druid believe the vision?"

"He did," Fiona said. "The queen summoned her Druid, and I explained the dream to him. He concurred that you were in danger but not from Cartimandua. He could not tell where the danger came from. That's when Cartimandua assured me she would do everything in her power to help you. She will send warriors to your aid when the time is right."

"She has said that before," Caratacus said.

"That is all the queen would tell me. She stood, approached, and slowly moved around to my back. She said, 'I ... we ... do not want anything to befall him.'

"This was embarrassing, but the queen pressed her form gently against my backside, and, feeling no resistance, cupped both my breasts, and with a moist tongue kissed the nape of my neck. I closed my eyes, in fear of what would follow.

"Cartimandua said, 'Did I not give my word to support him against the Romans?' The queen's hands fell slowly down my waist, and that's when I broke away. I flushed and said, 'He ... wants you to come and see him.' She said, 'We will discuss that later, tonight.'"

Fiona had departed the next day, relieved that her purpose had been accomplished and that she fled from the clutches of the queen. Cartimandua had promised she would journey to Caersws and see Caratacus. But she'd refused to say when. "The queen said she feared something would befall you, my lord. She knew not what or why or when."

* * *

One week after Fiona had returned from Eburacum, a vicious storm raked the Valley of Caersws the afternoon Havgan the Druid and his escorting acolytes and body guards arrived from the Isle of Mona. Because Havgan's prophecy of a victory over the Romans had proven to be wrong, when Caratacus's army was defeated at the River Medway, Havgan had been replaced by Owen as Caratacus's arch-Druid. Although the older man had fled in disgrace to the Druid sanctuary, he was allowed to return to Caratacus's holdings periodically when the arch-Druid of Mona had information on Roman activities.

Caratacus and his hunting party had been caught in the downpour and arrived at about the same time as the Druids. Coming from the direction of the nearby hills, the king and his men had barely escaped the River Sabrina's raging flood waters.

The king greeted and immediately invited the priest into the Great Hall. Havgan still shivered from the cold rain even though a servant came forward and placed a heavy blanket around his bony shoulders.

"My lord, Caratacus," the Druid said as they sat in chairs facing the comforting fire of the center hearth. "It is important that I have a word with you, now."

"Of course, Havgan. What news do you bring us from the Sacred Council?"

"The council is alarmed by the Roman landings along the coast of the Silurians; soon the Sacred Island will be in jeopardy."

Caratacus knew the Roman legions were moving up the Wye, making coastal landings along the Bristol Channel in an effort to encircle and isolate him.

"That's why I am raiding Roman positions wherever they are established," Caratacus said. "So long as Brath and his warriors keep them busy, you'll have little to worry about."

Caratacus's reports said the Silurians, whose kingdom the Romans had invaded to the south of Caratacus's stronghold, had raised so much havoc that the Romans had only conquered a small part of it during the last two years.

Havgan scrunched his wrinkled forehead and, while holding the blanket by one hand, pulled lightly at his well-trimmed, white beard. "But for how long? Our sources say otherwise."

Caratacus understood Havgan's meaning. The Druids used their extensive intelligence network to keep track of Roman Army movements. An invasion of Ordovician territory was a serious threat to the Isle of Mona just off its coast. Roman infantry could sweep across the muddy flats, reaching the island during low tide. If his forces didn't hold, Mona would be next. The Romans, in hatred, would slaughter the Druid priests and destroy the sacred sanctuary.

"We also know," Havgan continued, "the Roman general, Scapula, has fewer troops since the Twentieth Legion started campaigning against the Silurians in the south."

"That's in our favor."

"Aye, but we have learned Scapula has decided to concentrate all remaining forces against you. He has only one objective. Your death!"

Caratacus grabbed the hilt of his sword. "Ha! That is nothing new. Scapula knows where we are. If he wants his battle, it will have to be here. We move no farther."

"They will arrive at any moment."

CHAPTER 18

SEPTEMBER, AD 50

It had been evening, and the flaps to the front entrance and the side of his home had been left open to allow in the light from the setting sun and to alleviate the stifling heat. Light from the small hearth and oil lamps hanging from iron tripods filled in the shadowy gaps.

Caratacus sat bare-chested, while Dana and Macha wore light, short-sleeved and knee-length, plain tunics as they finished eating their evening meal by the center hearth. The aroma of bread and the tangy smell of beef stew lingered in the air.

One of the female servants had removed the cauldron from the hearth and took it outside to clean.

The king's eyes searched their wattle-and-daub home, a little bigger than those in which the rest of his people lived. In the shadows, he noted the belongings Dana had packed for her and Macha in several goat-skinned and cowhide packets and bundles. If the Romans overran Caersws, he wanted his family safely away. The Ordovices pledged to fight alongside Caratacus if he was forced to withdraw, but he shook his head and thought of once more retreating.

Caratacus took a drink of corma and washed down the last piece of bread. He let out a low belch. Macha laughed, and Dana smiled. Relaxing, he sat back on the bear-skin rug and closed his eyes for a moment.

Macha, who had been sitting between Caratacus and Dana, crawled onto Caratacus's lap and clung to his side, which pulled him out of his thoughts. *She is heavier than I remembered,* he thought as he felt her weight on his lap. Despite the lingering heat, her bright, sunset hair smelled of being freshly washed, her light, freckled face, newly scrubbed.

The little girl narrowed her intelligent, emerald eyes as she looked upon Caratacus's face. "Why do Mum and me have to leave in the morning, Da?"

"I want you to be safe from the Romans, my little darling," he said. "You and Mum would be in danger if you stayed here. You are going to a secret valley where you will be safe."

"A secret valley?" Macha asked.

"Yes, the Romans don't know about it."

Dana smiled.

Caratacus winked at her. He and Dana realized that it was known only to the local people. He only hoped the Romans wouldn't learn about it until much later. He feared the Romans would *persuade* them by means other than mere questioning.

"Why are the Romans so mean?" Macha asked. "Why do they hate us?"

Dana leaned over and lightly touched Macha's freckled face. "It's a long story."

"Don't worry, they won't hurt you, I promise," Caratacus said. He kissed her cheek, lifted her off his lap, and sat her next to his left side. "Now, I need to ask Mum something."

Caratacus motioned Dana to move closer. She slipped next to his other side. For a few seconds she rested her head on his shoulder. With the two he loved the most so near, he felt a moment of contentment. *Why couldn't this last a lifetime?*

He allowed himself to relish the closeness for a few minutes before he asked Dana, "Have you packed everything needed for your journey?" He already knew the answer. He still hated to see them leave.

"Everything has been," Dana answered. "Don't worry, all will be well with us. We are ready to leave."

"You realize that as my wife and queen, the families and my escorting warriors will look to you for leadership," Caratacus said.

Dana pursed her lips and nodded. "I know. And as their queen, I will do my best to lead them, but I will consult with the captain of the guard on matters of safety."

"Good thinking."

Caratacus had already planned the journey. The refugees would travel by foot. Not many horses and mules or other beasts of burden were available, and they were used only to pull the wagons and carts needed to carry the supplies. He could spare only a couple companies of warriors to provide an escort.

His eyes focused on Macha, and he grinned. He turned back to Dana and looked deeply into her large, hazel eyes. "I know I haven't said it enough, but I love you and Macha very much."

Dana raised a hand and placed a finger to his chapped lips. "I know, and so does Macha. I have prayed to Mother Goddess that one day this shall all be over." She lowered her hand, reached up, and gave him a lingering kiss on the lips.

* * *

A week had passed since Dana and Macha had departed with the other women and children for the hidden valley. Now, beneath the hot, midafternoon sun, Caratacus, Fergus ap Roycal, Venutios other minor chieftains, and escorting warriors rode their mounts along the base of the fortress wall inspecting the lower defenses. Caratacus, bare-chested, wearing red, plaid breeches, leather boots, and a bright-green, tartan cloak hanging about his shoulders, reined his gelding to a halt. In the distance he spotted the churning dust of a fast-approaching rider. The horseman raced along the rutted trackway, forded the muddy river, and hurried up to the entourage, the clatter of hooves echoing off the side of the stronghold's wall. Caratacus signaled for his group to halt.

"The Romans are approaching, Great King," the messenger reported to Caratacus, his horse seeming uneasy, smelling of sweat, white foam dripping from its mouth. Caratacus beckoned the messenger to draw closer to his mount.

"How many and how far away are they?" he asked.

"Parts of two legions and as many auxiliaries, maybe fifteen thousand," the sunburnt warrior said. "They're about a day's march from here."

Caratacus scratched his stubbled chin. "Which Legions?"

"Fourteenth and Twentieth, High King," the scout answered.

The king nodded and twisted about in his saddle toward his chieftains. "That makes sense. I know that Scapula has detached several cohorts from both legions to garrison the watch forts guarding his rear. We have inflicted much damage and killed thousands of his men."

"Aye, and our Silurian allies have done the same to the east and south," Venutios said, from his mount next to Caratacus's.

"Well done," Caratacus said to the rider and dismissed him.

Earlier that morning Venutios had received reports of Roman cavalry patrols not more than ten miles distant in the direction of the hills on the other side of the valley. Yesterday, they were thirty miles away.

Fergus spat from his shaggy, gray mount. "By now the shit-eaters are scouting about the hills."

"My warriors are searching but haven't sighted the Romans yet." Venutios tightly clasped the hilt of his sword secured to his waist. "I'll send out more men."

"Don't!" Caratacus said. "I want them to ride closer."

"What!" Fergus exclaimed. "Are you mad?"

Caratacus shook his head and grinned. "Fergus, my old friend and comrade, I haven't lost my wits."

Fergus's craggy face looked toward the river, and then he glared at Caratacus. "Convince us!"

"All warriors, except posted sentries, will stay out of sight for the rest of the day." Caratacus pointed toward the valley. "The Romans will believe we're no more than a miserable little force of bandits."

Venutios raised a hand above his brow to protect his eyes from the glaring sun and peered across the river. "The Romans aren't fools. Their spies have told Scapula the size of our forces. They'll see the defensive ditch and stakes."

"Aye, and the wall of stones in front of them," Fergus added.

"Scapula doesn't know with any certainty how massive we are," Caratacus said. "He can guess right up to the last moment, when we retaliate!"

A black-toothed smile crossed Fergus's face. "Clever like a wolf. Those pissing Romans will wish they'd never heard of this place."

"When the Romans appear tomorrow," Caratacus continued, "they'll see that we're as thick as mosquitoes in a swamp."

Fergus made a slashing motion across his throat. "And we draw a lot more blood."

Caratacus glanced about, down to the river, and then to the walls. "Now, there is one other matter that must be discussed." Fergus, Venutios, and the others watched him with quizzical eyes. "In case we are forced to withdraw—"

"Withdraw!" Fergus roared as he waved his hands. "We'll wipe out those thieving bastards before they reach the first wall."

"Nevertheless, I'm not taking chances," Caratacus said.

"Our warriors will fight far better knowing their women and children are safe," Venutios said in a reassuring voice.

In addition to the more than fifteen thousand warriors within and camped outside the fortress, there had been over three thousand women and children and other camp followers. Caratacus couldn't forget the sick and wounded and the five hundred cattle left for food. They slowed any retreat. He had decided one week before that the families and the sick must be moved to a more secure location. It would be difficult enough to defend the fortress as it was, without families being in the way, placing their own lives at risk.

It was just as well, the stench from the latrines that were rapidly filling, and so many unwashed bodies would soon make the stockade unlivable. The important thing was to defeat the Romans. The Crone would stay behind to attend to the wounded, but ready to flee if need be.

Owen had insisted on staying. Knowing that the Romans would show no mercy, Caratacus told him he did so at his own risk.

178

The hidden valley on the eastern slope of the mountain beyond Caersws provided ideal protection. It had already been stocked with provisions —a wise move.

Caratacus raised his hand above his head and made a circling motion. He turned his mount in the direction of the fort's entrance, kicked the horse's side, and moved out, his retinue following.

For seven years Caratacus had wreaked havoc among the Romans. He had forced them to drain away several cohorts of legionaries to protect their inner lines of defense by building dozens of watch forts, all the while losing many men. But the delaying actions Caratacus had taken couldn't continue. The Roman supply lines grew ever stronger as material and reinforcements continued to flow in with each passing day. His army was running out of places to go. He hated being cornered like a rabid wolf. *The running stops here.*

"At dawn, when the Romans appear, have your chieftains rally the men into a frenzy," Caratacus spoke out loud again. "Remind them if they don't destroy the Romans, their women and children will be raped and tortured. Either they'll win back their freedom and lands and be rid of the Romans once and for all, or they'll be enslaved forever."

Indeed they will be enslaved, we'll all be enslaved, Caratacus thought as he entered the fortresses main gate. *I will not see my wife and daughter enslaved by the Romans.*

* * *

Roman legions Fourteenth Gemina and Twentieth Valeria had arrived in the area late the night before. On a low rise above the river, soldiers built a stockade marching camp in the form of a large square, complete with ramparts. A defensive ditch lined with menacing wood spikes called "lilies" jutted upwards from within the deep trench.

Porcius, along with the rest of the general's staff, Centurion Bassus, and other cohort commanders of Fourteenth and Twentieth Legions, had been summoned to the banks of the River Sabrina early that morning to confer with General Scapula.

Nearby, men from the engineers detail, under the watchful eye of a snarling centurion, unloaded heavy, wooden planks and thick posts from ox-drawn wagons. The troops dropped them noisily to the sandy ground in preparation for bridging the River Sabrina.

The legions and their auxiliary troops had assembled in front of the camp, in formation, covering the small plain, waiting for the signal to cross the river. However, General Scapula had not yet made the decision to construct a bridge across the river or to chance fording the clear but swift running waters.

Porcius was proud to see that Bassus had risen to the rank of *Hastatus Prior*, commanding centurion of the Second Cohort, one of the best fighting units in the legion and perhaps better than the First, the general's personal outfit. Bassus's experience in battle and political intrigue, along with his knowledge of Caratacus, had earned him the right to a command in his old legion.

Once again, Porcius followed the Roman Army on campaign, this time with General Scapula. At age sixty-two, painful rheumatism had seeped into his knee joints, which he felt with every step he took. His excessive girth did not help either. The Roman's personal physician had advised him to use a cane or walking stick, but he had stubbornly refused. "I am not a cripple yet."

His uniform consisted in part of a linen corselet and bronze cuirass that covered a tunic and ankle-length breeches, which, despite the heat, he insisted on wearing like a Briton. It had been altered to fit across his ample belly.

Last spring Porcius had received a secret message from Emperor Claudius, sent through his secretary, Narcissus, the freedman. The Greek informed Porcius that the emperor had ordered him to report to General Scapula, Commander of the Fourteenth Legion, where he was to be part of his staff with the rank of legate, or inspector general. Scapula would receive a separate order as confirmation. It would be Porcius's duty to send Claudius independent reports in addition to those received from Scapula. The old ruler wanted an unbiased outside opinion regarding the true progress of the campaign against

Caratacus and the Britons. Scapula had been in command for the last three years, and Claudius was dissatisfied with the commander's progress against the wily barbarian king.

When Porcius had reported to Scapula at legion headquarters, the general had been in a foul mood and didn't offer Porcius a seat. As the Roman saluted, the general shoved the letter he had received from the emperor across the desk into Porcius's face.

"I received this so-called order this morning," Scapula said, his face flushed and breath reeking of sour wine. "Obviously you know I have been ordered by the emperor to add you as a legate to my staff, which is bad enough. But I must allow you the privilege of working independently of me as you see fit, making your reports directly to the emperor. In other words, you're a damn imperial spy!"

Porcius flushed, sweat poured down the side of his face, a result of the morning heat, which grew more intense with each passing minute. *I must carefully choose my words.* He gestured broadly with a hand. "General Scapula, I assure you it is not by my choice."

Scapula snorted. "It is obvious you have the emperor's ear."

Porcius cleared his throat. "If that were the case, I would still be in Rome and not in Britannia. Believe me, I would much rather be working at home in the garden, when my knees allow it, than here on a wretched, mosquito-ridden campaign where I am risking my life."

"Your risk is no greater than the rest of us. If anything, it is less. You won't be fighting in the ranks."

The general raised a silver cup of wine from the portable table and swilled its contents. He slammed down the cup.

Porcius winced.

"Nevertheless," Porcius said, "the emperor has commanded me to observe all battles that will take place on your forthcoming campaign against Caratacus. It may require that I observe the fighting at close range. In that event, I will need an escort of your Praetorians to protect me and the secretaries who will ride at my side. After all, they will need to write down notes as I dictate them during the heat of battle."

That hadn't sat well with Scapula, but Porcius knew the general had little choice. He had done the same thing years ago at the Battle of Bagshot Heath when the army of Caratacus's uncle, Epaticcos, had fought the warriors of Verica. Of course, Porcius had been kidnapped and most likely would have been killed if Caratacus hadn't saved his life. Porcius wasn't about to mention that to Scapula.

Porcius hated having to travel with the legion on campaign, but as long as he could bring along a few luxuries, slaves, and freedmen to make his life a little more comfortable, he would tolerate the inconveniences that went along being on march.

* * *

At about noon, Porcius and Bassus watched Scapula as he paced back and forth along the Sabrina's sandy bank. The general gazed at the sight of Caratacus's defensive position, with its dark, overhanging cliffs across the river. He dropped to one knee and scooped up a clump of earth in his right hand. For a moment, he examined it as if he would an expensive piece of jewelry. He opened his fingers, letting the soil sift through them, and stood looking about. Scapula motioned to his orderly to fetch a cup of dark wine undiluted by water. As he gulped it down, he studied Caersws' defensive positions.

"Jupiter's balls," the general said, "the walls are nearly impregnable. I never encountered positions this strong in Germania."

"His Roman deserters built the walls and lined the ditch with defensive stakes, sir," Figulus, the brawny, pig-faced tribune in charge of engineers, said in a droning voice.

The general glared at Figulus. He glanced to Porcius and Bassus and back to the tribune. "Don't underestimate the abilities of any barbarian," Scapula counseled. "They're not stupid, we have the losses to prove it."

Porcius and Bassus grinned. The centurion nodded with the other cohort commanders.

Figulus is a fool, Porcius thought. The young officer had recently arrived in Britannia and had a great deal to learn about the Britons.

Scapula motioned to the burly *Primus Pilus*, the legion's senior centurion and second in command. "Send out cavalry patrols on both flanks. See if there is another way the infantry can bypass those walls."

* * *

Two hours passed before the patrols returned. They reined up their mounts in front of the headquarters tent. Scapula and his staff were underneath the outside canopy looking over a map of the area. The squadron commander dismounted and reported that his riders found no other approaches to the citadel.

Scapula dismissed the commander and turned to Figulus. "Are you certain we have to bridge the river?" Scapula inquired. "It doesn't appear that deep."

"The bottom is too unstable," Figulus answered. "We need the bridge in order to bring artillery across, they are out of range. That along with men and horse alike will be hopelessly mired without bridging, sir. I'd stake my reputation on it."

Scapula sneered. "You mean your rich senator-father's reputation. If it weren't for his influence, you wouldn't be in charge of my engineers. I should have given the order earlier to your second-in-command to go ahead with the bridging instead of listening to you."

"Figulus is an idiot," Bassus whispered to Porcius.

"Just like his father," Porcius said.

"I have an idea," Bassus said to Porcius.

Bassus stepped in Scapula's direction. "General, may I make a suggestion, sir?"

Scapula eyed Bassus and then Porcius. He raised an eyebrow, and Porcius nodded. The general turned to Figulus, and then again to Bassus. "By all means, Centurion. At least you're a man of common sense."

Bassus motioned toward the stream. "Send an auxiliary cavalryman across. The combined weight of horse and a fully armed trooper is a good test for the bottom and the depth and current."

Bassus ignored Figulus's piercing glare.

183

Porcius smiled at the young tribune.

The commander crinkled his eyebrows together as he glanced to the engineer. "It's so obvious, why didn't you think of it?" Then he snapped, "Never mind!" before the engineer could answer. Scapula summoned a runner and sent him to the nearby Thracian cohort. Moments later a trooper wearing overlapping, fish-plated armor and riding a bay gelding appeared and was ordered to cross the river.

The Romans watched the javelin-wielding soldier carefully ford the Sabrina. Mid-channel, the water reached no higher than the lower part of the animal's chest before he bounded to the far bank.

"Send across a couple of auxiliary infantrymen," Scapula ordered. A nearby centurion motioned to a courier and gave him the order.

Minutes later, two chain-mailed Vascones arrived. Holding their shields and weapons above their heads, they waded into the stream. Although the current was swift, they managed to keep their balance and completed the crossing.

Porcius slapped Bassus on the shoulder and grinned.

"Well done!" Scapula shouted. He turned to Bassus and the other officers. "Centurions, return to your cohorts. We cross the Sabrina."

"But what about the artillery? Figulus asked.

"Damn the artillery!" Scapula snapped. "We don't have time to waste on building a bridge. We'll take the bloody fortress without it!"

CHAPTER 19

"What in Teutates's name?" Fergus ap Roycal blurted. "They're crossing the river!"

"Man the walls!" Caratacus ordered.

Wolf-headed trumpets blared raspy warnings, and within minutes warriors covered the barricades, all carrying extra javelins, slings, and stones. Emerging from behind every rock and boulder and along the ramparts, they brandished weapons, whooped, and shouted profanities at the oncoming Romans.

Caratacus stood on the parapet with his chieftains, Fergus ap Roycal and Venutios. All of them wore tartan tunics and breeches, covered by protective chain mail. Each carried an oval shield with an iron-center boss and a longsword hooked to a chain-link belt. Except for his long, drooping moustache with flecks of gray, Caratacus's scarred face was clean shaven. An iron helmet with wide cheek guards crowned his head of shoulder-length hair. Behind his leaders stood a dozen retainers, trumpeters, and a standard bearer holding upright a wooden pole bearing the image of a wolf made of brass that shimmered in the sunlight.

The king searched the far side of the river and caught a glint of golden light reflecting from the Roman horseman's armor who rode along its bank followed by an escort of Praetorian Guardsmen. Although several hundred yards away, he knew it was General Scapula. The cavalry rode small barbs and Spanish nags. Only the general rode a huge, black Zeeland from German Batavia. Over a white, linen tunic, the general's golden cuirass, trimmed with a wide, red stripe, gleamed in the bright sun.

"Who is that fat Roman riding next to the general on the undersized horse?" Venutios asked.

Caratacus squinted. "By Teutates, even at this distance, I recognize Porcius. Gods, he has put on weight—he is punishing that poor horse."

"If I have my way, that poor nag won't be carrying that shit-eater for long," Fergus said.

"The question is, why is he here?" Caratacus said, more to himself than to the others. "He is not a soldier." *Porcius had stirred up a lot of trouble among the tribes, but he had cautioned the Romans against invasion. He knew how costly it would be. I'm not sure if I want to see him die.* Caratacus frowned. *Gods, am I growing sentimental?*

The legions massed along the opposite bank, divided into dozens of cohorts, each containing nearly five hundred men. Legionaries formed centuries, their lines eighty men long and six deep, into protective, interlocking walls of shields. Their iron-tipped javelins, short swords, and segmented armor glistened in the morning sun, nearly blinding the defenders. Chain-mail-clad auxiliary troops from Spain and Gaul, wearing knee-length breeches and carrying oval shields and longswords, formed several cohorts in front of the Romans.

In the distance, from behind the troop's ranks, trumpets blared, signaling the advance. Scapula remained on the other side with the reserve forces.

Raising their shields and weapons above their heads to keep dry, the auxiliaries, including archers, followed by the legionaries, forded the Sabrina en masse. As they noisily splashed across to the snarling curses of their centurions, soldiers churned and muddied its clear waters, crossing without incident. Forming a shield wall to their front, the Spaniards from Asturia moved forward with drawn swords. They clattered them methodically against the metal edges of their shields as they climbed over and moved down the weed-covered defensive berm and crossed the ditch that encircled the fort. Behind them came a century of their comrades carrying dozens of scaling ladders protected by a shield-carrying escort.

A line of Syrian archers, wearing ankle-length tunics and conical helmets, moved to the top of the first berm. A century of Spaniards followed and stepped between the ranks of the bowmen and placed protective shields to the front.

Caratacus spotted them as they appeared on the berm's summit. He turned to Venutios. "Get your men here, now! They have to protect our bowmen with their shields."

Venutios shouted an order to one of his captains on the wall. They raised their shields above the bowmen, and together they kneeled and hunkered down against the base of the wall.

The Syrians drew back the arrows along the edge of their bows, raising and pointing them skyward. On the command of their Roman centurion, they shot a murderous barrage of arrows over the troops and down onto the wall of defenders. The rain of arrows, which filled the sky like a black cloud, arced and fell back on the defenders.

Caratacus's retainers had formed a protective covering of shields above and around him and the other chieftains. Arrows whistled and crashed upon the Britons like a massive wave on a shoreline. The deadly missiles slammed into shields, bodies, and exposed limbs. Screams and shrills of agony and death rippled along the catwalk like a rushing tide. Caratacus hunkered down as arrows slammed through the shield's leather-covered planks of oak with loud thuds, knocking him back upon the wooden catwalk. Two more arrow points sliced within inches of his eyes and face. His muscles tensed, and sweat poured from every pore as fear pervaded his body, not so much for himself, but concern for his companions and warriors. *How many have died? How many survived! What about my leaders?* He sneaked a look beneath the edge of his shield. Another arrow struck his shield, shoving it down upon him within a hair above his chest

Minutes later the barrage halted. Caratacus stepped out from under his shield and peeked over the wall. Despite the injuries, many more waves of arrows flew over and beyond the wall, harmlessly striking the hard-packed dirt parapet that curved down and away from the stockade.

He looked for Fiona, who slipped out from beneath her captured Roman shield about ten paces away. Head protected by a conical helmet, she wore a shirt of ringed chain mail over her striped tunic and breeches. Her armor had been recovered from a dead Gaul's body in an early skirmish.

"Captain!" Caratacus shouted."Get your bowmen up and wait for my command."

"Yes, sire." She turned and gave the order, which was passed along the parapet. Her archers grabbed their weapons and stood at the ready. Most of the warriors had also been protected by battered shields stripped from the bodies of dead Romans and auxiliary troops.

"Sire, the enemy is in range," Fiona shouted over the screaming warriors who once again taunted the oncoming Romans. "We'll cut them down like wheat in the field."

In the glaring sun, he surveyed the line of archers, men and women of his own people, and the rest, Roman deserters and foreigners from Germania. They were equipped with an array of captured armor and weapons. Some of the ex-Romans still wore segmented armor, now dull and dirty. Their bows of yew were knocked with arrows pulled back to their ears. He glanced to the right and left checking the bundles of arrows, stones, and spears stacked on the wooden walkway every twenty paces, along with barrels of water for drinking and dousing fires. He turned about and quickly focused beyond the hard-packed, dirt ramp way toward the black smith's forge near the granary and storage pits. He spotted the stacks of spare swords and shields, many of them captured, in reserve. Satisfied, he turned toward Fiona.

"Wait for my command."

The short, scar-faced woman nodded, her lips pressed together in a thin line. A few steps away a bowman fidgeted nervously for what must have seemed an eternity.

Grim-faced, the front auxiliary ranks, their hob-nailed sandals clattering on the rocky slope like galloping horses, raced toward the main wall and threw up a line of shields at its base and raised them high above their heads. The ladder men ran forward, and with escorting troops on both sides using shields to protect them, they slammed ladders against the wall with an echoing thud.

Caratacus pointed his right hand toward Fiona. "Captain, when I give the signal, your bowmen are to clear that ridge of the enemy archers." He turned to Venutios and Fergus ap Roycal. "At the moment I give Fiona the command, your men are to concentrate on the infantry with spears and stones." The three left the king and raced toward their warriors standing behind the bowmen the length of the wall.

The king nodded to the trumpeter a few paces away, who blared a raspy tune from his upright, wolf-headed carnyx. Signal torches were raised at intervals along the ramparts. "On my command!" he cried. "Now!" He dropped his arm, and the torches followed.

Fiona's bowmen and women fired a murderous stream of arrows straight into the line of Syrian archers. The rest flung an avalanche of javelins, small boulders, and slingstones onto the advancing cohorts of Gauls and Spaniards. The crashing impact echoed through the valley as they decimated ranks of Spaniards and Syrians alike. Seconds later the air resounded with the screams of wounded and dying. The barren soil turned dark from the spilled blood of troops. Fallen bodies lay strewn at the bottom of the ditch and ridge top in a contorted disarray, riddled with arrows and spears. The surviving soldiers raised shields above their heads but wavered and halted. Up and down the ramparts a victorious cheer erupted among the Britons.

Caratacus grinned. *No soldier in his right mind would advance further into that storm of death.* Again, he signaled for another volley of arrows. "No time to celebrate!" he shouted to his warriors. "Keep up the pressure, wipe them out!"

* * *

Porcius, along with his retinue, including Cyrus, sat on their mounts behind a cohort of infantrymen as they waited with Legion Twentieth Valeria for their turn to cross the river. Although he watched from a distance of nearly five hundred yards, the devastating rain of arrows, spears, and slingstones that poured down on the ranks of the auxiliaries left him aghast. The assault had been so intense that more than fifty of the Syrian archers had been downed by enemy arrows. The Spanish cohorts who were climbing the ladders, had been cut down, rolling back on the advancing ranks. Although he could not directly see it, Porcius saw in his mind's eye the dead and dying, shields and bodies, splattered with blood at the bottom of the ditch. He looked about and noticed the pale and cringing looks of his freedmen and slaves. Porcius shrugged. He was just as frightened as the rest of his entourage, but he couldn't let his people see that. He had to keep a sober face.

Earlier, before the troops began their assault, Porcius had been present when General Scapula gave Bassus's cohort the order to carry small picks and shovels tied to their waistbands. In case the auxiliaries failed to reach the top, they would mine the fortress wall. So far, they had failed.

He prayed Bassus's unit would succeed as they moved at the double-quick toward the decimated troops.

Then Porcius saw Bassus raise his vine cane and shout something he couldn't hear because of the noise of battle. The order became apparent when the soldiers formed into the turtle formation.

* * *

Caratacus and his warriors had killed the last of those few Spaniards who had managed to climb over the battlement, and shoved the remaining ladders crashing to the ground. Fiona's archers had slain most of the Syrian bowmen.

Sweating and thirsty, Caratacus's mouth felt as if it was full of sand. His muscles and arms ached from the fighting, his face and armor covered in blood. He looked about, seeing his own wounded and dying leaning against the wall or lying on the deck. Most of the injuries had been inflicted by the few surviving auxiliaries who had made it over the barrier. He ordered his warriors to throw the dead Spaniards down the dirt ramp to the back. Other warriors carried their injured to a dressing hut at the rear of the fort, manned by the Crone and her assistants. Caratacus stepped to a nearby barrel and drank water from a ladle attached to the side. Although tepid, it satisfied his thirst.

"More Romans are coming!" someone shouted.

Caratacus moved to the wall and saw the approaching cohort of legionaries snaking over the first berm behind the downed Spaniards. Seconds later, they changed from a standard skirmish formation six deep to the oval turtle. He knew the tactic well. It had been used during the River Medway battle to rescue the Roman general Geta. Soldiers raised shields, banged them together above to protect their heads. The outer ranks placed their's along the sides to cover their bodies. Moving forward again, a rhythmic clanking sound echoed off the battlement's walls as shields clattered against one another

"Ha! They don't have any ladders like the Spaniards," Fergus said. He had reported back to Caratacus after deploying his men. "What do they expect to accomplish with that maneuver?"

"The ramparts are too steep, and so far we have killed every man reaching the top," Donn said.

"They have more than one flea in their ears," Caratacus replied. "They're planning something." He motioned to Venutios. "Get your best spear and bowmen and concentrate them against that formation." He turned to Fergus. "Bring your sling men over here and another supply of rocks." He motioned to the foot of the rampart. "Smash it!"

* * *

As Porcius watched from the back of his horse, the cohort stepped over and around dozens of broken bodies at the top of the ridge. The stench of expelled bodily fluids from the dead drifted on a hot breeze. Carrion birds drifted in circles overhead. He spotted the turtle formation, commanded by Bassus, moving out of the ditch between the berm and fortress wall and climbing to its base under another barrage of missiles. Although he couldn't understand the muffled sounds being shouted from within the closed formation, Porcius believed he heard the words, "Closer!" being shouted. They pushed further up the rocky, weed-covered berm at the wall's base.

"What are they doing?" Cyrus asked as he sat on a mule next to Porcius.

"Centurion Bassus must have given his cohort an order to break from the turtle formation and form into ranks six deep," Porcius said.

Quickly, the front three lines raised their shields high over their heads, and the last three ranks went down on their knees and crawled between their legs.

"Why are they doing that?" Cyrus asked.

"They are mining the wall with their picks and shovels, the purpose is to bring it down."

"That could take hours while we suffer in this miserable heat," Cyrus said. He wiped his dark, bearded face with a scented handkerchief before placing it back in his waist belt.

"I couldn't agree with you more, my Persian friend."

From then on, at fifteen minute intervals, the front bottom ranks of legionaries, who were digging, would be relieved, and as they backed out, this allowed the rearmost ranks to move forward under the protective shields, to continue the mining.

The wall must be breached!

CHAPTER 20

After elements of Legion Twentieth Velaria had finished fording the river, Porcius received the order to cross. "It's about time," he said. Hot and sweating, Porcius took a drink of water from the canteen handed to him by Cyrus. When finished, he returned to the Persian and motioned for his retinue to follow him as he forded the Sabrina.

"Perhaps the wall will collapse before we near it," Cyrus said as he rode along Porcius's side.

Porcius sniffed. "No matter, we'll stay out of range of Caratacus's bowmen until then. I'm in no hurry to die."

The deafening noise from the shouts and screams and metallic banging of sword against sword, the thudding of arrows and stones against the fortress wall, and troops' shields grew louder as Porcius and his retinue neared the battle. The salty smell of blood mixed with the sickening odor of filth seemed to swirl about him and his retinue. He pulled a perfumed handkerchief hidden in the sash that girdled his large waist and, for a moment, covered his nose. Porcius looked back across to where the formation of three legionary cohorts stood in reserve. He regretted that he and his people couldn't have stayed with the reserves. But the emperor required an unbiased eyewitness account of the battle. Porcius had no choice but to risk his life. Still he had no intention of getting closer than need be even if it meant stretching the truth about Rome's forthcoming glorious victory. If Bassus survived this battle, he would get a first-hand account from him.

* * *

Caratacus hurried to Fiona's side as she urged her people to keep up the barrage of arrows.

"Fiona!" he shouted above the noisy din, "tell all your bowman to turn their attention to the approaching Romans on the berm. Cut them down. Leave the spearmen and rock throwers to kill the Romans below."

Fiona nodded. "Yes, sire!"

"See what they're doing?" Fergus called to Caratacus, his position further down the wall. He pointed to the soldiers at the wall's base as he hiked toward the king.

Caratacus had been pacing back and forth on the rampart, urging his warriors to keep up the fight. Fiona's men and women continued firing arrow upon arrow at the wall of shields only to watch them careen away with a thud. Thrown by Fergus and Venutios's warriors, they kept hurling large rocks and small boulders as they attempted to smash through the shield barrier, but to no avail. The Roman wall held. Another century of Syrian archers mounted the outer berm and fired a murderous volley of arrows at the wall top, disregarding the Romans below. Again, Caratacus's warriors had to shield themselves from the torrent of arrows plunging down upon them. British losses started to mount. One by one his warriors were struck down by the deadly rain of arrows.

"Can the Romans undermine the wall?" Fergus looked from under his shield toward Caratacus, who squatted beneath his and those offered by his retainers.

"The foundation is deep enough, but the Romans are well disciplined," Caratacus said. "They can do it if they have the heart and drive. That's why they must be halted—now!"

The Britons continued the intensive barrage, but the Roman formation held. Six legionarie cohorts, almost three thousand soldiers, joined in extending the excavation along a forty-foot section of a wall near one side of the gate. Those who did not have digging equipment resorted to using daggers and swords. Despite the furious onslaught of British weaponry, thousands of Roman hands continued digging at its base for the next couple of hours.

* * *

"Caratacus, the rampart!" motioned Venutios with a javelin. "A huge section is giving way!" Twenty yards to the right, choking dust shot up into the sky followed by screams of those caught by the crushing fortress stones below and above.

Thirsty, Caratacus licked his lips and wiped the sweat from his face. His stomach knotted, and he gritted his teeth. *Damn the Romans; will nothing stop them?* "Withdraw to the hilltop."

"Caratacus," Fergus said, "I have enough men to give you plenty of time to retreat. Why don't you do that? We can hold them while you lead the rest of the forces."

"But I need both of you," Caratacus said.

"Pah!" Fergus spat. "You've got Venutios and Fiona. I've lived a long time. I'm ready to go to Teutates as a warrior should."

"He's right," Venutios insisted. "Don't stay here. Leave the fortress

"Don't waste the army here," Fergus pleaded. "The Ordovicians want you in the north. Caratacus, for the sake of an old friend, take your warriors and go!"

"Aye, and when the Romans reach the top," Venutios interjected, "we'll be gone like a spirit in the night."

Caratacus swallowed the lump rising in his throat. He attempted to smile, but only shook his head. "Even the God Teutates could find no warriors more loyal than you, my friends. I won't forget this." Caratacus turned and headed for the hilltop at the rear of the citadel.

* * *

Porcius and his retinue reached the summit of the outer berm just as the defensive wall crumbled away. An echoing roar raced along the front wall, followed by the tumbling center layer of crushed gravel and the collapse of the inner protective wall. A blinding cloud of dust shot up more than thirty feet, following on the heels of falling rock. Legionaries scattered to avoid the path of the choking grime and crushing stones. A forty-foot-long section tumbled down the steep hillside leaving a gaping fissure.

He spotted Bassus motioning with his short sword where he stood on a small rise near the collapsed wall's opening and shouted an order Porcius couldn't hear. The remnants of six centuries reacted instantly amidst the clanking of armor and jostling of legionaries for position and forming ranks of about sixty to seventy men across and six deep. Behind his cohort, another one had reformed. Bassus raised his sword and shouted another order and ran forward, the cohorts followed. The Vascones, who had been on Porcius's left flank, moved out in front of the Roman at the double-quick, along with other fast-moving auxiliaries on the wings. They flooded through the same wide opening in the wall, while Bassus's cohort led the legion's advance.

Perspiring, Porcius sat in his saddle, his large bottom sore from the long wait. His protective scarf didn't prevent the chafing of his neck from his hot, brass cuirass. Cautiously, Porcius motioned his people to follow him. He kicked the side of his mount and rode forward to the squeaking of saddle leather and jingling of brass pendants hanging across the horse's chest. He had ridden far enough that from his saddle he looked over the heads of the auxiliary troops in front of him and watched as the defending Britons hurtled themselves against the moving barrier of Roman shields and short swords inside the wall's opening. The bloody fighting raged at a furious pace. Screams of the wounded and dying echoed across the valley, and the gore of body parts and unholy fluids slimed shields, armor, and faces of Celts and Romans alike. More legionaries died, but nothing halted them. He could not see every detail, but his imagination would later fill in the rest if Bassus did not survive.

At that instant, Porcius watched Bassus slay a huge, craggy-faced, heavily armored warrior. The centurion's blood-splattered face glanced to the right and left flanks.

Porcius realized the real fighting still loomed at the hilltop where Bassus might encounter Caratacus. If so, it would be a horrendous fight to the death. True, Caratacus had spared his life on the first day of invasion seven years before. But Porcius knew that Bassus understood. He would do his duty as a Roman soldier.

* * *

Sweat-stained and dirty, Caratacus had moved to the top of the hill with Venutios and their retainers. One of his men handed him a goatskin full of water, which he drained before handing back. He watched from the hilltop at the fortress's rear as the Romans burst through the first battlements below. In spite of the savage fighting before them, the Romans slowly advanced across the long, wide slope. They wavered here and there, adjusted the lines where necessary, but continually moved forward.

More than a thousand Britons lay butchered in their wake. And yet their comrades rallied again and again, exacting vengeance upon the legionaries.

Bodies choked their advance, and the Roman line broke. A horde of warriors in purple tattoos swarmed forward, exacting a deadly price for discipline's failure and, in turn, died.

Torn between rejoining his men, where he knew he would meet certain death, Caratacus realized he must flee as Fergus ap Roycal had urged. His warriors would continue to fight to the death if he allowed it. But Fergus was right. There was nothing left to prove. He looked about and saw that hundreds more warriors had fallen. The Romans steadily moved forward, advancing up the slope. Uncertainty rose within Caratacus. He longed to follow his instinct to charge and follow his brother kings to the world beyond.

"Venutios," Caratacus said, "if meaning is to be given to this battle, you must take the bulk of our forces north. You'll be welcomed by the Ordovician king."

Venutios turned his head. "Aren't you coming with us?"

"I will later, after I go to Eburacum."

Venutios's eyes widened. "Don't be a fool, Caratacus! Cartimandua will hand you over to the Romans."

Caratacus bristled, his muscles tightened. "She promised to side with us. I'll convince her the time is now. With her support, we can still drive the Romans out of Britannia. From what my spies and the Druids tell me, the people hate the Romans, especially her chieftains." *Gods, I hope that is true.*

Venutios gestured wildly toward him. "Impossible! She's bought and paid for with Roman gold, like the whore she is."

"If that is true, then I will kill her. Her chieftains don't want to be Roman lapdogs."

Venutios exhaled and shook his head. "Her shield bearers won't let you close enough to her."

The king looked at Venutios then down the hill toward the Romans. "I'll find a way. I know at one time she wanted

me for her consort. Maybe I can persuade her that I want
to be one now."

"That is a big risk. Do you think she will believe that?
So long as you are married to Dana, I doubt she will.
Cartimandua loves Roman gold and herself too much for
you to take a chance."

"I'll speak before the council and persuade them to
follow me."

"If you went to her victorious from today ... maybe. But
in flight? Whatever happens, I wish you good luck,
Cousin."

"I know."

They clasped one another's right forearms in friendship
and farewell.

"Should anything happen," Venutios added, "know this,
I will continue the fight. I refuse to give in to these dogs."

"Sire!" a blood-stained Fiona exclaimed as she
approached the leaders. "Fergus was slaughtered by the
first Roman through the wall, a filthy centurion."

Caratacus clenched the hilt of his sword. His face
tightened. "Shit! A warrior's death is what he wanted, but I
still don't have to like it. Damn!"

"My warriors and I will hold the Romans here while you
make good your escape," Fiona said. "Then we'll follow."

Caratacus's eyes held Fiona, both knew it would likely
be the last time they would meet. "May Andraste and
Teutates be with you."

He faced Venutios. "Withdraw your men and go to our
Ordovician allies." The king turned his horse away from the
battle.

* * *

It was late afternoon. Porcius had waited just inside the
fortress walls as the Romans were mopping up the last
resistance by the Britons when Scapula rode up with his
escorting Praetorians. Bassus, smeared with blood and,
covered in dust, trotted back down the hill from the far
side of the bastion to make his report.

"They've vanished, sir," Bassus said to Scapula.

"Impossible!"

"It's true. Gone," Bassus said and motioned back
toward the slope. "We fought our way to the top, but by the

time we got inside, most of Caratacus's forces had scattered. They escaped through a hidden gate and underground passageway at the rear of the fortress."

"How can more than ten thousand men escape?" the general spat. Scapula surveyed the area seeing the bodies strewn about the ramparts and defensive perimeter.

"By the looks of their clothing, most of the dead are German mercenaries and Roman deserters," Scapula commented. "Good riddance to the lot!"

Dark clouds of buzzing flies gorged upon the torn and gutted corpses. Already the sweltering heat reeked of bloating and decaying flesh, the earth a muddied pinkish-brown.

"We've found tracks indicating the direction of the enemies' travel." Bassus pointed to the mountains beyond the hillfort.

Scapula paused and walked away from his commanders. Porcius, Bassus, and the other commanders stood by uneasily as they always did when awaiting orders from him. His heavy drinking and frequent drunkenness made the general moody and unpredictable. Sometimes brilliant, but often erratic, they never knew what to expect from him.

Scapula turned and faced the officers. "These barbarians' tracks lead us where?" he asked as if addressing himself. "Into ambush? Or is it what it appears to be, a simple rout?"

"No, sir," Bassus answered. "Caratacus is too cunning. He must have known we would prevail against him."

"If that's true, then what do you think his next move is?" Scapula asked.

"He's leading us away from their women and children," Bassus said. "They must be hidden somewhere nearby."

"Search for them." Scapula turned his head for a moment and viewed the mountain behind the fortress. "The question is," he continued throwing another look at Porcius and the other officers, "should we find and enslave them? Would that provoke his return to a final fight?"

"That'd bring 'em back sure as I'm standing here," the chief centurion commented. "I'd like to finish off the bastard once and for all."

"NO!" Scapula exclaimed. "That would be our worst mistake. There are too many details over which we have no control. They would surely fight like demons to the death and perhaps win. Better to let them run with their tails tucked."

"As long as they flee, sir," Bassus interjected, "they run from us in defeat."

"Defeat, Centurion? That bastard broke our advance as clearly as if we were all slaughtered." Seeing his puzzled look, the general explained further. "Look, we no longer can advance blindly into his traps. We need reinforcements. It takes time to bring up men to fill our ranks. Our supply lines are still spread too thin, and he has destroyed them time and again. And time is what can finish us here. I hope Caratacus believes he was defeated today."

"It's when they turn upon us unified, as only rescuing their families can provoke them, that we could lose," Bassus said.

Scapula smiled, apparently pleased that his lesson sank in. "Yes! Centurion Bassus is right. Their families can wait. However," Scapula paused and turned to one of his tribunes, "I don't want him escaping our grasp. Dispatch cavalry patrols immediately. There must be a pass he's following through that range. Find it! I can't have them rebuilding their forces."

* * *

Dusk had fallen before Bassus finished a detailed report to General Scapula. The general glanced up from the wax tablet. Porcius, who had been present, had also read the document. "Do you realize that you are eligible for the Palisade Crown?"

"I never gave it a thought, sir," Bassus said. "You don't think about heroics in the middle of battle. You simply do your duty."

"Nevertheless, Bassus, as the first centurion over, or in this case, through the rampart, you are entitled to it."

"Thank you, sir."

A medal is worthless to a dead man, and almost useless if you live, Porcius thought.

"Your idea to mine the wall was exceptional. Many lives were saved. The emperor shall hear about it in my next dispatch."

And no doubt you'll take all the credit as generals do, Porcius wanted to say. *I'd wager this is what Bassus is thinking.*

Bassus grinned.

At that moment a rider from one of the patrols returned.

"Yes, courier, what news do you bring?" Scapula inquired.

"We've captured the barbarian supply train and their families, sir. Among them is the wife and daughter of the bandit Caratacus!"

CHAPTER 21

"I hear horses, Lord Caratacus," barked Alfyn, their Brigantian guide.

"They're Roman," Caratacus answered. "No Briton is that noisy."

The guide nodded.

Alfyn furrowed his bristly, red eyebrows as he turned from side to side on his shaggy pony. "Can't tell the direction they're coming from."

The hilly forest hemmed in Caratacus's band of ten warriors on all sides, causing sounds to bounce like a skipping rock on a pond's surface. They had followed narrow, twisting animal trails in a northeasterly direction from Caersws for the last five days. Before leaving the fortress, Venutios chose Alfyn, a pock-faced veteran of twenty-five, to be Caratacus's guide to Eburacum. He was from a western Brigantian village and knew the area well. Another week's journey lay ahead of them before reaching the Brigantian capital.

"We've got to shake them off our trail," Alfyn warned. "Look! Over there!"

Caratacus strained his eyes. "Where? I don't see—"

Alfyn pointed. "Up there, the side of the hill."

Caratacus spotted a jumble of big, interlaced spider webs, partially covered by a huge bush. The great orb spread like spokes of a hundred wheels, across the tall underbrush and hillside of huge cedars and oaks.

"There's a cave there," Alfyn said. "We can hide there until the Romans pass."

"Where is it? I don't see anything."

Alfyn nodded toward a rocky path around the far end of the bushes. "This way. I know these woods. Did a lot of hunting here when I was a lad. Follow me."

The group rode about two hundred paces up the
hillside, when the guide raised a hand signaling a halt. He
turned his mount back toward the group. "Dismount here.
We'll lead the horses the rest of the way. Cover the trail
behind us. Hurry!"

Quietly, they led their mounts around the side of the
hill. Upon approaching the web, Caratacus saw hundreds
of black spiders crawling across its sticky surface.

"Careful," Alfyn warned. "Hug the bank as much as you
can, and don't touch the web. Otherwise, the Romans
might investigate."

The spiders weren't poisonous, but Caratacus figured
as superstitious as the Romans were about these woods,
they wouldn't know that.

Alfyn stopped and took an oiled rag from his saddlebag.
He picked up a broken oak branch laying nearby and
wrapped the rag around the top. Taking a piece of flint and
steel from a pouch tied to his waist, he struck them
together. This caused a spark to ignite and create a
burning torch.

Alfyn motioned to the band to gently pull back the
branches holding the web. As if knowing they were being
disturbed by intruders, hundreds of spiders, one from each
web, skittered to the tiny, funnel-tube nests along the edge
of the web and disappeared. Cautiously, the group edged
its way into the huge cavern. When everyone was through,
the branches were eased into their original positions
without damage to the web.

A gust of chilly air from within the cave slammed
Caratacus's face as they entered, followed by the foul smell
of bat droppings. Caratacus had never seen anything like
the huge cavern. In the shadows, created by the pulsating
torchlight, hundreds of grayish icicles of stone cascaded
from the invisible ceiling. More reached for the ceiling from
the cave's damp, rocky floor. Caratacus touched one with
his hand. It wasn't as icy as he first believed, but damp
and coarse, like gravel. Beads of water ran down one side,
across his palm, and inside his wrist.

Alfyn pointed his torch in another direction, the light
swallowed by the vastness of a corridor. "This way. About

thirty paces on there's another cavern. It's drier, and there's enough room for all of us, including the horses."

Approaching voices came from outside the cave. Alfyn extinguished the torch against the cavern wall. "No time to move."

"Quiet!" Caratacus ordered in a loud whisper. "Muzzle the horses!"

"By Jupiter himself," thundered the foreign voice. "Look at the size of them."

From the cave's dark recesses, Caratacus watched a lanky cavalry trooper approaching the big webs.

"Never knew they grew so big or so close together," the soldier continued.

"You city lads wouldn't know a spider web from a mattress," taunted an unseen voice.

"Kiss my arse," the first trooper snarled.

For a moment he studied the radiating nets. "Look!" He pointed to the biggest orb. "There's a live bee caught in the strands. I won't let them blood suckers get this one." He stepped closer and reached for the bee.

"I'll see if I can pluck it out before that pissing vermin gets it." A lone spider below bravely left its protective cone and scurried towards the trapped insect.

"Get away from there, shit brain!" roared a husky voice. "Don't you know those demons are poisonous? You'll die in seconds."

A big spider dangling from its invisible drag line dropped onto the soldier's face. He recoiled as his hand shot up and swatted it away, knocked off his helmet, and sent it careening down the path. He reeled about and entangled himself in the patchwork of sticky webs engulfing his face and mailed armor. He broke loose and stumbled down the hillside cursing and swatting away other spiders that had jumped onto his clothing.

No sooner had the soldier fled when dozens of the black creatures converged on the damaged portions and began respinning the family of webs. The Roman voices and the sounds of their horses faded as they widened their search.

* * *

The band of warriors spent the night in the cave. Caratacus sat brooding in the blackness long after everyone fell asleep. He'd sought solitude deeper within the cavern. *Death must be like this.* Perhaps it might have been better if he, too, had died at Caersws, like Fergus ap Roycal. No, never! He had to think about Dana and Macha. For what seemed to be the hundredth time, he wondered if they, along with the other women and children, were still safe. Had Venutios and his men escaped from Caersws? Did he gather up the refugees from the hidden valley and flee with them to the land of the Ordovices? Its king had pledged to resist the Roman onslaught. Caratacus prayed that all of them had escaped the Romans.

Then it occurred to him, a thought that was almost horrifying: did he actually fear dying? After all his battles and raids, why should he now fear death? He lived with death all his life. Why did it suddenly bother him?

He was forty-one summers old and had lived longer than most men. He didn't fear dying in battle. He feared old age. The fear that he would lose his memory as did his father. Caratacus vowed never to allow that to happen to him. He would take his own life rather than become a helpless invalid.

The small fire had long since flickered out, yet the faint warmth of charred coals touched his nakedness as total darkness chilled his backside. The only sounds were his own breathing and slow heartbeat. A beat he imagined he could slow to match the unseen drops of water plopping within the dark bowels of the cave. He knew there must be a pond like the cave he used to play in as a boy. Yet, he felt the touch of a draft from the darkness above. From the invisible ceiling drops of water fell from a place too high to be seen by torchlight.

Although there were ten others sleeping within shouting distance, Caratacus felt alone in the cavern's abyss. Again, he thought of death and knew when he held his breath, the sound of his heart was, to his mind, the only presence of life. If his heart stopped, there would be no difference between total darkness and total death. He no longer feared death.

* * *

Caratacus and ten followers had traveled twisting mountain trails, ridden across open plains, and dodged

Roman patrols for ten days after fleeing Caersws. He prayed he would succeed in persuading Cartimandua to ally her warriors with his. Cold winds swept across the barren moors, driving before them the fleeting warmth of the morning sun. Caratacus gripped the woolen cowl closer to his body, attempting to keep out the biting chill. His guide, Alfyn, reminded him that the Brigantian Plain was the Land of Two Winters, white and green.

The group halted upon a ridge of a grassy limestone hill. They smelled of pungent horse sweat and leather, their mounts foaming at the mouth after a hard ride. In the distance, down the slope, stood Eburacum, crossroads of northern Britannia, on the bank of the placid River Ouse. Nearly twenty river barges and coastal merchant ships were beached along muddy banks or docked at its overcrowded wharf. A small flock of curlews flew across the plain toward the river for another day of feeding, while others skimmed its murky surface. Their loud, dual-pitched calls drifted on the breeze.

"Alfyn, before we enter," Caratacus said, "ride on ahead and see what you can learn about Cartimandua's activities."

The pock-faced warrior rubbed his hands together and blew on bluish fingers. "Aye, easy enough, especially after I warm meself by a cooking fire," he said. "Today's market day, and everybody from the countryside will be trading the latest gossip from the outside world."

"As a precaution, take this." Caratacus handed him a leather pouch. "This will loosen a few tongues."

Alfyn opened it and pulled a silver coin from the bag. He furrowed his bristly, red eyebrows. "This is Iceni."

"Tell them you were a mercenary for the Iceni. For all they know, you could have been on any one of the ships on the river. That will explain the questions and money."

* * *

In the late afternoon that same day, Alfyn returned to Caratacus's camp in a grove of sycamores on the opposite side of the hill from Eburacum.

"What news do you bring?" Caratacus inquired as they huddled around the small campfire.

"Unless you be counting the merchants, it's been nearly a year since they've seen a Roman. But everywhere I turned, the people spoke your name. You're their hero."

Caratacus frowned. *I'm not a hero to anyone.* "What do they say about the queen?"

"No one speaks openly against her. But people whisper she's a Roman puppet. She's a cruel woman who deals harshly with traitors and has executed many rebels from the western tribe."

"Anything else?"

"They know about the defeat at Caersws. But they aren't sure what to believe. Rumors say you're dead, have escaped, or been captured. But ...," for a moment Alfyn hesitated averting Caratacus's eyes, and scanned the slate-gray sky, "there's another rumor you must know."

"Go on."

"They say ...," Alfyn bit his lower lip and swallowed, "they say your wife and daughter and all the women and children have been captured."

Caratacus flinched. His stomach tightened. He waved his men into silence. Heat rushed to his face. "Do you place any truth in the rumors?"

"Who can say?" Alfyn shrugged. "No one knows what to believe. The news came from passing merchants. What will you do, sire?"

For a moment Caratacus remained silent, pondering his next move. He glanced around seeing nine pairs of tormented eyes on him.

"We go to Eburacum," he said after a moment. "I'll learn from the queen the truth about our families."

"But won't she arrest you?"

"I won't slink away like a cur. We'll see what the people really think about me."

* * *

An hour later Caratacus's retinue, riding horseback, reached the city gates, and four sentries attempted to block their way with crossed spears.

Caratacus, his face set, waved his hand in a wide swath before him. "Clear the way! I am Caratacus, King of the Trinovantes and cousin of Queen Cartimandua!"

The guards glanced to one another and back to the scarred and weather-beaten figure, wearing chain mail and a scarlet and gold, tartan cloak.

The king's calloused hand gripped the hilt of his sword. "I've killed fifty Romans with my bare hands. They were ten times the men you are. Clear the way, or I'll personally cut down the lot of you, too!"

The sentries moved aside, and the entourage proceeded. As Caratacus rode through the gates, the word passed among the market crowd, "It's Caratacus!"

Soon people chanted his name: "Caratacus! Caratacus!" Dressed in cloaks and furs to ward off the cold, they crowded and jostled for a place close to the band of horsemen riding down the dusty street between the trading stalls. People reached out to touch him. Women held up their babies for him to see, asking for his blessing. The mob kept thronging about until his party reached the Great Hall.

Sentries, posted outside the hall, attempted to block his passage.

"Tell the queen," Caratacus commanded, "that her cousin, King Caratacus, Scourge of the Romans, requires an audience immediately! I will count to ten, ten times. If I don't hear any word by the time I finish, I will storm the hall! She *will* see me!"

* * *

Caratacus's eyes adjusted to the dimly lit meeting room. Smoky torches in sconces lined the walls. Passing the central hearth, he approached Cartimandua, who sat in a purple-cushioned, high-backed chair on the dais, a foot above the mosaic floor. Two husky shield bearers stood behind her along the back wall. Despite the dim light, the queen's gown was ablaze with spirals of blue and green, twisting lines of red and silver, and circular strands of orange hemmed by gold thread; truly befitting the Queen of Brigantia and her reputation for extravagance. *She is deep in the money pouches of the Romans.*

As he stood before her, he looked about the chamber. No Romans.

Cartimandua's rouged face did not hide the cruelty with in her. Her aqua eyes focused on him like two daggers.

"Welcome, noble Cousin and warrior," the queen intoned formally. "Were you someone else, your impertinence would warrant death. But since you are our cousin and true king of the southern tribes, we grant your audience."

"Forgive my boldness, but the times we live in call for boldness." *Perhaps it was a fool's errand coming here.*

"Indeed. We know of your exploits against the Romans," Cartimandua answered, her voice softening.

"The question is, are you impressed enough to join us, Cousin-Queen?"

"I, too, am concerned with what the Romans have done to our tribes." She motioned to Caratacus to take the low-backed chair to her right. "I was alarmed when I heard you, the Scourge of the Romans, had been defeated," she continued after he was seated. "We received word that you were dead. Thank the gods you survived."

He ignored her mocking tone. "Tell me, is it true? Are Dana and Macha Roman prisoners?"

"I'm afraid so," Cartimandua sighed. "I wish it weren't. I truly loved my sister." She pressed her full lips together and shook her head.

You despised her. "Where have they taken them?"

"I don't know. But I only know they're safe. My information came from reliable merchants."

"They'll be used as hostages to lure me into a trap." Caratacus bunched his fists, attempting to suppress his growing anger.

Cartimandua looked down at the two gold bracelets on her left wrist. She pushed them farther up her arm with her other hand. Then she tugged at the necklace around her neck before she returned her gaze to Caratacus. "Be careful. Don't allow yourself to be drawn into such a situation."

The veins throbbed in Caratacus's temple. He loosened his fists and took a deep breath. "I won't. But I need your help."

A spasm of irritation crossed her face. "I will, if I can."

"Most of my army escaped and is in the northern lands of the Ordovices. If your forces joined mine, we could push back the Romans."

Cartimandua nodded, her eyes focused on her cousin. "No doubt we could. You must have heard the rumors that I am sympathetic to the Roman cause?"

"Aye, so I've heard."

She leaned closer. Her eyes narrowed like a cat's. "It's an act," she whispered. "I had to keep the Roman dogs from overrunning my lands."

"And the money and your expensive clothing?"

"It's true, I took their gold and the western lands, they're rightfully mine." The queen paused and touched her cheek. She turned and glanced to her bored shield bearers, standing at a discreet distance and back to Caratacus. "But I've protected my people. And, I say this in all sincerity, I have been with you since the day the Romans stepped upon the shores of Britannia."

Caratacus eyed her skeptically. *Cartimandua doesn't care for her people. Surely she is lying. I must be wary.* "Then are you ready to join us?"

"I believe the time is right." She smiled broadly.

"Then it's settled."

"Your arrival could not have been more timely. I have called for a war council with my chieftains for tomorrow morning. All of them are present for the feast I am giving this evening. You shall address them this evening. I know deep in their hearts they have supported you all along." She grazed his forearm with her hand. "They will listen to you."

"You flatter me, Cousin. "It has been many years since I addressed your council, I'm looking forward to having them as allies once again."

"Well, it's growing late, time for the evening meal." Her face brightened. "You shall join us as an honored guest."

* * *

Caratacus sat to Cartimandua's right on the ornately carved wooden dais. Her arch-Druid, Erfig, was on the left. Seven chieftains of the queen's council were divided, with four seated along the dining table on Caratacus's side and three with the Druid. Prior to dinner, the queen had introduced Caratacus to them. Sitting along rows of dozens of tables below them were members of the nobility and their wives, dressed in their finest clothing. Wealthy merchants, lesser Druids, and Caratacus's followers, including Alfyn, sat behind them with captains from Cartimandua's army. As the queen and her guests waited for dinner to be served, they conversed among themselves while drinking cups of corma or Roman wine. A strolling bard played a lively tune on a small Celtic harp, blending with the voices of talking and laughing diners.

Ensconced in the surrounding walls, the quivering light of dozens of torches smelling of pitch illuminated the hall. Mixed with the smoky light's oily smell, drifted the aroma of mutton and venison roasting in two fire pits and the central hearth.

Caratacus and Cartimandua had been making small talk when the queen's steward approached. He bowed and informed her dinner was ready.

Cartimandua took a sip of wine and set her cup down. "Dinner will wait—I will tell you when to serve."

The steward bowed again and backed away.

The queen raised a hand, and a hush fell over the hall. All eyes turned to her. "As I told Lord Caratacus earlier today, the time has come for us to support him. We must drive the Romans from our lands, from Britannia."

Caratacus looked out of the corner of his eye towards Cartimandua. *Does she mean it?*

A murmur erupted among the diners. The clan chieftains looked at one another.

"It's about time," one noble on the main floor said.

Cartimandua raised an eyebrow so slightly that it seemed to Caratacus that no one but he had noticed.

"Why now?" another said. "The Romans will kill us!"

Arguments sprang up throughout the hall, the noise rising to a deafening level.

Cartimandua's nose flared. She raised a hand. "Silence!"

Within the length of half a dozen heartbeats, silence enshrouded the room. A few people coughed and cleared their throats.

"It's time for Lord Caratacus to speak." The queen lowered her hand.

Caratacus nodded to her and stood. "I thank the queen for her generosity. However," he paused and motioned with his head towards the chieftains and back towards the diners, "I came here not only to ask her support, but yours as well. As sure as I'm standing here, the Romans will invade your lands, if not now, certainly later. Is that what you want?"

"No!" several chieftains and diners, including Alfyn and Caratacus's men, shouted.

"That's a lie," one noble on the floor roared. "No Romans will invade our lands, we have their promise."

"You're a damn fool if you believe that," barked another.

Other men shouted in agreement.

Caratacus nodded to the audience and chieftains. "We can stop them with the aid of your warriors." He sat.

Cartimandua glared at the men who had objected to supporting Caratacus. She shook her head. "Lord Caratacus is right. By combining our forces with his and the Ordovices, we shall defeat the Romans and drive them from Britannia."

"My loyalty has always been to my queen," Kyncar, a chieftain in his midforties said. Dark, owlish eyes stared in Cartimandua's direction from a face covered by a blotchy, wine-colored birthmark. A gray, drooping moustache covered his thin upper lip. "I agree and praise her wisdom in this matter." He jabbed his right hand, which was missing a little finger, toward a couple of chieftains to his left, Donaut and Uric. "Unlike some present, I will never swear allegiance to the Romans."

The chieftains' eyes flashed in anger, frowns crossing their weathered faces.

"You dare call us traitors?" Uric growled. His scarred hand grabbed the hilt of his dagger.

"Enough, Lord Uric!" Cartimandua ordered.

Uric lowered his hand.

Kyncar nodded to the queen. "So long as the Romans stay out of our lands, I will obey my queen's commands." He paused. "Should they step one foot across our border, then, with all due respect, Great Queen, I will have to disobey you. If need be, I will fight to the death."

For a split second, Cartimandua stiffened, her eyes darkened.

The chieftain faced Caratacus. "But since the queen has agreed to an alliance with Lord Caratacus, that won't be necessary. It will be my honor to fight along your side."

"So will I," said Gadeon the pig-eyed leader sitting next to him. He scratched his flat, broken nose.

"He places us in great danger," Donaut the pock-face chieftain said. His fierce, brown eyes spotted with yellow flecks peered from beneath protruding brow ridges like a hawk. His dark beard failed to conceal blackened teeth that showed through the overbite of his upper lip. "He cannot be allowed to stay. When the Romans learn that Lord Caratacus is here, they will order you to arrest him, Great Queen."

Again a loud murmur raced among the chieftains and diners.

"No Roman orders me to do anything," Cartimandua said in a voice full of venom. "It is I who decides if he stays or departs, and I say he stays."

"Rome would accuse you of harboring an enemy," Donaut said.

Cartimandua jabbed a finger in Donaut's direction. "You leave the Romans to me. Caratacus is our guest, my cousin, and friend." She sighed and touched the gold bracelet on her wrist. "His wife Dana is my beloved sister. She and her daughter, Macha, my niece, are Roman captives. I will not allow them to languish in captivity. We shall find a way to set them free."

Inwardly, Caratacus shuddered. *This reeks of a trap. How would she free Dana and Macha? Her spies will inform the Romans.*

Three other chieftains besides Kyncar and Gadeon, who up to this point had kept sober expressions, spoke up in support of Caratacus. Uric, who sat beside Donaut, had remained silent after Cartimandua had rebuked him.

Donaut and he are probably in the money bags of the Romans. Is Cartimandua testing her chieftains' loyalty?

* * *

Late that night, Caratacus sprang awake, his body shuddering. He pulled away the heavy, wolf-skin blanket and sat upright on his pallet, trying to recall the dream that had startled him from sleep. A warning. A faceless

213

woman with golden hair blowing in the wind stood on a barnacled rock in a raging sea. The surf pounded around her, but she remained untouched. She beckoned him to flee! He shuddered.

The warning was obvious. He must leave Eburacum. But he never placed any credence in dreams. They had many interpretations. Charlatans flooded the land making a living foretelling what their customers wanted to hear.

Caratacus knew that Cartimandua was probably lying, but he was willing to take the risk. *Perhaps she no longer receives her annual payments from Rome.*

He had to learn what she really wanted, promise her that and more. Concede something to her she would never have dreamed possible. And then turn her murky promise into one of granite.

* * *

At dawn the next day, a groggy Caratacus was summoned to the Great Hall. Upon getting dressed and strapping his sword to his waist, he was escorted by Cartimandua's shield bearers. He was hungry but was given no time for breakfast. The giant captain of Cartimandua's shield bearers said it was urgent that the queen see him immediately. And no sooner did he realize something was amiss when he entered the torch-lit room. Porcius, stone faced, but fatter than ever, stood near the queen's throne.

Caratacus bolted for the hallway passage to the outside.

"Seize him!" Cartimandua commanded. "I want him alive!"

Three guards confronted him at the hall entrance. In an instant, he sliced up two with his longsword, spattering blood and limbs against the stone walls and mosaic floor. The third used his shield skillfully, fending off Caratacus's blows.

As soon as Caratacus saw the entrance was clear, he raced for the doorway. He faced the third guardsman for a split second. He didn't see it coming from a fourth. A searing pain shot through the back of his head as he slumped to his knees. Standing above him was the captain of the queen's shield bearers, gripping with both hands a long, black hardstick horizontally across his thighs. Caratacus slowly toppled to the cold floor, unconscious.

* * *

After a bucket of icy water splashed his face, Caratacus regained consciousness. His head burned like a hot iron. The right side of his face throbbed, and he barely opened his eyes. His teeth felt as if they had been smashed with a sledge hammer. He rolled his tongue around the inside of his burning mouth, touching the jagged edges of broken teeth. He swallowed warm, salty blood while more flowed from his mouth, dripping on his tunic and the glossy, mosaic floor. He realized his hands were tied behind his back as he staggered to his feet. Twice he stumbled, nearly falling to the floor. Water dripping down the side of his face did nothing to ease the pain.

He turned and spotted Cartimandua standing five steps away guarded by one of her retainers. Next to her was Porcius, grim-faced, peering at him.

"Is this how you treat your people, you traitorous bitch!" he rasped.

A guard slammed him to the floor.

"Leave him be!" Cartimandua commanded, rising to her feet. She glared at Porcius. "His words are nothing."

After Caratacus was yanked to his feet, she continued, "You're a bigger fool than I first believed. Did you really think I would support your fight against Rome?"

"I was warned to stay away," Caratacus gasped through broken teeth. *How could I have believed her lies last night!*

"Fortunately for us you didn't," Porcius interjected.

"I knew you had a part in this, Roman pig!"

"Aren't we touchy?" Porcius said in a mocking voice. "You've been a menace to Rome for more than seven years. We knew one day you would seek the queen's help. We prepared for this moment."

Caratacus turned to Cartimandua. "Why did you conspire with this dog?"

"You are a defeated man, dearest Brother-in-Law," she said in a silken voice. "Rome is too strong for both of us."

"With your warriors we could have won."

"You mean we could have been crushed," she answered sharply. "Siding with you would have meant disaster.

215

Count the thousands who followed you to their meaningless deaths."

Porcius nodded to Cartimandua. "Wisely spoken." He turned and for a split second studied Caratacus's face. "She knows we would replace her with someone else."

"Another Roman puppet!" Caratacus spat.

"Call me what you like, Cousin," Cartimandua answered. "What matters is that I survive and so do my people. And now I know who the traitors are among my chieftains. I arrested all who expressed their desire to fight with you."

"Kyncar and Gadeon and the others are patriots. It is you and your lackeys, Donaut and Uric, who are the traitors. The people have never mattered to you," Caratacus retorted. "You have thought of no one but yourself and your Roman luxuries." He spat a bloodied, broken tooth at the queen, which fell inches from her feet.

"What she gains from us, Caratacus, is security," Porcius counseled. "We promise not to enter her realm, so long as she recognizes our supremacy over Britannia and pays us an annual tribute."

"Tribute from the blood of her people," Caratacus growled as the pain in his head subsided to a pounding ache.

Cartimandua quickly raised her hand to stay the guard's blow. "As soon as your military escort arrives, Senator Porcius," the queen said, "we will release him to your custody. Your arrival last night was timely. Otherwise, I would have had to find some other way of detaining him."

"I appreciate your keeping it a secret from Caratacus. After his defeat at Caersws, I was certain he would flee to your kingdom—that's why I came here as quickly as I could."

"You realize there was a chance that Caratacus might not flee to my capitol?"

"Yes, but the risk had to be taken. Thank Castor and Pollux, gods of good fortune, that he did."

Damn your good fortune, Roman pig! Caratacus thought.

Cartimandua turned to her shield bearers. "In the meantime, take him away."

"Before he goes, I would like another moment with him," Porcius said.

Cartimandua nodded to the guards to wait.

"I have something else to say, Caratacus," he said in a quiet, private tone.

"You have said enough," Caratacus spat.

"Nevertheless, I must say it." Porcius shook his head and sighed. "Why did it have to come to this, Caratacus? Perhaps I'm growing sentimental in my old age. It never had to be this way, all this bloodletting. We could have been friends. You and I, Rome and Britannia."

"Friends? Not as long as the Romans remain in our lands!"

* * *

As the guards escorted Caratacus from the Great Hall, Porcius watched silently until they disappeared, relieved this Briton was a Roman prisoner. He turned to Cartimandua and caught her staring at him.

"He has royal blood," the queen said. "The consequences of an untimely death or public humiliation could undo all the good of his capture and drive my people into rebellion."

"Come now, my Queen. Do you really believe that I have waited so long just to see him executed like a dog—the man who saved my life?"

"Nevertheless, I warn you, Senator Porcius. You alone are responsible for his safety."

"You have nothing to fear. He is worth far more alive than dead."

She locked eyes with Porcius for a moment. He noticed something he wouldn't have believed possible with this woman. Tears were welling up at the corner of her dark, green eyes. She quickly turned away. He remembered once she said Caratacus should have been her rightful husband. "Rest assured," Porcius said, "I will see that no harm comes to Caratacus or his family."

I wonder if the treacherous bitch believes me.

CHAPTER 22

NOVEMBER. AD 50

The wagon halted at the edge of the Forum where the prisoners were rousted by the guard. The crisp night air sent a shiver through Caratacus's chilled body as he dropped to the cobblestone pavement. He stretched his stiff, sore limbs. There had been no room to lie down or spread their legs, and sleeping was nearly impossible.

Dana pulled the cowl of her cloak over her greasy, tightly curled hair and retied the garment in front. Soggy clothing clung to her slender body like a wet rag. She huddled close to Caratacus, clutching a sleepy Macha dressed in a filthy tunic.

"Where are we?" Dana whispered, her breath rising as a cloud of steam in the freezing air.

"We're in Rome," Caratacus whispered in reply.

Caratacus looked at his wife and daughter. His face tightened at the sight of their miserable appearances, which grew with each passing day.

After Caratacus had been captured, he was returned to Caersws and reunited with his family. The three were confined in an iron cage, outside, exposed to scorching heat and freezing rains for a week before they left for Rome.

The journey from Britannia to Rome had taken nearly six miserable weeks. The bloody Romans had shackled him, Dana, Macha, and five captured chieftains and as many noblemen, including Kyncar and Gadeon, for the entire duration. Bathing was limited to buckets of water thrown over their heads, and dirty clothing. They were fed only enough rations to survive. Caratacus's shoulders tightened at the memory of Dana pleading with their captors for something additional for little Macha.

Fortunately, one of the guards took pity, and when he was on night duty would sneak Macha extra bread every evening after taps. Caratacus had nodded his thanks. Under heavy guard, they traveled in a cramped and creaky wagon down the middle of Gaul to the Port of Messalia, where they sailed for Italy in a leaky, rat-infested merchantman.

They arrived at the Port of Ostia in a pouring mid-November rain. Even then, the guards refused to unchain the drenched, freezing prisoners, who had been quartered topside under a flimsy canopy. It hadn't mattered that Dana, Macha, Caratacus, and the chieftains were shivering so hard their teeth chattered. After disembarking on the slippery quay, the trembling and sneezing detainees were stuffed into another cramped, covered wagon for the twenty-three mile journey to Rome. Clothed in drenched, burnt-red cloaks that protected the troopers' mail shirts, tunics, and breeches, two squadrons of Praetorian cavalryman provided escort. A flag bearer, carrying a scarlet banner emblazoned with the image of a gold scorpion, led the way. One *turma* of thirty horsemen, each carrying longswords hooked to their sides and hexagonal shields and covered by protective oil cloths strapped to their backs, rode ahead of the prisoners wagon. The other turma acted as a rear guard.

Caratacus spat in their direction. Fortunately, the troopers were too wrapped up in their own misery to notice.

It was the first hour after midnight before the captives passed through the Ostian Gate and entered the Capitol of the World. The drenching rain had relented only to be replaced by a numbing wind that careened off the city's ancient walls and whistled through the deserted entryway.

"Your new home is over there," the duty centurion said, jolting Caratacus from his thoughts. "Get moving!"

In the bouncing torchlight, Caratacus spied the black silhouettes of hundreds of statues on pedestals dotting the Great Plaza. Tall colonnaded buildings stood in the gloomy shadows bordering the square's four sides. Although Caratacus caught only a few torch-lit glimpses as they trudged up the hillside, he immediately recognized the

Rostra. Porcius had described it years ago, but he had not believed his bragging. The elaborate platform, framed by a magnificent, marble balustrade, adorned with exquisite, bronze statues of Roman heroes, and iron beaks from captured warships, could not be mistaken for anything else. Yet he was too weary to be impressed. The craftsmanship of Britannia's silversmiths and bronze workers was as good, if not better, than any Roman's.

Beyond the Rostra, halfway up Capitoline Hill, they stopped alongside a small, brick building with a vaulted roof. Caratacus, his family, and the others were herded into a musty-smelling, torch-lit chamber. Not ten feet away in the tufa stone floor was a wide, black pit. A large, wicker basket big enough to hold five people sat near the ledge.

"Welcome to Tullianum Prison," said the lizard-faced turnkey in a snide voice.

A muffled scream shot from the darkness below, and Macha sobbed. "I'm afraid, Mama."

Caratacus turned to his daughter, bent his knees, and looked into her hazel eyes. "I know, my brave, little one, so am I. One day we will go home." *Do I really believe that?*

Dana hugged her. "It will be all right, sweet. Da and I won't let anything happen to you, we promise." Her reassurance soothed Macha.

"That's right," Caratacus said as he stood.

The basket, which took the captives to the lower level of the prison, was only big enough to hold five prisoners. Three trips were required to take Caratacus and the rest below. Caratacus, Dana, Macha, and the two remaining chieftains, Kyncar and Gadeon, were sent down on the final trip.

Two husky turnkeys winched the prisoners to the bottom in the rope-held basket on a series of squealing pulleys.

As Caratacus traveled downward past stone walls of rotting, blackish-green moss, an agonizing scream drifted upwards from the pit's invisible floor. It must be coming from the infamous torture chamber he had heard so much about from the guards during the voyage. All confessed before its notorious rack masters, even if it meant fabricating stories to stop the bone-crushing, limb-stretching pain. He prayed that wouldn't be their fate.

The basket reached the bottom of the torch-lit pit where they were met by the jailer and three guards. The prisoners were ordered out and Caratacus and the rest stepped to the dusty floor.

They were led along a bleak passageway barely high enough to stand. The deeper they went, the fouler the air grew. Water dripped from crevices in the ceiling onto their faces. A pained voice whimpered from an unseen cell. Muffled chains slithered across a reed-covered floor.

The detail halted before a single rusty, iron door containing a lone, tiny window. To the side a miserable little torch jutted from an iron stanchion in the wall. The jailer unlocked and opened the creaking door.

"In you go," he ordered.

Caratacus, Dana, Macha, and the chieftains were shoved into the nearly black cell, stumbling and cursing. Immediately, they were hit by the foul stench of filth, urine, and feces. For a moment they choked and gagged as they groped about in the shadowy darkness that enshrouded every corner.

"There's no room," Kyncar said, "I can smell the sump hole, I must be right over it."

"Where? Gadeon asked.

"In the corner," Kyncar answered.

"Well, get away from it, or I'll shit on you," Gadeon said.

As his eyes adjusted, Caratacus held his hand before him to find the walls and to make sure Dana and Macha were close to him. He took a few steps when he touched the rough, slimy surface of the wall. Along one side, he felt Dana's skeletal body through her ragged clothing.

"Caratacus, is that you?" Dana asked.

"Yes, it's me, glad you stayed close. Is Macha with you?"

"Where are you, Mama? I can't see," Macha said.

"I'm right here, darling," Dana said. "Here, take my hand, can you feel it?"

"Yes, Mama."

"Can you feel the wall?" Caratacus asked.

"I can," Dana said.

"This is as good a place as any, let's sit down," he said.

"Bloody fucking Romans treating us like dogs," Gadeon said. "If I could get my hands on a sword—"

"They'd slice you like a melon before you could blink an eye," Kyncar said.

"Enough!" Caratacus said. "Everyone spread as best you can."

The chieftains grumbled as they tried to find a spot to sit.

"We have to make the best of it," Caratacus said.

"Best of what?" Kyncar asked. "While we wait for our deaths?"

Caratacus had no answer, he knew the man was right.

Despite the darkness and cold, sweat rolled down Caratacus's body. His tattered clothing, like everyone elses, reeked of filth and crawled with lice. His body itched from flea bites, and his hair was a greasy mat.

As his eyes adjusted to the darkness, he saw the shadowy outline of rats boldly padding along the floor and leaping over the chieftains' bodies to their curses.

Macha screamed. "Rats! I want to go home, Mama!"

Dana hugged Macha close. "It's all right, I'll make certain they don't bite you. I'll kill them first."

* * *

More than a week passed before Caratacus and his people saw the light of day. The captives received news they were to be shackled and publicly paraded through the streets of Rome. Afterwards, they would proceed to the Praetorian Barracks, where Emperor Claudius waited to render judgment.

The morning, growing warmer with each passing minute, greeted the prisoners as they were lifted into the daylight and left Tullianum Prison surrounded by Praetorian Guardsmen.

Caratacus's eyes needed a moment to adjust to the sunlight. The sky was as blue as lapis lazuli. *The Roman gods must have decided the emperor should receive his prisoners only on the brightest of days.* He gazed down upon the crowded Forum as he, Dana, Macha, and the chieftains trudged down the hill.

222

"What are they going to do to us, Caratacus?" Dana whispered. "Will the Romans kill us?"

"I won't lie, if they don't today, they may later on. Who knows what the Romans have waiting for us?"

Dana gasped. "Even Macha? Surely, they will spare her? She is only a child."

Caratacus shook his head. "You would think the Romans would show her mercy, pray that they will."

"Shut up, savages!" a guard snarled.

Gods, why must Dana and Macha suffer my fate? I would gladly give my life if the Romans would spare them.

Dana sighed, her shoulders slumped, and she lowered her head as if resigned to her situation.

All Rome, from the perfumed nobility in their finest togas and silk gowns to the penniless, smelly mob in ragged tunics, waited for the triumphal procession to begin. Cohorts of the Praetorian Guard assembled at the front of the parade awaiting orders to begin the march. Behind them followed wagons and pallets, filled with war booty, and then came the filth-encrusted prisoners in shackles. Caratacus was ordered to walk alone, behind his wife and daughter, who in turn followed the chieftains. The fine, sandy hair raised along the length of his purple-tattooed arms and chest. The chains chafed his wrists and ankles, and he had to slide his feet along as he walked. The heat from the cobblestone streets burnt through his worn leather shoes, his feet already sore.

At the sound of the trumpet fanfare, the parade wound its way through guard-lined streets and plazas to the cheers and jeers of the populace. A century of drummers beat a heart-thumping cadence that rivaled the cheering and vibrated deep into a man's soul. Caratacus determined to maintain his dignity, if anything, showing his disdain for the mobs, being held back by spear-wielding city guards.

He locked eyes briefly with a jeering merchant, who froze his foreign curse in midsentence. Moments later, he stared at the monumental buildings with their great archways and pillars, porticoes and domes. Never had he seen so many buildings crammed together in one place—all built of burnt, red brick, marble, and stone. Nearly all were painted in an array of colors—many coated in gold and silver. Hundreds of buildings and thousands of toga and tunic-clad spectators lined the avenues. For a moment, he closed his eyes to clear the dizziness he felt at seeing so much in such a crowded area.

As they traipsed through the forum, Dana and Macha grew more frightened with every step. Macha started crying, followed by Dana's weeping. She turned to Caratacus. "Caratacus, I don't know how much longer I can endure this. The crowds are terrifying, and the city, it's so big."

"You must stay calm."

"Calm? I was calm throughout our journey and endured that horrible prison," she answered in exasperation. "I don't know how much more I can take."

"We must not show fear—that's what the Romans want to see—cowering *barbarians!*"

"I can't. I just can't." Her face tightened and tears filled her eyes. She turned away, but even through the noisy crowd's din, he heard her weeping.

Macha clutched her mother tightly. Dana turned to Caratacus and shouted to be heard above the mob. "We must do something! Nothing can happen to Macha!" Caratacus looked away.

"Have mercy on us!" Dana cried in Latin, appealing to the crowds. "Please save us! Ask the emperor to spare our lives!" She repeated the lament, and soon Kyncar, Gadeon, and the other captives picked up the cry and made similar appeals.

Caratacus tightened, his face growing hotter with every step. He glowered at Dana. *I can't believe my own wife would stoop to groveling. Not before the Romans!*

"Hush, woman," Caratacus growled. "We ask no mob for mercy. We've done nothing wrong, we've defended our lands!" Had he not been manacled, he would have slapped her, something he had never thought of doing before.

The crowd jeered and laughed at Dana's pleas.

"If it is the will of the gods that we die," Caratacus shouted above the noisy din, "so be it! We cower before no one!"

"Don't let your foolish pride get in the way, Husband!" Dana snapped out the words. "You don't want Macha to die anymore than I do. No daughter of mine should die like this!"

"Must you let the mob know that! We're still Britons!"

Caratacus looked about in disdain, ignoring further appeals for mercy by his family and chieftains. *If my courage as a warrior-king is known throughout the Roman Empire, I will do nothing to diminish my reputation here.* Caratacus held his head high, pondering what he should say to the emperor to save his daughter's life. *I will never show any sign of fear to these filthy Roman dogs.*

They left the forum and soon passed through the gate at the northwest corner of the city wall. Ahead stood the Praetorian camp. The great fortress dominated the low hillside, its huge walls constructed of brick and concrete, crowned with battlements. The central gateway, through which they entered, was covered with fine, marble sculptures worthy of a great king. No, an emperor.

Inside the fortress, across its gigantic field, five thousand six-foot-tall Praetorian Guardsmen stood on parade wearing scarlet and white tunics beneath segmented, armored cuirasses. Their crimson and gilded shields and iron javelins glistened in the midafternoon sun. Caratacus smiled to himself as he lumbered by their ranks. *Am I so dangerous that Rome needs this army of troops to contain me?*

The prisoners shuffled by the mass of buildings in the fortress center to the front of a small temple, where Emperor Claudius, the Empress Agrippina, and their retinues waited. Silken, purple flags and streamers fluttered faintly in the light breeze.

Caratacus prayed the emperor would show mercy, if not for himself, then for Dana and Macha. He steeled himself for whatever fate awaited him.

CHAPTER 23

After the tribute and plunder were paraded before the imperial couple and the assembled multitude, the prisoners followed. Caratacus and the other prisoners were commanded to halt.

Twelve guardsmen marched forward and escorted Caratacus, with Dana and Macha following, to the plum-carpeted stairs below the dais. The emperor raised his trembling right hand, and they stopped.

Claudius sat in state on the tribunal under a protective purple and white canopy. He wore the purple cloak of the Praetorian Guard over his white, linen toga. The emperor appeared older than Caratacus had imagined. Jaundiced skin, drawn tightly over his face, exposed blue veins in his fragile cheeks and jaw, his head crowned with short, scraggly, dead, white hair.

Agrippina, dressed in a chlamys of cloth covered with gold, sat conspicuously nearby on another dais. No more than thirty-five, her heavy rouge harshened otherwise soft features. A hard-fixed glare shot from dark eyes, and a sneer crawled across the curve of her full lips as she stared at the fallen prince.

Behind the imperial couple stood dozens of toga-clad senators, including Porcius, his face impassive.

No doubt he's gloating, looking forward to my execution!

"We shall speak to the prince," Claudius said in a clear but deep voice. "He is to come forward, alone."

There was a stir amongst his entourage. Probably because the emperor was placing himself in jeopardy by allowing the barbarian to approach so closely without an escort. Claudius turned and glared them to silence.

Caratacus had heard that Roman emperors did not recognize Celtic or German leaders as kings. In their eyes, they were considered barbarians not worthy of a title higher than prince. As he mounted the top step, he looked about, puzzled. First to his wife and daughter, and then to the aging ruler. It seemed the whole parade had been carefully staged. He wondered the purpose. Months before he had learned that the emperor was attempting to strengthen his position with the Roman people. But he had been proclaimed Conqueror of Britannia years before, and was already the most powerful ruler in the world. By all rights, there wasn't anything left he could desire.

Caratacus slowly passed his eyes over the opulence of the surrounding buildings and the city beyond. He paused as the old emperor studied him.

"You have been brought before us for judgment. Do you have anything to say in your defense?" Claudius inquired in an even tone.

For a few moments, a silence fell, broken only by the snapping of fluttering streamers. The purple canopy billowed gently, bathing the emperor in its filtered light, casting a dream-like effect about him.

Caratacus nodded.

"You are to address the emperor as *Caesar*, barbarian!" admonished some petty official standing nearby.

"L-l-let him b-be!" stuttered the emperor. "Is it t-true you speak Latin?" he asked with interest.

"Yes, Caesar," Caratacus answered in a clear, firm voice. He had heard rumors that Claudius had stuttering fits when least expected.

"S-s-speak to us then," Claudius commanded.

Caratacus waved his manacled hands in the direction of the city. "When you have all this, *why* do you envy us Britons, our poor lands, and homes?" His voice echoed across the parade field. "I come from a line of great kings and warriors. Had I not chosen to defend my people and our lands from Rome's aggression, you would have invited me to this city as a friend rather than a prisoner. You would not have scorned a peaceful alliance with one so nobly born, the ruler of so many nations. As it is," he paused, studying the emperor's impassive face and those in attendance and continued in a lowered voice, "humiliation and defeat is my lot, glory yours. I had horses, men by the thousands, arms, and a sea of wealth. Are you surprised I am sorry to lose them?" His voice rose again. He drew a deep breath. "If you want to rule the world, does it follow that everyone else welcomes enslavement? If I had surrendered without a blow before being brought before you, neither my downfall nor your triumph would have become famous. If you execute me, they will be forgotten."

He looked back towards Dana's tearstained face, her chin uplifted in pride and Macha's who clung to her waist.

Caratacus continued, "Had I but glimpsed the might and majesty of Rome, I would have never challenged you. But as a man, a mortal, I would have still defended my family." He gestured towards them. "Spare me, and I shall be an everlasting token of your mercy." He bowed his head in silence.

Claudius turned to Porcius, who stepped to the front of the emperor's retinue, then to Agrippina, and back to Caratacus. Briefly, he sat in silence as if considering the prince's words.

Exhausted, his mouth parched, and his tongue like sand, every muscle in Caratacus's body ached. The speech had drained nearly every bit of energy. Now, it was up to the emperor to decide his fate and that of his people.

"Rome was founded," Claudius spoke a minute later without further stuttering, "on the principles of fortitude, justice, temperance, and wisdom. But these ideals are not exclusively Roman. They are found in all peoples, be they Roman or Greek, civilized or barbarian." Claudius paused and glanced to Agrippina and his retinue, including Porcius.

"Prince Caratacus, ruler of the British people, you have proven a worthy opponent of the Roman people, and we hold you no ill will. My triumph and your people are worthy of remembrance. Let the world know the power of Caesar and the justice of all that is Rome. Therefore, we hereby grant you *pardon*."

A gasp shot through the retinue. Again, Claudius gave them a scathing look. "You will be honored," he continued, "and granted the privileges of any visiting foreign prince. Our only condition is you shall remain in Rome for life."

Caratacus stood motionless for a moment, stunned by the emperor's words. *No execution?* He swallowed hard, went down on one knee, and bowed his head in supplication. *No matter how much I hate Rome, I must think of my people and our lands. Nevertheless, I will do whatever necessary to return my family to Britannia.*

"Strike their chains," the emperor commanded, "bathe and clothe them befitting their station and rank."

Dana and Macha ran to Caratacus's side, weeping in gratitude and relief.

"Come to us," the emperor said in a gentle voice.

The three approached Claudius and once more knelt at his purple and white, silk-covered sandals.

"May your gods and mine praise you for this day, Lord Caesar," Caratacus said. "History will not forget your mercy."

"Bravery such as yours is very rare in these turbulent times. It deserves mercy," Claudius answered. He turned to Narcissus, his Greek freedman and secretary. "See that proper quarters are prepared for the prince and his family immediately."

"Yes, Caesar."

"In the meantime," the emperor said, returning to Caratacus, "you and your wife shall join us for a feast tonight. Many of my guests are eager to meet the Wolf of Britannia."

Claudius nodded to Agrippina, who frowned and looked away. Within the space of a few heartbeats, she turned back and gave a terse nod. "Now, pay your respects to the empress. She, too, deserves your homage."

* * *

The sun had dropped below the hills of Rome before Caratacus and Dana were led from their new quarters to the great dining hall by one of Claudius's freedmen and two serving slaves. Their new residence, located in part of the empress's quarters, was on Palatine Hill opposite the emperor's palace, where Claudius and Agrippina could easily keep an eye on them. No matter, their apartments were clean, airy, and spacious beyond their wildest expectations. Ten slaves were attached to the new household—no doubt spies.

Caratacus looked about the airy, open hall lined with high columns, still marveling that he and his family had gone from imprisonment and certain death that morning, to the emperor's pardon, and now were noble guests for dinner. However, he noticed four toga-clad men wearing army sandals who walked a short distance ahead of them. Outlined under the clothing, swords hung below their left arms. Caratacus turned his head and spotted six more a little ways behind.

As Caratacus's family and escort continued down the corridor, he leaned toward Dana and lowered his voice. "We may be the emperor's guests, but we are still prisoners."

"What do you mean?" Dana said.

"Those tall men in togas in front and behind are Praetorian Guardsmen. They have the bearing of soldiers and carry hidden weapons."

Dana squinted in the direction of the guards walking to the front of them. "I shouldn't be surprised. At least we are no longer in that horrible prison. Actually, my mind is still spinning. Everything is so different here. The tall buildings, I never dreamed anything could be so big. And the crowds —so many people—and what an awful smell."

"Are you sure that wasn't us you smelled as they paraded us like animals on the street?" Caratacus said.

"No! It was the mob—they stank!"

Caratacus turned his head back and forth. "And here in the palace everything is clean, perfumed, and with much space."

"At least we were allowed to bathe and given decent food and allowed to live!"

He clenched his hands and glanced about. Realizing that he might be watched, he opened his hands. "Considering how the Romans starved us, we deserve it."

"I hate leaving Macha behind while we dine with the emperor—it's too soon after coming here to our new place. She's afraid we won't return."

"Do you think the young slave girl left with her will keep her occupied?"

Dana tightened her lips for the space of a heartbeat, then clucked. "I hope so, she seems like a sweet, young woman—she's barely more than a child herself. Maybe that will help having someone closer to her age."

"Well, she's a Gaul, and her language is similar to ours, that should make it easier." He leaned close to Dana again. "She's probably a spy like the rest of the slaves serving us."

Dana sighed. "I suppose you're right. So long as she treats Macha kindly, I will tolerate her presence. But I shall keep a close eye on the woman."

He surveyed the freedman in front of him, who at that moment glanced over his shoulder. The dark-haired Greek kept a blank face and turned his head to the front.

"Caratacus, please," Dana whispered as if guessing what he was thinking. "Don't even think about escaping, they would kill you in an instant—they would kill all of us!"

He nodded and whispered, "I know, but I still hate being here and will always hate Rome."

They passed beneath a lofty archway, framing the entry to the Grand *Triclinium*, over which was pedestaled a splendid quadriga bearing a godlike charioteer riding off to the underworld.

Hundreds of people, bejeweled and dressed in costliest silk and linen clothing, reclined on numerous couches. Thousands of oil lamps gleamed from colonnaded walls and on alabaster and bejeweled ebony tables, glittering, dazzling, and intoxicating the great room. Pots of roses perfumed the air.

Caratacus viewed the countless number of statues among the columns, their limbs painted so pink they seemed to be alive, representing Rome's multitude of gods and heroes. Among them stood a gigantic statue of a naked god looking down on the throng. It reminded him of the god Lugh, framed like gold in the sparkling lamplight. Yet, the images were foreign to him. The gods he knew were set among nature in the form of animals or other natural objects. Apart from Lugh, few were represented in human form.

The couple reclined near the emperor's couch, treated by attending slaves as his special guests. Claudius and the empress had yet to arrive. The other diners stared at them, none approaching. *Perhaps protocol required the emperor to*

*recognize Dana and me first. No doubt they will surge
forward once the emperor arrives.*

Caratacus observed Porcius a short distance away,
bedecked in a white, silk toga with a wide, scarlet border,
conversing with a fellow senator. He overheard him
commenting that the Senate had earlier convened, giving
many long and tedious orations in honor of Claudius and
compared him to heroes like Scipio Africanus, conqueror of
Hannibal. General Scapula was also awarded an *Honorium
Triumph.*

"It's without precedent," Porcius continued in a loud
voice, "an imperial consort sat in state today and received
the homage of the Praetorian Standards. It shows the
degree of power that Agrippina wields."

The senator cautioned Porcius to hold his tongue,
saying the pillars contained unfriendly ears.

Porcius shrugged. "I'm already in her disfavor." He
turned in Caratacus's direction and waddled towards him.

"Ah, good evening, Prince Caratacus and Lady Dana.
Your new clothing becomes you both."

Caratacus wore a linen tunic, trimmed in gold and
purple, and soft, leather boots dyed red and white, like a
senator's. The slaves had bathed and scoured him,
washing and trimming his hair to the nape of the neck.
They had shaved his face, except for the drooping
mustache that contained flecks of gray.

Dana, freshly scrubbed, wore a powder-blue, silk gown
trimmed in gold. A small, pearl diadem framed her tightly
woven hair. Her face was lightly rouged and lips reddened
with the juice of pomegranates.

Porcius cleared his throat. "I know you'll find this hard
to believe, Prince Caratacus, but I've never wanted your
death. Truly, I was very relieved when the emperor granted
your pardon."

"Is this another one of your lies?" Caratacus wanted to
spit in Porcius's face, but dared not.

Dana crinkled her nose and frowned at the Roman.

That's quite all right," Porcius said, "I'm not surprised
you believe I'm lying. Perhaps in time you'll realize that I'm
sincere."

"I doubt it," Caratacus said.

"I know you're bitter and have every right to be. But know this." Porcius paused, stooped, and whispered, "Had it not been for me, you would have been tortured and left to languish in that filthy hole—among other things."

A chill ran down Caratacus's back. *Is this some sort of Roman trick?* "Why did you help us?"

"I believe in repaying old debts."

The prince narrowed his eyes. "What debt?"

"Have you forgotten? You saved my life, for which I'm eternally grateful."

For the space of a couple heartbeats, Caratacus remained speechless. He slowly shook his head and exhaled, "Gods, that was an eternity ago, when my Uncle Epaticcos warred against Verica. I was so young."

"And courageous." The voices of the listening diners fell, every ear straining to hear.

"If it hadn't been for you," Porcius added, "Verica's son would have killed me. But enough of that."

Caratacus decided to reward him publicly with a sop for helping him in prison. "What you said is true, but the honor you show me is all the more valued knowing that you, too, have claimed the head of a warrior in single combat."

An anticipated ripple of excitement swept the assembly.

"So it was true," one senator called to Porcius. "I remember you displaying that foul-smelling box containing a head prize at your villa when I visited your home some years ago. If I recall, it was just before you left for Britannia."

Porcius nodded to the senator, pleased. He turned back to Caratacus. "We shall talk again soon at greater length. My lady." He nodded to Dana and shuffled away, head raised high.

"Caratacus, you never told me you'd saved him," Dana said in disbelief.

He shook his head and snorted. "At the time, it meant nothing to me."

"Obviously it did to him." Dana softly stroked his cheek with her almost child-like hand. "Thank the Three Mothers you saved him."

Caratacus nodded. Although he would never tell Porcius, he held a grudging respect for the old Roman. He appreciated what Porcius had done for him and his family, but he couldn't allow the bloody Roman to know how much, at least not at this time. Caratacus hated being on display, like the emperor's favorite pet. Humiliated before all the world or the part that counted—the nobility. He loathed the thought that he and his family were expected to live the rest of their lives in so-called honorable confinement with no escape except through death.

"Caratacus, you're shivering. What's troubling you?" Dana asked.

Caratacus leaned over and whispered, "I swear by holy Lugh that one day I will escape, no matter how well they treat us!"

Dana looked about. "Don't say that, not now," she whispered. "Don't even think it! Please, for Macha's sake!"

He looked away, putting forth his best smile for the nobility.

A short time later, Centurion Bassus appeared, dressed in his finest white toga, but wearing the hob-nailed sandals of the army. Unlike the Praetorians, there was no bulge protruding from beneath his clothing under his right arm, which indicated a weapon. Like everyone else, the emperor's guards checked him for arms before entering the dining area. He approached Caratacus's couch.

"Greetings, Prince Caratacus. I congratulate you on your release. As one warrior to another, I bear you no ill will."

"Nor I, you." Then, as recognition presented itself, he added, "My fight was never with you, but with Rome. You fought against us bravely and fairly."

Dana nodded.

"I'm in Rome for a short time." Bassus glanced toward the main entrance of the dining hall and back to Caratacus. "Then I'll be posted to the legions in Syria. Would you mind an old enemy dropping by for a visit?"

"If that's all, of course."

Bassus chuckled. "I'm no spy. I've gained too much respect over the years for you and your people."

Caratacus gestured with a hand toward Bassus. "You, I believe."

"Lady Dana," Bassus nodded his respects and walked away, heading for a nearby group of Roman officers.

Caratacus turned to her. "There goes an honorable soldier."

Minutes later, the court chamberlain pounded his hardwood staff on the marble floor, the sound echoing through the dining hall. He formally intoned, "All rise for your Lord Caesar, Tiberius Claudius Drusus Nero Britannicus, Conqueror of the Britons, and his wife, Lady Agrippina."

Caratacus's muscles stiffened. *Conqueror of the Britons? The fight isn't over yet!*

The guests noisily rose in unison and bowed as the imperial couple strode to the dining couches at one end of the room, draped in purple.

He turned to Dana, his jaw tight.

She shook her head and whispered, "I know what's on your mind, don't say it."

"I won't," Caratacus whispered in reply, "but I don't have to like it." He looked about. Fortunately, no one else seemed to have heard them.

The emperor wore a white toga trimmed in gold and a purple cloak hooked above his right shoulder with a white enamel broach in the form of an eagle. An olive wreath crowned his white hair.

Agrippina's hair was built up into an elaborate semi-circular mound in front with plaits and ringlets stringing behind. Long, ivory hairpins kept the tresses in place. A coral gown, trimmed in gold, covered the empress's slender frame, while two strings of pearls circled her neck. She glanced about the dining hall, and a bored look crossed her powdered face.

Emperor Claudius whispered to the chamberlain, who had earlier followed behind the imperial couple to their couch. The man nodded and turned in Caratacus and Dana's direction. "Prince Caratacus and Lady Dana come forward."

A murmur erupted from the guests, and everyone turned heads in Caratacus and Dana's direction.

The two looked at one another. Caratacus shrugged, and, with a nod to Dana, walked the ten paces from their dining couch to that of the imperial couple, where the two halted and bowed.

The emperor, reclining on his left side next to Agrippina, studied the couple through pale but alert brown eyes. "I bid you and your wife, welcome," he said formally without a hint of stuttering.

"Lord Caesar, it is an honor," Caratacus said in a strong voice. He hated speaking the words, but had been instructed earlier by the chamberlain to say them. They were a sign of respect. Had he refused, he would have placed his and the lives of his family in jeopardy. Dana, Macha, and he had to survive.

"Your new clothing becomes the both of you," Claudius said. "You are worthy of nobility."

Agrippina raised an eyebrow, and a buzz arose from the diners.

"Caesar is kind," Caratacus said. *Does he think I believe his rot?*

"Are your new quarters satisfactory?"

"Yes, Caesar," Caratacus and Dana answered in unison.

"We are pleased," the emperor said. "Since you will be our guests indefinitely."

Inwardly, Caratacus winced, but what the emperor said was true.

"We will see that you and your wife are treated as the worthy couple that you are," Claudius continued. He raised a hand and gestured toward them. "Now, turn and face the rest of our guests."

They did.

"Noble guests," Claudius said, "may I present to you our new friends, Prince Caratacus and his wife, Lady Dana. They are to be treated with the utmost courtesy and respect worthy of the friends of Caesar. You have our permission to come forward and introduce yourselves."

Being considered *friends of Caesar* was a high honor and meant being under his protection, but Caratacus knew that his and Dana's status could change with a whim. They had to be careful.

Now that the emperor had formally introduced Caratacus and Dana to the gathering, the diners eagerly approached them.

One senator's wife pulled Dana aside upon learning that she spoke Latin. During the ensuing conversation the wife disdainfully commented on the morals of British women.

"But isn't it true," Dana inquired, "that some of the wives of your senators and knights ran away with actors, gladiators, and slaves?"

"Of course, my dear," the matron replied, gazing down her nose, "but only for a little diversion."

"Then what right do you have questioning our morals?" Dana retorted. "In Britannia, we consort openly with the best of men, while you Roman women allow yourselves to be debauched in secret by the vilest."

Caratacus grinned as the woman turned on her heel and stormed through the milling crowd of diners. "Well said, Dana, she got what she deserved."

"It's true, you are the best," she answered, giving him a light kiss on the cheek. "The nerve of that painted cow. I'd rather associate with slaves than the likes of her."

"Unfortunately, you'll have ample opportunity. Our freedom is little more than comfort in the confines of Rome," he said with a sigh. "For now, we must learn Roman ways if we are to survive. But we'll keep to our own. We will make new friends, people who may be of help to us in the future. And most importantly, we must do nothing to offend the emperor."

But he swore one thing to himself. No matter how long it might take, one day they would see Brittania again.

CHAPTER 24

JULY, AD 60

Caratacus stared blankly across the wine-dark waters of Mare Tyrrhenum to the edge of the horizon. Only a tiny slice of the setting sun's fiery orb remained and reflected like twinkling stars on the gentle swells. Minutes later, it slid beneath the sea's murky depths. He loved the Italian coast and its mild sea breezes, especially Antium, where he lived thirty miles south of Rome. Nine years before, one year after coming to the imperial capitol, he had obtained a small villa, purchased for him by friends. Much to his relief, Emperor Claudius had loosened his reins, allowing him to settle south of the little fishing village. *Thank the gods for that, I hated the city's stench.*

It was an older home, plainly built, but ample for Caratacus's family needs. Although the settlement was dotted with palatial summer homes of the rich, his house sat isolated along a dirt track beyond the end of the Severinian Way. Snuggled inland among the pinewoods, the home bordered a wide, sandy beach, and at night he could hear the waves gently lapping against the shore.

During the evening, when he walked the pathways, he almost felt the freedom of his homeland.

He stooped, picked up a stone, and hurled it into the foaming surf as it crashed onto the rocky beach. *So much has happened since we were brought to Rome.* Following Caratacus's pardon by Emperor Claudius, Porcius had made at least three attempts to befriend him. Twice, Caratacus rebuffed him. The turning point with Porcius came during the third visit when he informed him that he had petitioned the emperor to transfer Caratacus's former guide, Alfyn, to the ex-king's new home. After the young

Briton had been taken prisoner, he and many British warriors had been pressed into the Roman Army as auxiliary soldiers and sent to garrisons on the Danubus frontier.

When Caratacus asked Porcius why he was doing him the favor, the Roman replied he did this as a show of friendship. Despite the invasion of Britannia, he still had a high regard for the British people. He wanted to be Caratacus's friend as he had been to his father, Canubelinos.

So far, Alfyn seemed happy to be serving Caratacus again.

Caratacus continued his stroll along the shore, inhaling the salty air carried by the gentle, summer breeze swirling about his face. His musings continued. Claudius had died four years after their arrival. Caratacus had heard rumors the emperor was poisoned by mushrooms fed to him by his fourth wife, Agrippina, so her son, Nero, could ascend the throne.

Through it all, Caratacus lived a quiet life. He had been careful not to stray from the limits set by Claudius and prayed he had not come to Nero's attention. It went against his character, but if he were to survive, he had to live with it. One day he would escape.

Caratacus's once-long, tawny hair was rapidly being replaced by a legion of gray strands. His drooping mustache had faded years before, and hairline receded at the temples. When he read books or messages, he had difficulty focusing on the parchment unless held at arm's length.

A screeching sound pulled him from his reverie. Close by, he saw the shadow of an unknown seabird gliding over the water's surface in the growing darkness. Another breaker, growing higher from trough to crest, toppled and broke, crashing on shore in a thundering mass of foam and spray. He sighed. Little more than a year had passed since Dana died. The wasting sickness struck her down, and within six months after becoming ill, she passed away. The grief he experienced plunged to the depths of his spirit. Had it not been for his daughter watching over him, he might have taken his own life.

"Lord, your daughter and her husband are here," his retainer, Alfyn, said, jolting Caratacus out of his daze.

Caratacus shook his head, puzzled. According to an earlier message, he had not expected a visit from Macha and Titus for at least another two weeks. "How long have I been standing here?"

"Not more than half an hour," Alfyn answered. "Looks like the tide's coming in."

Caratacus eyed his boots, covered to the ankles by the foamy surf. A chill raced through his soaked feet and up his legs. He shivered. "So it is. I was so deep in thought I hadn't noticed. Gods, the salt will ruin the leather. When did they arrive?"

"A few moments ago, sir. I didn't think you'd minded me disturbing you."

"Under these circumstances, no. Macha's the only one I'd see anytime. My one consolation since losing my wife."

Caratacus turned eastward studying the purple-black outline of the Alban Hills, rising gracefully in the distance. Hundreds of winking lights, emanated from the white-walled villages and towns nestled among the vineyards on its slope.

He exhaled deeply. "Alfyn, tell them I'll be along shortly."

After hugging Macha and greeting his son-in-law, Titus, with a hand shake, Caratacus called for wine, and they strolled to the atrium.

"This is an unexpected pleasure," Caratacus said heartily. "I hadn't expected the two of you until the end of the month. What brings you to Antium so early?"

Macha smiled. "Oh, you know how boring and hot Rome is in July."

Titus winced.

Dressed in a green gown, covered by a yellow and blue stola, Caratacus's long-legged and willowy daughter turned to her husband and then back to her father. "Seriously, Da, we have good news. Titus has received his appointment as tribune in the army."

"Congratulations," Caratacus answered as a grin crossed his face. "You've waited some time for that, haven't you?"

"Yes, sir," the tall, smooth-faced, dark-haired, young man answered. Dressed in a white tunic, trimmed in red, with a small sheathed dagger strapped to his waist, Titus was no more than twenty. He hesitated for a moment. "But it means Macha and I are leaving Rome."

Caratacus studied Macha. With each passing day, she favored her mother more. "I thought as much. You can't serve the army in Rome. Besides, she'll be with you."

Titus straightened slightly at the indirect compliment.

"Where are you going?" Caratacus inquired.

"Germania. Moguntiacum, on the Upper Rhenus," Macha replied.

Caratacus frowned as he turned to Macha. "I'm going to miss you, both of you," he added as an afterthought. "How long will you be gone?"

"At least two years," Titus said. "I'm being posted to Legion Fourth Macedonica. After that I'll decide whether to make the army my career or return to Rome and follow my father into imperial service."

They walked in silence as Caratacus considered the posting. As son of a senator, Titus would eventually inherit his father's position in the Senate. In Caratacus's mind, being an army officer was safer than a politician. At least a soldier knew who his enemies were.

"When do you leave?" Caratacus asked.

"Next week." Macha glanced at Titus and then her father. "We'll miss you, too, Da. Are you going to be all right?"

"Of course, I will." He noticed that she seemed uneasy, as if there were something more she wanted to say.

"Mum's death was very hard on you, wasn't it," she said, slipping her arm about his gently.

"It was painful for both of us, only you've recovered sooner," Caratacus answered softly.

Macha shook her head. "I still grieve for her, Da. I loved her so much."

"Both of us did," Caratacus said.

"Actually, I'm still recovering, but I guess I have faster than you." She sniffled and cleared her throat. "I'll never forget her, never!"

"Nor will I. Now, I've grieved long enough, and it's time to put my life back together. I may be fifty-one, but I'm not an old man yet." For a moment he feared tears would flow if he met Macha's eyes. Dana's eyes.

Two slaves approached, one carrying a small amphora of Alban wine and, the other, three silver cups and a jug of water to dilute it. Caratacus motioned to the cushioned oak benches near the atrium's gurgling fountain.

The three sat around a small table. After pouring the dark, red nectar and leaving the jug and amphora on the stand, the servants departed. Caratacus raised his cup to the young couple. "Here's to your appointment, Titus. May the gods keep you safe on your journey and may your career be rewarding."

Although Macha had adapted to Roman ways, it pleased Caratacus that she was still fiercely proud of her Celtic heritage. Unlike most Roman women, she had a passion for horses and rode on a frequent basis, wearing the tartan clothing of her people. She worshipped the British Mother Goddesses and practiced using knives in self-defense as taught by her father. Crimson as the setting sun, her long braided hair indicated to the people of Rome that she was a barbarian.

It never stemmed the tide of suitors from coming to Caratacus's home when Macha came of marriageable age at fourteen. As custom dictated, he refused entry to the young Romans who vied for her affections, unless accompanied by their families. Like any other self-respecting parents, he and Dana would decide who Macha married. Many of Rome's most distinguished families visited him on a regular basis. Caratacus learned from these patricians that an alliance with the family of a former barbarian king, like his, was not to be disdained.

At age seventeen, Macha had married Titus, shortly before Dana's death. He was ambitious and a fine, young man of Gallic nobility. Because of his family's tremendous wealth, his father was a member of the Senate, his people among the first of several Gallic families, to be admitted by Emperor Claudius to that illustrious body. If Caratacus had to marry off his daughter, better to a Gaul than a Roman. At least Gauls and Britons were of similar Celtic stock. Now, at eighteen, Macha's life was set. She still spoke a little about her life in Britannia, but Rome had become her home.

"I was just thinking," Caratacus said, "as much as I'm going to miss you, it's as well that you're going to Germania. The current political climate in Rome is growing much too warm."

"I hesitated in saying anything with your slaves within hearing," Titus said, "but Nero grows more tyrannical with each passing day. Now that his mother is dead and his old tutors, Seneca and Burrus Afranius, are out of favor, he does as he pleases. His excesses will bankrupt the empire."

"I understand the nobility fears he'll turn on them," Caratacus said.

Titus looked about. Only the three of them present. "They're certain it's only a matter of time before he'll issue a proscription list. He's desperate for money. There is no doubt one day he'll arrest and execute members of the nobility, who are out of favor, on trumped up charges. Then he'll confiscate and sell their properties at auction."

"What about your father?"

"He isn't too concerned. He's very old, you know." He sighed. "He'll take his own life before submitting to arrest. Even the emperor won't dare confiscate property of one committing an honorable suicide."

"I'll pray your father isn't forced into that situation."

Titus nodded. He tossed off the remaining wine in his cup. "Although he's willed all his property to me, I'm in no hurry to receive it, at least not that way. Under the circumstances," Titus commented ruefully, "I'm happy to be going to Germania. Nero never visits the frontier. Perhaps he'll forget I exist."

"Not likely, but on the frontier, chances are you'll be out of political harm's way."

Aye, I'll take my chances with the Germans," Titus said.

"Let's drink to it, Da," Macha said.

Macha poured for the three of them, and they quietly toasted one another and drank.

"Titus," Caratacus said a few minutes later, preparing to voice what both men had hitherto left unspoken.

"Suppose someday you are posted to Britannia. How would you feel about fighting my people, Macha's people?"

"Such an assignment is not completely unlikely, especially nowadays," Titus answered at once as if having considered the question before.

"What would you do then?" Caratacus pressed.

Titus held eye contact with him and clenched his dagger. "Kill Britons."

The aging warrior measured the look in his eyes, recognizing that he was prepared for a fight and that Macha seemed alarmed. An icy silence descended upon the three. For the next few seconds only the distant sound of rolling surf, breaking on the shoreline, intruded on their thoughts.

Then Caratacus roared in laughter, melting the tension. "I would expect no less from my son. With luck, you can bring me the head of Cartimandua, my bitch cousin-queen."

CHAPTER 25

One morning, about a week after Macha and Titus departed for Germania, Caratacus sat on a wicker-backed chair in the garden under a vine-trestle canopy. Adjacent to the far end of the house and outside the area, the yard faced in the direction of the sea. He glanced to the tall, white-washed, stone walls bordering the other three sides. Installed in the middle fence hung an iron gate that opened onto a path leading to the beach. Every night when he returned from his evening walk he locked the gate, not trusting the slaves. He and Alfyn possessed the only two keys. Caratacus inhaled the perfumed scents of well-tended anemones, poppies, lilies, and roses kept behind a dozen latticed fences along the walls. Down the middle ran a graveled path bordered on both sides by a well-trimmed, low hedge and several cypress and plane trees.

The sun, a deep-orange-red disk, peeked over the Alban Hills. The racket of squawking gulls and the rumbling sounds of waves breaking on the beach beyond his home drifted on a light wind, the cool air stroking his face. He reflected on how much he already missed the young couple, especially his daughter.

He pulled a light cloak about his tunic and tighter around his shoulders. *Is this a sign of old age? This cold isn't anything compared to what I experienced while living in Britannia, and that bothers me.*

Footfalls crunched on the graveled path. He turned as Alfyn approached with a slave he recognized as belonging to Porcius.

"Sir, he brings a letter from Lord Porcius," Alfyn said.

Strange, I thought Porcius was still in Rome, not at his summer home north of Antium.

After the messenger departed, Caratacus sat straighter, unrolled the parchment, and read the message. His hands trembled, and he took a couple of deep breaths. He grabbed the cup of heated wine on the table next to his chair, gulped its contents, and slammed the cup down.

"Sir, is it bad news?" an alarmed Alfyn inquired.

"That depends on whose side you're on. Queen Boudicea of the Iceni is in revolt against Rome. She's slaughtered at least forty thousand people."

Alfyn screwed up his scarred, narrow face. "I hope they be Romans."

"Many were. Ten thousand were soldiers of Legion Ninth Hispana and its auxiliaries. Thousands of Roman sympathizers were killed in Camulodunum."

Caratacus finished reading the dispatch and tossed it on the table. "Many innocent Britons also died."

"Isn't there anything you can do? If only you weren't living in this foreign cage."

"There must be a way." Caratacus sat quietly, thinking. "Alfyn, my people need me, and whatever the consequences, we must go. But if we're to get out of here alive, we'll need help from someone we can trust."

Alfyn scratched the ridge of his broken nose with the stub of a forefinger lost in battle. "Only you have the influence to unite the forces of Queen Boudicea with Lord Venutios. The people would rally around you."

Would they? It has been ten years since my capture. Boudicea might consider me a Roman spy. He shook his head. *It makes no difference, I must leave. If we can defeat the Romans, the effort will be worth any future blood feuds.*

The question remains, who will aid in my escape from Italy and keep it a secret?

A slave approached Caratacus and announced the arrival of Porcius.

"What's he doing here? His message arrived less than an hour ago," Caratacus said.

The slave and Alfyn shrugged.

Dressed in a white toga and heavy mantle, but shivering, the seventy-two-year-old Porcius hobbled along the pathway until he reached and sat in the chair next to Caratacus. "I left Rome yesterday afternoon and have traveled all night so I could see you as quickly as possible," he said. Squinting, the Roman observed the parchment laying on the citrus wood table beside Caratacus. Alfyn and the slave stood at a discreet distance. "I see you've received the message."

"You had no reason to travel to Antium so quickly unless it was about this." He nodded to the scroll. "Am I right?"

"You are," Porcius answered softly.

Caratacus wondered if Porcius's presence was an omen. Over the years, Porcius and he had become friends. Porcius had given no indication of betrayal. *Now is the time I must take a risk and trust Porcius.*

"Why did you send me the news about Boudicea?" Caratacus asked.

Porcius glanced to Alfyn and the slave.

Caratacus dismissed the slave. "Alfyn stays."

The old Roman cleared his throat. "Very well. I wanted you to hear the truth, not wild rumors. I know you still care for your people."

"Then it's true?" Caratacus clenched his fist.

"As far as I can learn, yes. There's more, and that's why I came."

Inhaling deeply a couple of times, Caratacus relaxed his hands and leaned closer. "I'm listening."

"I will help you to flee Italy," Porcius said in a voice barely above a whisper.

Caratacus's heart seemed to jump into his throat, his chest tightened. *Am I dreaming?*

"But why would you help me escape?"

"My time is running out. Forty thousand souls were slaughtered in Britannia. Sooner or later, Rome will remember who you are."

"Has Nero issued a proscription list?"

Porcius's sagging face tightened, and he nodded. "His extravagances have become enormous. He needs new revenues to pay for them. He's marked at least one hundred senators for death, including me. I'm at the top of the list." Porcius went on with a sigh. "He's taking revenge on his mother's account for my indiscreet remarks."

"That was years ago," Caratacus said.

The Roman sniffed. "Even though he murdered her last year, he hasn't forgotten that I once called her *an incestuous slut.* It's a convenient excuse to confiscate my lands and revenues."

Porcius had once told Caratacus that he regretted some of the things he had done in his life, but most he didn't. His health was failing, and he had suffered from arthritis since his early thirties, crippling him more with each passing day. He walked haltingly at times. Most of his teeth were now gone. He complained his eyesight grew cloudier by the day and believed he would soon be blind.

I thought I would never see the day when I would have pity for the old man, but now I do. Pity, not contempt. "What does this have to do with me?" Caratacus prodded.

"You're a danger to Nero," Porcius answered, "even though you're not on his list yet."

Caratacus frowned and shook his head. "I've lived in obscurity since I've been in Italy."

"True, but because of the Boudicean rebellion, you're a threat." Porcius gestured with a trembling hand. "You could be a rallying point for the Britons. I don't know when he plans to arrest you, but you can wager on it."

"And yet, you'll help me flee?"

"Why not? If I'm going to die, I will have the last joke on Nero." Porcius steadied the reoccurring tremor of his left hand with his right. He paused for a moment. "Now, don't look so gloomy, my friend," he said, "it isn't so tragic."

"I didn't realize my face betrayed me," Caratacus answered, surprised by his own sadness. He wiped a sweaty palm on the sides of his breeches.

The corpulent Roman paused and, for a few seconds, closed his eyes and dipped his head before raising it again. "Regardless, I shall pray for your safe journey. Maybe the gods will speed you in time to help Boudicea. Suetonius Paulinus, the new imperial governor, is in the process of reorganizing the legions to counterattack, if he hasn't already.

"I regret to say," Porcius continued, "Rome deserves to lose. Had the government handled the British people with greater dignity, the rebellion would never have happened."

Caratacus turned his head toward the gate and path leading to the beach. From the distance, muffled by pines that bordered the beach, the pounding surf sounded like a hissing whisper on the breeze. A flight of gulls drifted overhead.

"I'll find Venutios, and we'll join with Boudicea."

Porcius jabbed a shaky finger toward Caratacus. "Be careful, my friend. The legions are well entrenched. They'll bring in reinforcements from Gaul and the Rhenus."

Caratacus slapped his thigh with the palm of his hand. "Regardless of what happens, I must go."

"And I'll do everything in my power to help you."

"What do you suggest?"

The Roman told Caratacus that a ship, the *Eyes of Kronos,* would pick him and Alfyn up from the beach near his home the following evening, about an hour before midnight during high tide, and sail to Britannia. "Once you are reported missing," Porcius said, "Rome will search for you by land and sea."

"I'm willing to take the risk," Caratacus said.

"Then it shall be done," Porcius said. He grimaced while twisting his bald, wrinkled head about. "I have it all worked out," he whispered. "In a few minutes, I will leave for my summer home. Once I receive the news that you have *disappeared,* I will order my slaves to draw a hot bath. As I relax in the tub, one of my slaves will play the *Hymn to Venus* on the lyre while I open my veins and fade away."

"I hate the thought of you taking your life and that monster Nero confiscating your property," Caratacus said.

A wry grin flashed across Porcius's fleshy lips. "Oh, did I not tell you, he won't."

Caratacus raised his eyebrows. "I don't understand, unless I'm mistaken, you don't have any heirs."

"Ah, until a few days ago, you would have been correct."

"And now?"

Porcius chuckled. "Our favorite centurion, Bassus."

"Bassus! What about him?"

"He doesn't know it yet, but I have secretly adopted him as my son and heir. I have dispatched a courier with the news to Judea where he is posted. He will automatically inherit my rank as senator."

Caratacus shook his head. "Incredible, and it couldn't have happened to a better man."

"Indeed. He will serve in my place with honor." Porcius winced as he got to his feet. "And now I must go. Farewell, my friend, may all the gods, yours and mine, be with you."

Caratacus slapped his thigh and exhaled. "Damn! I never thought I would see the day when I would be sorry to see you leaving like this, but I am."

"You know I must."

Caratacus nodded.

He shook Caratacus's hand and hobbled away, his sandals scraping along the graveled pathway, back to the house, leaving by way of the front door.

* * *

The following day, Caratacus made his rounds about the villa as he always did, maintaining the facade that all was normal in the household. As usual, Alfyn accompanied him. Casually, Caratacus spoke to a few of the slaves about their duties. He told the cook what he wanted for breakfast and dinner the next day even though he and Alfyn would be long gone.

He and Alfyn wouldn't bring much with them: a change of clothing suitable for traveling and fighting, boots, and a leather pouch containing a small amount of gold. They also possessed weapons, including a cavalry longsword and dagger, which had been given to them secretly months before by sympathizers. The night before, after Porcius had departed, Caratacus and Alfyn had hidden their gear. They buried it in a shallow hole, within a heavy clump of shrubs by the pines, behind the long sand dune that paralleled and overlooked the beach.

Caratacus took his regular evening meal. Upon finishing it, he hiked to the garden and sat by the fountain. In the center of the basin a bronze dolphin stood on its tail and spilled water from its beak, the gurgling sounds pleasant to his ears. A light wind blew in from the sea, the smell of salt on the breeze. He heard the "pic-pic-pic" of sandpipers scurrying across the beach.

A few minutes later, Alfyn approached him.

"Sir," Alfyn said, "there is a messenger from Lord Porcius, he is waiting in the atrium." Tension crawled through Caratacus's body. *Another warning?* "Bring him to the garden."

Alfyn returned, followed by the slave, a young Gaul, whom Caratacus recognized as belonging to Porcius. Sweat rolled down the youth's flushed face as he gasped for air. A light coat of dust covered his plain tunic. *He must have run all the way from Porcius's summer villa on the other side of town.*

"What word do you bring from Lord Porcius?" Caratacus said.

The runner gulped a few more deep breaths. "Forgive me, Lord Caratacus." He inhaled again. "My master says Praetorian cavalry have been dispatched from Rome to arrest you."

"Arrest? This is sooner than I expected."

"Yes, sir. They were last seen only a few miles north of Antium and will be here at any time."

"How many troops?" Caratacus asked.

"A squadron of thirty. My master asks that you flee at once and hide until the ship can pick you up."

"Do the Praetorians know of my escape plans?"

"No, sir, not that Lord Porcius is aware of. Except for me, he has forbidden all his people, free and slave, from leaving his villa until further notice."

"Very well, give Lord Porcius my thanks." He dismissed the messenger.

When Alfyn returned from seeing the slave out, Caratacus said, "Get ready to leave. Pray we won't have to wait long for the ship. Our movements must be as casual as possible. Since I haven't taken my walk yet, none of the slaves should notice—they'll believe that is what I am doing." *I hope.* "You will be with me, as usual."

"Aye, we can't leave anything to chance."

"Do you have your gate key with you?"

"Yes, sir, always."

"It's late, and most of the slaves should be in bed, but check the house quickly and see if anyone is still awake."

Alfyn nodded and headed for the house. A few minutes later he returned. "They're all in their rooms, lord."

"Let's go!"

The two left by way of the garden through the gate, which Caratacus locked behind them, and headed for the pines at the edge of the beach. "Locking won't do much good, but it will delay them, even for just a few precious seconds."

"It'll force them to go around the outside," Alfyn said.

"Stay off the path, we can't leave any tracks," Caratacus said. "There'll be a full moon tonight, the Romans could follow us easily."

They fled to the bushes above the beach and grabbed two small, hidden shovels beneath a clump of pulled up weeds. Carefully, attempting to keep the scraping sounds of shovels to a minimum, and stopping every few seconds to listen, they dug up their goat-skin-leather carrying bags and weapons. The two removed and placed oiled-cloth protective cloaks around their shoulders and strapped on their swords. Crouching in the thick brush on the lengthy sand bar, where the slope with high, overgrown sand-dune grass descended toward the pebbled beach, Caratacus and Alfyn waited for the arrival of the ship described by Porcius.

Caratacus's eyes searched the shadowy darkness of the Tyrrhenian Sea, barely seeing the outline of white-capped, black swells. "Gods, I pray the ship arrives before the Praetorians do."

The hissing surf receded back into the oncoming waves. White foam reflected in the light of the nearly full moon, as it rolled along the top of churning waves, curving along the edge, crashing onto the beach. Black clouds drifted across the moonlit sky. In the distance, a front of bruised thunderheads piled up to the stars, like an army preparing for battle. The smell of salt drifted on the night air as warm wind, a *sirocco,* rolled out of the south from North Africa. Caratacus's shoulder-length hair whipped about in the breeze, gritty sand stung their eyes.

* * *

Hiding for what seemed to be ages, but probably was no more than three or four hours, Caratacus and Alfyn's limbs and elbows ached from lying in the scratchy, weed-infested bushes. It was nearly midnight, and still no sign of the ship.

Did Porcius lie to me? Caratacus wondered.

Then sounds of screaming and shouting came from the direction of Caratacus's villa.

"Praetorians, they're at the house!" Caratacus blurted. "Don't they realize the slaves are spies?"

"The slaves are nothing to those butchers," Alfyn said. "They'll torture them for the bloody fun of it! At least the poor devils don't know our secret."

"Not yet."

More screaming.

"It's only a matter of time before the Praetorians search along the beach, they're not stupid."

Once more, Caratacus scanned the shoreline and the sea. "Look, there it is—finally!" He pointed at a boat, heaving and diving, manned by six oarsmen coming in through the rumbling surf. Squinting his eyes, he searched the churning waters beyond the boat, barely making out the silhouette of a ship's square mast in the center of a stubby merchant ship. *Pray this is The Eyes of Kronos and not a trap.*

The muffled sound of snorting horses and jingling pedants, hanging from their chests, resounded on the stony beach—the outline of at least a dozen helmeted riders on their mounts emerged out of the shadows from woods several hundred yards away. They spread out in a single line from surf to the tree's edge, walking, as if sweeping the area.

So far they haven't seen us! Caratacus thought.

He motioned to Alfyn. "Run for the boat!"

The two flung their bags over their shoulders and raced across the rocky beach.

Caratacus looked as the Roman troop reassembled into a double column, kicked their mounts forward, and headed at a canter in their direction. They angled toward surf where the sand was firmer and footing better.

The Briton's feet sunk a few inches in the soft sand as if they were slogging through mud.

Caratacus's leg muscles started to ache. *My gods—not now!* He doubled his efforts, lifting his legs high, pulling himself forward. *I swear by the gods, I will not let them take me alive!*

He turned toward Alfyn and saw him stumble and fall to the sand.

"Alfyn!" Caratacus stepped to his side, stooped, and pulled him up.

"Sorry about that, sir," Alfyn said.

"Never mind, get moving!"

The riders looming ever larger, hooves pounding and horses snorting growing louder with each passing second.

The two Britons waded into the cold surf up to their knees. The shock ran through Caratacus's body. Two seamen, manning the forward paddles, alighted from the boat and held it by its bow. The Britons tossed their clothing bags into the boat and pulled themselves aboard.

Pushing with all their strength, the sailors then shoved the little vessel into the breaking surf.

"Hurry, the riders are almost on us!" From behind Caratacus, an oarsman shouted to the sailors still in the water.

Just as the seamen rolled themselves over the sides, into the boat, the troopers rode their mounts chest high into the surf. In an instant four of them hurled their javelins at the boat. Two missed, but the other pair struck the sailor's backs. The two screamed and fell into the surf, dead. The Praetorians threw more javelins. Three struck the boat's hull with loud thuds, and bounced away. Another wisked past Caratacus's ear by inches before it dropped into the swirling eddies at the tide line.

The other four oarsmen hesitated.

"Your friends are dead!" Caratacus shouted. He motioned to the forward paddler. "We'll take their place. Now, get us out of here!" Caratacus and Alfyn sat on the wet, splintery, wooden cross seat. They grabbed the oar handles, lowered the paddles, put their backs and shoulders down to dig the oars deeply into the churning waters, and paddled through the surf, dodging more javelins. The boat crashed through another wave, drenching Caratacus and the rest in cold water as they moved out to sea. The cursing horsemen faded into the darkness, their deadly weapons no longer in range of the little vessel. Still heaving at their oars, Caratacus and Alfyn looked at one another in the moonlight, grinned and nodded.

* * *

Caratacus shivered while he leaned against *The Eye of Kronos*'s wooden rail. A fine mist sprayed his leathery face with a lingering taste of salt. He was certain a storm would strike the coast before dawn. Regardless, the ship's captain said he must sail to delay risked interception and capture. The Roman Fleet had weighed anchor that afternoon and sailed north. The old ship was too slow to outrun the navy's swift triremes.

Caratacus shrugged, knowing even as the purple-black outline of the Italian coast disappeared from view. He neither knew what the future held, nor if he would succeed in getting to Britannia safely, but he must take the risk to reach his native land.

Once I return, can I help Boudicea rally the people to her cause? Will I be too late?

No matter. Better to die in Britannia than in a foreign land.

THE WOLF OF BRITANNIA

AUTHOR NOTES

Very little is known about Caratacus, especially his early life. What little evidence exists indicates Caratacus was raised from childhood by his uncle, Epaticcos, King of the Atrebates. What I have attempted to portray in the early chapters is the typical right-of-passage experienced by Celtic youth. Many of the feats accomplished by Caratacus were expected of a young man desiring to become a warrior.

It must be noted that Celtic women had nearly the same rights as men. Many trained to fight as warriors from the time they were young girls. Women of the nobility obtained important roles within the Druidic priesthood, including arch-Druid.

From an early age, it appears Caratacus was heavily influenced by the Druids. Unlike his father, Cunobelinos, who was pro-Roman, he grew into manhood despising everything Roman. When his father became enfeebled, he seized power and drove his older brother, Adminios, and his cousin, Verica, from Britain. In turn, they appealed to the Emperor Claudius for help in restoring them to their tribal thrones.

Unfortunately, Caratacus made the mistake of demanding his brother and cousin's return as prisoners'. This sent Claudius into a rage and gave him the excuse he needed to invade the island and strengthen his position with the Senate. The devastating consequences can be seen in the story.

Caratacus was defeated at the River Medway and waged guerilla warfare for nearly eight years. He made his last stand at Caersws and fled into the traitorous arms of his cousin, Cartimandua, Queen of the Brigantes. History does not record whether it was days or weeks before she betrayed Caratacus to the Romans, but, eventually, she

THE WOLF of BRITTANNIA

placed him under arrest and turned him over to their custody.

Along with his wife and daughter, whose names are not recorded for posterity, Caratacus was paraded before the people in Rome and brought before the Emperor Claudius. The historians, Tacitus, in his *Annals of Imperial Rome,* and in Cassius Dio's *Roman History,* record parts of his impassioned speech, which I use in the story. Claudius was impressed and pardoned the renegade king.

At this point, Caratacus fades from history. Most likely he lived the life of a royal Roman captive. However, that would not preclude him from escaping Italy if the opportunity presented itself, especially during the Boudicean revolt. We will never know with any certainty if he did. I leave that to the imagination and speculation of you, the reader.

CPSIA information can be obtained
at www.ICGtesting.com
Printed in the USA
FSHW02n0635160718
50550FS